A Poisonous Pour

Books by Maddie Day

Country Store Mysteries

FLIPPED FOR MURDER
GRILLED FOR MURDER
WHEN THE GRITS HIT THE FAN
BISCUITS AND SLASHED BROWNS
DEATH OVER EASY
STRANGLED EGGS AND HAM
NACHO AVERAGE MURDER
CANDY SLAIN MURDER
NO GRATER CRIME
BATTER OFF DEAD
FOUR LEAF CLEAVER
DEEP FRIED DEATH
SCONE COLD DEAD
CHRISTMAS COCOA MURDER
(with Carlene O'Connor and Alex Erickson)
CHRISTMAS SCARF MURDER
(with Carlene O'Connor and Peggy Ehrhart)

Cozy Capers Book Group Mysteries

MURDER ON CAPE COD
MURDER AT THE TAFFY SHOP
MURDER AT THE LOBSTAH SHACK
MURDER IN A CAPE COTTAGE
MURDER AT A CAPE BOOKSTORE
MURDER AT THE RUSTY ANCHOR
MURDER AT CAPE COSTUMERS

Local Foods Mysteries

A TINE TO LIVE, A TINE TO DIE
'TIL DIRT DO US PART
FARMED AND DANGEROUS
MURDER MOST FOWL
MULCH ADO ABOUT MURDER

Cece Barton Mysteries

MURDER UNCORKED
DEADLY CRUSH
A POISONOUS POUR
CHRISTMAS MITTENS MURDER
(with Lee Hollis and Lynn Cahoon)

Published by Kensington Publishing Corp.

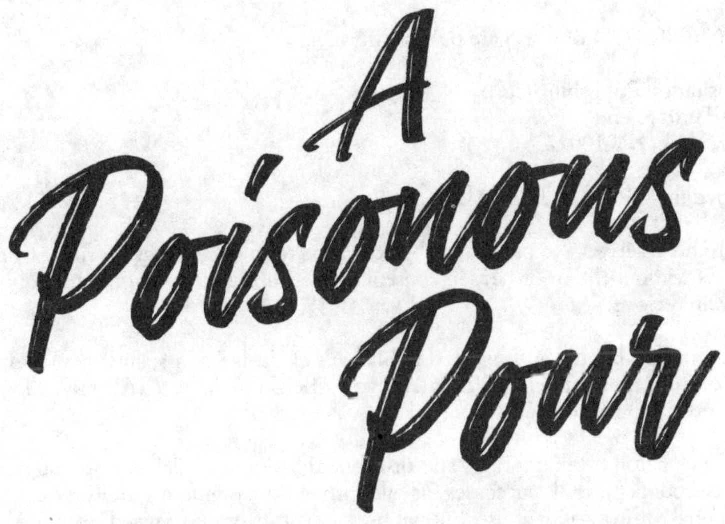

Maddie Day

Kensington Publishing Corp.
kensingtonbooks.com

KENSINGTON BOOKS are published by

Kensington Publishing Corp.
900 Third Avenue
New York, NY 10022

All Kensington titles, imprints, and distributed lines are available at special quantity discounts for bulk purchases for sales promotion, premiums, fund-raising, educational, or institutional use. Special book excerpts or customized printings can also be created to fit specific needs. For details, write or phone the office of the Kensington Special Sales Manager: Attn. Special Sales Department, Kensington Publishing Corp., 900 Third Ave., New York, NY 10022. Phone: 1-800-221-2647.

Library of Congress Card Catalogue Number: On file

KENSINGTON and the KENSINGTON COZIES teapot logo Reg. US Pat. & TM Off.

ISBN: 978-1-4967-4236-0
First Kensington Hardcover Edition: May 2026

ISBN: 978-1-4967-4238-4 (ebook)

10 9 8 7 6 5 4 3 2 1

Printed in the United States of America

The authorized representative in the EU for product safety and compliance
is eucomply OU, Parnu mnt 139b-14, Apt 123
Tallinn, Berlin 11317, hello@eucompliancepartner.com

For the memory of my cousin Kurt Maxwell Reinhardt, who died suddenly while I was writing this book. A creative, funny, and gentle son, brother, husband, and father, he was always part of my life and was an enthusiastic supporter of my writing. He left this world while sitting outside at the family vacation home overlooking the Alexander Valley. We all miss you, dear Kurt.

ACKNOWLEDGMENTS

My town's historical organization, the Amesbury Carriage Museum, hosts a gala fundraiser and auction each year, to which I once again donated the right to name a character in my next book. Local businessman and town benefactor Greg Jardis was the high bidder. He was excited to be included in a book about wine and California, both favorites of his, although he's a much nicer person than my fictional version. Thank you, Greg, and apologies. (The bit about him generously donating a big chunk of money to the local food pantry comes from real life here in Amesbury, and he's also been generous with the Carriage Museum, enabling the creation of their Industrial History Center).

A couple of years ago, when I was in the Alexander Valley on a research trip, Geyserville resident and family friend Victoria Heiges arranged for the two of us to take a tour of the Kendall Jackson wine production facility. Her friend Ed Robinson, the plant manager, generously explained the entire process. We saw two tons of just-picked grapes being dumped from a truck into a massive hopper (big enough to have a body at the bottom). Ed walked us all the way through to bottling. She and I both asked Ed lots of pesky questions about ways murderous mayhem could happen at the plant. I'm pleased to include some of that information in this book, and I'm grateful to both of them for their time. Any errors in the telling are mine.

The "Cycle of the Vine" poster I describe is a real poster produced and sold by Alexander Valley Vineyards. Mine hangs on the wall of my office and serves as a research tool no matter which season I happen to be writing about.

Any statements about the functioning of the Sonoma County

Board of Supervisors are entirely fictional, and the Alexander Valley District Organization is entirely fictional. The towns of Colinas and Las Madres also come from my imagination, although they might take inspiration from certain sights and structures in real neighboring towns. I also took several liberties in describing the actual Healdsburg Hospital.

I include mention of the Southern California fires of 2025, some of which burned areas close to where I spent my childhood and which destroyed the home of a family member. The volunteer artists of the very real Homes in Memoriam include author Ellen Byron's daughter. The artists created lovely paintings of many residents' incinerated houses as gifts, which I found touching beyond words.

I also slid in mention of the Seattle Spice Shop with an owner named Pepper, which I lifted straight from the fabulous *Spice Shop Mysteries* by Leslie Budewitz, a longtime friend. It's one of my favorite series.

Once again, fan-friend Jay Roberts supplied Jo with an appropriate heavy metal band T-shirt. I'm grateful to friend Pam Shaeffer for helping with medical details. Thanks to Gillian B., a fellow blog commenter over at Jungle Red Writers, for the poem about twins.

Since the subtleties are lost on me, I'm grateful to wine writer and mystery author Becky Sue Epstein for help with wine flavor descriptions, and to Geyserville resident Jo Diaz for filling me in on what plants are blooming as May turns to June.

Note to readers: The ideas and words in this novel were generated entirely by the author without contribution from an AI application. I wish I didn't have to include that statement, but you should know where your fiction comes from.

Once again, Amy Glaser gave this book a close read and vastly improved the story in all kinds of ways, for which I'm ever grateful. Many thanks to John Scognamiglio and Larissa

Ackerman as well as the rest of the expert team of Kensington publicists, artists, production staff, and salespeople. I also want to thank my talented graphics and social media helper, Jennifer McKee—you're the best—and my former agent, John Talbot.

I couldn't pull off this writing gig without my partner, Hugh, my sons, John David and Allan, my daughters-in-law, Alexandra and Alison, my sisters, Janet and Barbara, and of course the little grandgirl of my heart, Ida Rose. Continuing thanks to all the Reinhardts, my beloved Bay Area family, and to cousin-in-law Laurent Cruvellier, who filled me in on which farmers market produce would be available.

I hope readers will check out Mystery Lovers' Kitchen, where you can find a fabulous author and her original recipe every day of the month, including me on the second and fourth Fridays. Finally, huge thanks to all the enthusiastic readers, fans, librarians, and booksellers out there. I would be nowhere without you.

Chapter 1

The person who thought up the idea of a vintage car show paired with wine tasting should get the Brilliant Award. And on the Saturday of Memorial Day weekend? Even better—at least until the anger-fueled fireworks started.

I backed Blue, my sixty-six Mustang, next to the white pop-up tent I was sharing with Jo Jarvin for the day. Jo's forty-eight Chevy service truck was already parked on the other side of the tent, with JJ's Automotive magnetic labels on both doors of the red pickup. The mechanic greeted me from one end of the long table she and I had been invited to share.

"I was just starting to set up, Cece."

"Have you ever seen this many great cars in one place?" I gestured to the rows of cars, none made more recently than thirty years ago, with some dating back from the early years of the automobile. I pulled out a long black tablecloth and spread it on the table with Jo's help, then tied on a maroon apron bearing the logo of Vino y Vida, the downtown Colinas wine bar I owned and managed.

"Isn't it a gorgeous sight? I'd like to get my hands and tools on every one of those engines." Jo rubbed her hands together. She worked only on cars made before computers became a part of engine compartments.

"These people get up early." The hoods were raised on half the vehicles, and owners slouched in lawn chairs next to their pride and joy. I hoisted a case of Zelma wine onto the table and began pulling out bottles. "It's eight thirty, and they look like they've been here for hours."

"I think most of them have." Jo set out her business cards and a plastic stand holding a poster for her business. Next to it, she arrayed a line of branded key chains to give away. "Does the tasting start before noon?"

"The organizers didn't say, but I imagine so. If folks want to indulge in morning drinking, I'll pour for them."

The weather was perfect. The mercury had already climbed to the midsixties, and the day was forecast to reach into the high seventies with no fog or precipitation. You didn't get much better Northern California weather than that. I'd donned a pink Vino y Vida polo shirt and tucked it into newish jeans for the day. My pink tennies would keep my feet comfortable, too.

I unloaded the cooler, which I'd preloaded with ice packs, from my car. I selected a half case of white wines and laid them in the cooler on their sides.

"Cece Barton?" A tall man strolled up to our table. "I've been hearing about Vino y Vida. I'm Greg Jardis, the new owner of Colinas Hardware." He extended his hand. An older man who still had all his hair, he also wore a white Van Dyke–style beard.

We shook. "Glad to meet you, Greg. Do you also have a car here?"

"I do. Pamela the Pretty Porsche." He gestured at a sleek silver sixties-era Porsche arrayed in the first row behind him.

Jo glanced at the car. "Is that a sixty-five?"

"Good eye," Greg said.

"Greg, this is Jo Jarvin, owner of JJ's Automotive," I said. "You're going to want her to take care of Pamela."

The two shook hands. Jo handed him her business card.

"We almost share a last name. Did you move to Colinas recently?" she asked.

"Yes, this winter. I retired but found myself at loose ends, so I sold my place in Marin County and bought a new business." He shrugged with an abashed smile. "Go figure."

"Some of us love to work," she said. "I'll be happy to keep the Porsche in tiptop shape for you, from the routine to the more challenging issues."

"Thanks. I had an ace mechanic in San Rafael, but that's too far to go now."

The two began talking about Jo's truck and her business.

I finished setting out our tiny tasting cups and signage. Entrance to the show included being carded for legal drinking age, which meant I didn't have to worry about checking IDs. The high school soccer teams, both boys and girls, had set up a kids area at the nearby park and were offering low-cost babysitting so parents weren't excluded from the event.

Greg moved over to my area. He admired Blue and asked a few questions about the car. "Where'd you find her?"

"My father's grandparents gave him the Mustang for his sixteenth birthday."

He gave a whistle. "So she's always been in the family?"

"Indeed."

"Lucky. I had to buy mine." He gazed at my wine offerings. "I've been loving this rich wine valley. Can I taste the Twomey sauvignon blanc?"

"Sure." I poured and handed him the plastic cup. "It's quite smooth, and I have bottles of everything for sale. Sorry about the plastic, but I do recycle the used ones." I'd researched high-quality plastic stemless glasses that were easily washed and reused, but they were too big for sample tasting like I offered here.

He savored the taste. "That's good. I'd like to try the 2021 pinot noir, too."

"The Russian River Valley?"

"Yes."

After he tasted the red, he bought a bottle of each. "Thanks, Cece. See both you ladies around," he said as he headed back to his car to stash the purchases.

"Nice guy," Jo said.

"Seems so. And you might have picked up a new customer."

"I hope so. Thanks for the intro."

The show picked up, for both Jo and me. She schmoozed with show participants and others, while I explained wines and gave out tastes, plus Vino y Vida corkscrews to anyone who bought a bottle.

A trim, petite woman in a business pantsuit and heels stopped by and fingered one of the JJ's Automotive key chains. I gave her a quick look. That suit had to be either a designer brand or tailor-made, it fit her that well. The fabric was both soft and crisp. I wasn't a slob and tried to dress reasonably well, but I would never look that good in my clothes.

I turned back to a trio of ladies wanting to taste everything, laughing and saying their husbands were looking at engines while they got the good stuff. Pantsuit must have moved on, because she didn't visit my side of the table.

An hour or two later, I glanced up at the sound of raised voices. A woman stood face-to-face with Pantsuit. The fifty-something woman's face was red, and walnut-colored hair was flying loose from the knot on top of her head. As I peered at the pair, I realized the other one was my part-time employee Dane Larsen, who was also a local artist. I'd never seen her irate before.

Jo also looked over. "That doesn't look good, at least not for Dane."

"Who's the woman in the pantsuit?"

"You don't know?"

I shook my head.

"That's Regan Greene," Jo said. "She's the director of AVDA, the Alexander Valley District Association."

"I've heard it's a powerful group."

"Yeah, and Regan holds most of the power. At least she'd like to."

"Too bad we can't hear what they're saying," I murmured. "Dane looks like she wants to slug her. I wonder if I should intervene."

Dane shook her head, hard, before spinning on her heel and stalking away.

"I guess you don't have to," Jo said.

Good. I checked the time on my phone and groaned. It was twenty minutes after noon, but Dane was supposed to be at work at Vino y Vida at twelve thirty. Should I call over there to see if my regular weekend guy, Dev, was already there setting things up? *No.* He was super reliable. Dane, not so much, although when she did make it to work, she was great with customers and knew her wines.

CHAPTER 2

My feet hurt after five hours of standing on pavement, but my bank account was a fat, happy camper. One of my supplying wineries had delivered reinforcements in the form of three more cases. We'd had a nearly nonstop flow of tasters and schmoozers straight through the lunch hour, many of whom had purchased a bottle or two to take home.

Jo had a good event, too. She had given out all her key chains to interested vintage auto owners. Plenty of them also added their names and email addresses to the sign-up sheet on her clipboard so they would receive her newsletter.

The show's official closing time, for cars and wine tasting, was at two o'clock, a half hour from now.

"Did you save me a glass?"

I glanced up to see my fraternal twin, Allie, approaching arm in arm with her husband, Fuller Halstead.

"Of course," I said. "I have a full bottle of red and two of white waiting to be tasted by both of you." I came around the table and hugged them.

"Thank you, Cece, but I'll hold off for now." Fuller pushed up his glasses and ran a hand through his dark, curly hair. He sounded more subdued than usual, not that he was ever super effusive except with their boys.

"Whatever you want," I said.

"I'm going to go check out that Porsche." He squeezed Allie's arm and headed across to Greg's car.

"Al, what would you like?"

"I'll start with the chardonnay." Her gaze followed Fuller's progress.

"I know it's tiny, but refills are free." I handed her a full little cup. "I think I'll have a sip to keep you company. The show's almost over."

"Your first wine of the day?" She turned back to me and smiled.

"Yep. Come around the table and sit in Jo's chair. She's off wandering the grounds."

Allie plopped down next to me.

"Where are the kiddos?" I asked her. Franklin and Arthur, Ali and Fuller's fraternal twin sons, were now eleven and were two of my favorite people in the universe.

"Fuller's dad took them for the day, bless his generous heart. Which means they probably baked banana bread and are now somewhere fishing." She raised her cup. "It doesn't make much sense to clink plastic, but cheers."

I sipped mine. "Mmm. Nicely creamy with fruit notes of apple and citrus and a medium mouth fill."

"I thought 'buttery' was the way to describe this wine," Allie said.

"That's a common descriptor of oaked chardonnays, and it works. One day I'll pour you an unoaked. The Burgundian chardonnays can be leaner and more complex, with an interesting minerality."

"You lost me." She rolled her eyes. "Where's Jo?"

"Handing out business cards to car owners, I imagine."

"She has a captive audience." Allie pointed with her chin. "Uh-oh. I'd say trouble's brewing."

I glanced in that direction. A few yards away, Regan Greene

stood facing Colinas mayor Malia Gutierrez. Regan's arms were folded on her chest, and Malia glared and gestured as she spoke, her curvy figure in a wraparound red dress.

"What do you know about Greene?" I asked Allie.

"She's director of AVDA, and she's a power grabber. I'm pretty sure she has her eye on a higher office than what she's in, maybe county supervisor or something statewide. Richard has a new article out about her that's going viral."

"My Richard?" I stared at her. Richard Flora was my ninety-something neighbor who'd had a long career as a journalist and author. Usually we chatted in our back gardens about plants and growing things, but sometimes it veered into local politics. "He hasn't said a word about it."

"Ask him next time you see him. I haven't seen it yet, but he apparently wrote an exposé about the association and Regan in particular."

"You bet I'll ask." I finished my chardonnay while gazing at the two women. "She and Malia don't look particularly happy with each other."

"They have a bit of history, those two." Allie drained her little cup. "Can I have a refill?"

"How about the pinot noir?"

"Hit me."

I poured red wine into both our cups. "What's the story?"

"I only know the dribs and drabs I've heard, and part of it is as mundane as love and jealousy."

"Classic. What, did one of them steal the other's husband or lover?"

"Something like that." She clamped her mouth shut as Greg Jardis sauntered up.

"Afternoon, ladies." He flashed Allie a big smile and proffered a hand. "I'm Greg Jardis."

Allie actually blushed, which wasn't like her. She pushed up to stand and shook his hand.

"Alicia Halstead."

"Allie's my twin, and the best real estate agent in the county," I said. "Greg owns Colinas Hardware."

The two chatted for a minute while I watched Malia and Regan's continuing standoff. They'd moved nearer and raised their voices.

"You can't do that to Colinas." Malia now had her fists on her hips. Despite being in her fifties, her wavy dark hair had hardly any silver adorning it.

"Actually, I can. It's in my job description."

Greg and Allie fell quiet. He shook his head. "Please excuse me." He made his way to the women.

"Ladies, ladies." He didn't exactly step between them, but he got close and held up both palms. "What seems to be the problem?"

Regan whirled to face him. "Butt out, Jardis," she growled. "We don't need you interfering, you of all people."

"Whoa." His tone seemed to mock her, but he took a pace backward. "Yes, ma'am, Madam Director."

"We'll be in touch, Greene." Malia lifted her chin, spun on her heel, and strode away with measured steps.

Regan didn't respond to the mayor, keeping her stare glued to Greg. "Seriously. Haven't you done enough damage?"

"Who, me?" He dropped his facetious smile. "Can't we be friends, Reenie?"

Reenie? I glanced at Allie, who rolled her eyes. Regan couldn't have looked less like a Reenie. That's what you called a little girl. No way it was the nickname for an ambitious valley official.

"Don't call me that," she hissed. "Why did you move to Colinas, anyway? You knew it was in my district."

Greg shrugged. He gestured around. "What's not to like about the place? Charming small town, friendly people, excellent wine." He paused, waving toward where Allie and I sat.

Regan gave herself a little shake and turned away from him. She pulled out an asthma inhaler and took two puffs, then plastered on a smile as she approached.

"Afternoon, Ms. Halstead." She held out a neatly manicured hand to Allie. "I don't think we've met, but I recognized your picture from various real estate signage. I'm Regan Greene, the director of AVDA."

"I'm glad to meet you at last." Allie shook her hand. "Do you know Cece?"

I stood and held out my hand to shake Regan's. "Cece Barton. I'm Allie's sister, and I own the Vida y Vino wine bar."

"Charming place. I've been in, but not when you were behind the bar, apparently. I hope you're a member of AVDA."

"All the adobe businesses are," I said. That is, I had joined when I began managing Vino y Vida, which was housed in one of four historic adobe buildings, but I never became involved.

"Good." She fished out two business cards and handed one to each of us. "If there's ever anything you need from the association, I'm only an email away."

"Thanks," I said. "Would you like to sample any of the wines?"

"Do you have any without sulfites?"

"We don't, sorry."

"In that case, I'll decline. Ladies." She turned away.

Greg had disappeared, wisely moving back into the crowd. Regan continued down the line of booths but didn't appear to taste wine from any of them.

"What was she arguing with the mayor about?" Fuller suddenly appeared. "I could hear them from a row away."

"We're not entirely sure," Allie said. "Did you see some good models?"

"Yes." He pointed his thumb over his shoulder. "I'm coveting that pretty Porsche, though."

"Greg Jardis owns it," I said.

"Does he? He took over the hardware store. Nice guy."

"It's too bad," I said. "You missed him by a minute."

Fuller smiled. "I know where he works."

I wasn't surprised I hadn't met Greg at the store. I knew why. My small house was finally in good shape, over a year after I bought it. Lightbulbs never burned out anymore, and I had all the garden tools I needed. I hadn't needed anything Colinas Hardware sold for half a year.

Now I wanted to go back in search of Greg's history with Regan and maybe with Malia, too. Or not. It wasn't any of my business, as far as I knew. It might be Allie's, what with her real estate dealings. She'd let me know if I could help.

For now, I had a late-arriving crowd of thirsty and curious wine lovers to pour for.

I smiled at the group in front of my table. "Red or white to begin?"

CHAPTER 3

Jo and I set to packing up at about three o'clock. The show had officially been over for an hour, but the customers kept coming. The antique cars began pulling out, one by one, and the flow of browsers finally ebbed enough for me to turn my back on them.

"Did you collect good prospects?" I asked Jo.

"You bet I did." She ran a hand through her short hair. "If they all pan out, I'm going to have to hire another vintage mechanic."

"Maybe you can train up a teenager, like somebody from the voc-tech high school."

"That's an idea." She slid her last piece of literature into her bag. "Need a hand with your stuff?"

"No, that's okay."

"I'd better get over to my mom's and relieve her of Ouro duty. He'll be missing me." Her golden retriever Ouro was a sweetheart and well behaved but completely attached to his human.

"Go. Are you going to the town picnic Monday?"

"I doubt it." Jo eased open the door to her pickup. "A social event with a bunch of folks I don't know? Not really my scene, Cece."

"I heard there's going to be a great bluegrass group playing, and a beer tent, too."

Jo snorted as she climbed in behind the wheel. She twisted toward me, pointing to the front of her black T-shirt that read "AC/DC Back in Black."

"Also not my scene. Take care." She started up the truck's engine, which purred, and eased out of the spot.

True. Bluegrass was about as far as you could get from heavy metal. Benjamin Cohen, the man I was seeing, and I both liked traditional acoustic music. We'd already planned our picnic meal for Monday.

I hoisted the two cases partly full of unopened bottles into the Mustang's trunk and slid the three open bottles of red wine into their own case. I switched off the tablet, which doubled as credit card reader and email address recorder. A number of today's customers seemed eager to sign up for my newsletter.

As I worked, I thought about the arguments I'd witnessed earlier. Regan Greene had clashed with Dane, Greg, and the mayor, and those were only the conflicts I'd witnessed. The AVDA director seemed to have a talent for rubbing people the wrong way.

I perked up when Malia Gutierrez approached my table. We'd met last year at a local business meet and greet event but hadn't had much contact since.

"Darn, Cece. It looks like I'm too late to sample the wines you were offering."

"For you, Mayor Gutierrez, I will pour." I smiled. "Red or white?"

"A cool white sounds perfect, but only if you call me Malia."

"It's a deal." I fished the open bottle of sauvignon blanc out of the cooler, grabbed a clean cup, and poured to nearly the brim. "Enjoy. Have a seat if you'd like."

She came around the table and sank onto the other chair. "It's been a day." She took a sip and followed it by another.

I poured myself a cup, set the bottle on the table, and sat next to her. "Cheers."

"Likewise." She wore a chunky silver necklace featuring different colored beads, including turquoise, and matching turquoise earrings.

"I love your jewelry," I said.

"Thanks. They're a few of my better pieces."

"You made the earrings and the necklace? I'm impressed."

"I did." A tinge of pink colored her cheeks. "It's a hobby, but one I love. So, you had a good show?"

"Very much," I said. "Vintage car fans—and owners—seem to like a little wine with their wheels, and I was happy to oblige. The show was your idea, I heard." The banners had proclaimed "Mayor's First Annual."

"It was. I hope it'll continue. Starting a tradition like this would be a nice, albeit minor, legacy to leave Colinas."

"It's good for the town. If the show keeps going, I'll be back with wine and my vintage car every year."

"I appreciate that." Malia's shoulders slumped. "My dad offered me his sixty-seven Volkswagen bug when he was getting a new car, and I very much regret not taking it. It was still his only vehicle thirty years after he bought it. He taught me how to drive in that little thing."

"But you couldn't accept the car?"

"No." She let out a long breath. "My life was complicated at the time. But what a beauty of an automobile it was. Simple, straightforward. Like yours, on a smaller scale." She tilted her head toward Blue.

"Blue is all of that."

"I picked up an old bug at JJ's recently, but it's kind of a wreck. It'll need work before I show it at a place like this."

"Earlier I saw you and Regan Greene having some kind of disagreement." I took another sip and refilled her empty cup. "Is everything okay?"

"Not exactly," Malia said. "She thinks as the head of AVDA she can take over powers reserved for the town. She wants a cut of our taxes to support the association, and she's made other egregious demands."

"But aren't those kinds of things specified in the law, or the city bylaws, or wherever?" I asked.

"They are." Her nostrils flared. "Unfortunately the association's board seems to support her."

"I heard there's an article by a local author exposing some of that." I was pretty sure she didn't know Richard and I were neighbors.

"Yes. Mr. Flora has done his best."

I watched more old cars putt single file toward the exit including a Bailey, an electric car from the early 1900s. Around me the last wine vendors and exhibitors were packing up. I was eager to get home and talk to Richard about his article, and I knew the organizers wanted to clear the area and take away their tents and tables. I also didn't want to cut short this unusual conversation with my adopted town's mayor.

"Do you know Regan outside of town or valley business?" I asked.

She tensed and twisted to look at me. "How do you know about that?"

"I don't know anything. I was simply curious."

"Oh." She narrowed her eyes for a second, then relaxed. "Ms. Greene and I have a little bit of history, that's all. It doesn't matter."

I dropped the topic. She wasn't going to tell me.

Malia drained her little cup and stood. "I'd better get along."

A few yards away, a Thunderbird that looked like an early seventies model was the last car left in the closest row. A convertible with the top down, its sleek green paint job was as pristine as the creamy leather interior. I hadn't seen an owner hanging around it schmoozing with other proud car enthusiasts or explaining anything to casual viewers.

Now the T-bird's engine roared to life and the car turned toward us. The color rose in Malia's face when the convertible approached.

"Cheers." Regan raised a hand from behind the steering wheel. She gave us a perfunctory smile before driving on.

Malia watched her go and muttered, "I'd like to . . . well, never mind." She pressed her lips into a line, tearing her gaze away from Regan's car. "Thanks for the wine, Cece."

CHAPTER 4

I drove home slowly with the top down on my convertible. I considered dropping off the wine at Vino y Vida but decided not to. I'd bring it in when I went to work.

Maybe at home I could dig up a bit of past dirt on Regan and Malia. Except it was too nice of a day to hunker down inside over a phone, table, or laptop. The temperatures would only warm from here on out through early fall. Today had probably hit a high of eighty. With the weather now in the low seventies plus a mild breeze, I was entirely comfortable.

I thought about driving to the nearest beach on the coast but nixed that plan. A gorgeous Memorial Day weekend like this would present me with packed roads, distracted drivers, and full parking lots. No, my lovely backyard right here in Colinas was the place to be. Bonus points if Richard was home.

Once Blue was safely parked in the garage that adjoined my house, I washed up and changed into leggings and a T-shirt. I brought a refreshing glass of iced tea and a bowl of nibbles out to my patio. Junior cat Mittens dashed through the open door after me, while Martin made his feline way out with his usual nonchalance.

"Did you guys miss me?" I asked my four-legged friends.

Neither answered. Not a problem. I sipped and munched

and did my best to stay in the moment. I was lucky to have found this house a little over a year ago, with its private back garden and an attached garage for my beloved—but old—car.

Hummingbirds zipped in and out of trumpet flowers. Three California quail ran along the top of the fence, looking as goofy as always with their curly topknots. A skinny lizard did push-ups next to orange golden poppies as if pumping itself up for more dashing. Martin tensed and crouched, then raced at the reptile. The cat didn't stand a chance of catching the little guy.

After the winter rains, we were now back in the dry season verging on drought that was becoming the norm. Drip irrigation lines kept the vegetables in my raised beds alive. Otherwise, the mostly Mediterranean herbs I grew loved it hot and dry. Rosemary and oregano came from sunny, rocky places. They were right at home here.

Being in the moment in my garden seemed to be futile right now, as my thoughts kept straying to Regan, Malia, Greg, Dane, and what I witnessed earlier in the day. I'd remembered a few minutes ago that Richard was out at a family gathering at his brother's for the day. A chat with my neighbor would have to wait.

I looked down at the bowl of cut-up carrots and radishes in my lap. I was going to need supper sometime, and these weren't cutting it as a snack, no matter how healthy they were. I stood. Five o'clock wasn't too early to venture out for dinner. With any luck, I'd inhale some juicy gossip.

"Come on, kitty-cats. You can have an early supper, too."

They both raced ahead of me into the house. As I followed them in, locking the sliding door behind me, a text pinged my phone. I smiled when I read the message from my employee and friend Mooncat.

Join me for an early bite at Hoppy's?

Why not? Hoppy Hills brewpub had great bar food and fabulous microbrews. I'd been thinking of heading to Edie's

Diner, owned by my friend Ed Ramirez, but a meal and a glass of suds with Mooncat would be equally as good.

Sure! See you in 15.

I swapped out the T-shirt for a long top and laced up my tennies. A bit of lip gloss, a brush through my crazy thick hair, and a small purse slung across my chest later, I set out, sweater in hand. The bar was only a few blocks away, and it wouldn't be dark until seven thirty. I wanted to move my legs after standing most of the day.

Plus, Mooncat was a wise and experienced woman who'd lived in the area forever. She was fun to be around, and she might even know something about Regan Greene.

CHAPTER 5

Mooncat and I opted to sit outside on the patio. We were lucky to get a table in the fresh air on this holiday weekend. Tourists and locals alike came here for a beer, a nosh, and casual conversation. After dark, the hop-shaped lights strung all around gave a warm and welcoming vibe. In daylight it was fun to watch the vigorous hop vines that climbed up the strings that ran from the tops of twenty-foot posts down to the huge planters on the ground. The brewery pulled down the strings and harvested the cones in late August, then started over.

Once we had our draft beers, I ordered a fish sandwich, while Mooncat went for a bowl of beef chili, loaded.

"Anything to start?" our much-tattooed server asked. They also displayed studs or rings in their pierced ears and eyebrows.

"Absolutely," Mooncat said. "The deep-fried artichoke hearts, to share."

"You got it." The server turned away.

"Cheers." I held up my pint to my friend. She'd already been on the payroll when I took over the wine bar last year, and I couldn't run it without her.

"How was the car show?" asked Mooncat, who at seventy always said age was just a number, and today wore a short knit dress with turquoise leggings and knee-high boots. The dress fabric, a riot of big flowers in psychedelic pinks and greens, could have come straight out of the sixties—and possibly did. She'd woven turquoise and pink ribbons through her long gray braid.

"I'd say it was a big success," I said. "Tons of tasting, and I sold lots of bottles. We have a pretty good margin on them. It was definitely worth doing."

"You shared a table with Jo, right?"

"I did. She made plenty of contacts, too."

"I thought you might call me during the day for reinforcement," Mooncat said. "I offered, you remember."

"I know you did, and I appreciate it, but I was fine. I didn't want to bother you on your day off. Zelma Vineyards brought over a few more cases when I ran low. We did fine."

"Good."

After our appetizer arrived, I dipped a crispy golden morsel into the lemon aioli and nearly swooned as I bit into it.

"That good, huh?" Mooncat laughed.

I could only bob my head. I swallowed and took a sip of beer. "If that's what heaven tastes like, save me a spot."

Her mouth full, she nodded her agreement.

"But listen, speaking of work, Dane was at the car show at about midday."

"Wasn't she due to open the wine bar?"

"Yes, and I think she was late. She was arguing with a woman I found out is a mucky-muck in the valley."

Mooncat's lip curled. "Regan Greene?"

"That's the name. Sounds like you know her."

"Unfortunately, yes."

"Do you know what history Dane has with Regan?" I asked.

"Huh. I don't. That could be an interesting addition to what I do know."

"I'm dying to hear more."

She wiped her mouth and sat back. "It could take a while."

"I don't think they close here until ten." I flipped open my palms and grinned. "As long as you'll give me a ride home after dark, I'm game."

"You're on. So, it's been a few years." She clamped her mouth shut and frowned, apparently at the sight of something or someone behind me.

I twisted in my seat. *Oh*. Greg Jardis sauntered toward us, hands in his pockets, a little smile playing around his lips. The little smile grew into a beam when he spotted us.

"Ugh," Mooncat muttered. "Good thing we're at a table for two."

"Well, hello there, lovely ladies," he said, smooth as silk, when he reached us. "Twice in one day, Cece? I'm a lucky man. And it's always a treat to see Ms. Mooncat in the flesh." He winked at her as he leaned against the low wall separating the patio from the sidewalk.

"Hi, Greg." She folded her arms over her chest. "Did your date stand you up?"

"No, not at all. She's, ah, running a little late." He glanced at the gold watch on his wrist.

A Rolex or a knockoff? I couldn't tell.

"How does Reenie feel, you dating someone else?" Mooncat gave him a level gaze.

"Now, honey, you know that thing was over long ago."

"Unlike some women, Jardis, I'm not your honey," Mooncat said. "I never have been and never will be."

I felt like I was watching a table tennis match, following this conversation. What would he volley back next?

Our server arrived holding our orders.

"If you'll excuse us?" Mooncat said to Greg. She thanked the server.

"As you wish." Greg lifted his chin. "Oh, look, here's my lady now."

A slender woman in spotless white Capris, red heeled sandals, and a short denim jacket approached. I pegged her for about my age, somewhere between forty and forty-five, which meant his date was at least twenty years his junior. She had one of those perfectly cut, perfectly streaked hairdos that I happened to know costs well over a hundred bucks every month or two.

"We have a reservation inside," Greg said before she reached our table. "Enjoy your dinners." He hurried over to the woman and steered her the other way, laying a proprietary hand on the small of her back.

"Ladies' man much?" I raised my eyebrows.

"The very definition."

"He's been in town only about as long as I have, right?"

"Even less, but I think he had ties here before he bought the hardware store." She stared down at her bowl of chili overflowing with chopped onions, grated cheese, dabs of guacamole interspersed with sour cream, and thin slices of pickled jalapeño peppers. A basket of house-made tortilla chips had been delivered next to the bowl. "I'm ravenous. Let's eat." She dug in with enthusiasm.

My batter-fried fish was sweet and crispy. The same aioli that came with the artichoke dip coated the toasted roll, and shredded cabbage gave it the perfect amount of crunch. The fries were perfectly crunchy and crisp, but if I ate them hot, the sandwich would get cold, and vice versa. I went for the fish first.

"Help yourself to fries if you want," I said after I came up for air.

"I have plenty of food, thanks."

The sun sank behind the tall sycamore trees across the street. I shivered and pulled on the cardigan I'd brought. The nights still chilled to fifty degrees or below. I might get too cold to stay out here until ten, no matter how good Mooncat's story was.

Chapter 6

Mooncat's story hadn't been that long, after all, I mused as I cradled my first cup of coffee the next morning at eight. She was a retired astrophysicist in the aeronautics industry. She'd known Regan Greene a decade earlier when Regan was an aggressive salesperson for a company that made a part critical to air navigation.

"That woman is one of the most ambitious people I've ever met," Mooncat had murmured. "Pretty sure she has her sights set on national office."

"By ambitious, do you mean power hungry?" I'd asked.

"Exactly."

"It sounds like she and Greg dated for a while."

"They did. But really, who hasn't he dated?" She'd laughed and we'd left it at that.

Here on my patio, in the fresh cool of the morning, ambition and a hunger for power seemed distant and silly. Unlike my twin, I'd never been much of a go-getter. My simple goals were to maintain reasonably good health, enjoy a modest degree of happiness, and make enough money to pay my bills with a little left over. Some people apparently wanted a lot more. Not me.

What in a person's background gave them that kind of drive? In Allie's case, it was in her nature to want to succeed.

She was good at everything she tried. Doing well had been easy for her. But power wasn't part of the equation for her, unlike with Regan.

I finished my coffee and stood. This garden needed a touch of TLC. I turned on the drip irrigation. I wandered around pulling weeds here, clipping a couple of dead stems there, and tying new shoots of one of my tomato plants to their stake.

"Knock-knock," Richard called from his side of the six-foot-tall fence.

"One second." I hurried over and unlocked the gate in the wall. He didn't care if it was secured, but his yard was open to the street on the other side. I'd had an attempted break-in from the back in the last year, and I cared deeply about restricting access to my yard.

"Good morning, Cece." He leaned on his cane, and his smile was a paler version than usual. "I thought I heard you moving about out here."

I returned the greeting. "Shall I come over there?" He was usually more comfortable in his own cushioned patio chair than in mine.

"That would be fine, thank you." His turn away was slow and deliberate. He picked his way along the path and sank onto his seat with a sigh.

"You look like you're hurting, Richard." I sat on the bench facing him.

"I'm not having the best of days, but that's neither here nor there. Tell me what you've been up to." He flashed his adorable snaggletoothed smile.

"Mostly the usual, except we had a booth at the vintage car show and wine tasting yesterday. According to the mayor, it was the first annual."

"And you did well?" he asked. "Displaying Blue along with wine, I assume."

"Yes to both. But listen, I hear congratulations are in order.

You have a new article that's going viral, and you didn't tell me?" I kept my tone gentle.

"So I do." He rubbed his brow. "I'm afraid it's attracting rather more attention than I expected."

"That's what going viral means. Tell me about it."

He stretched out his legs, clad today in his usual gardening khakis complete with grass stains at the knees and years of dirt worn into the frayed cuffs despite laundering. He tented his hands under his chin.

"I've been concerned about power imbalances for many years, Cece, on many levels of the government," he began. "Since my retirement, I've found the so-called voluntary district associations to be particularly egregious in this regard."

"Go on." I leaned my forearms on my knees.

"In smaller states, power is more evenly divided between the towns and cities and the state. With the size of California, the counties take on part of that burden. For example, homicide investigations are carried out by the county sheriff, not by the city or state, unless it's one of the big cities like LA or San Francisco."

"I know all about that." In the past year and a half, after murders with which I'd somehow been connected, I'd cooperated with two different Sonoma County detectives.

"I should think you do. Also, the county board of supervisors holds at times more power than they should, but the district associations are worse, especially AVDA."

"Speaking of AVDA, I met Regan Greene yesterday at the car show."

His eyebrows rose. "What did you think of her?"

"Cold. Entitled. She got into disagreements with three different people, including Mayor Gutierrez, and those were only the interactions I witnessed."

"Entitled is a good way to put it," Richard said. "She thinks she can have anything she goes after and doesn't mind slashing and burning whatever's in her path on her way."

"Mooncat says she knew Regan in the past," I said. "Malia seems to have, as well."

"I'm not surprised. At any rate, my article focused on Regan. Colinas is one of the valley towns in the district association." He brought his hands to his lap and studied them.

"You said the article has been drawing attention. Who from, and where was it published?"

"It first came out last Sunday on the opinion page of the *San Francisco Chronicle*, but since then it's been picked up by the *Los Angeles Times* and even the Gray Lady."

"The *New York Times*?"

He nodded. "Not to mention in digital form nearly everywhere. I've been plagued with requests for interviews. Ms. Greene's lawyer has been in touch, as well, threatening me with libel."

"Wow."

"I was simply telling the truth about power, as I have done for my entire career. I'm ninety-one, as you know. I wish only to putter in my garden, enjoy the company of my lady love and my family, and occasionally scribble my thoughts. This onslaught might well be the death of me."

I stared at him. I hoped he didn't mean that literally. "You have a good lawyer, I assume."

"I do. And I have taken my landline telephone off the hook, so to speak. But if any reporters come to your house, please do me the favor of saying 'No comment' and shutting the door."

"I promise. Scout's honor." I reached over and patted his hand. "Luckily, we still have a free press in this country, or mostly. We'll get you through this."

"Thank you, my friend. Would you like a copy to read?" He set his hands on the arms of his chair.

"Yes, but stay put. I'll find it online."

"Very well." He closed his eyes.

"I'm going to get going, Richard. I'll stop in after church, shall I?"

He opened his eyes. "You don't need to. My great-nephew is coming by to do a few chores for me, and after that we plan to play board games the rest of the afternoon."

"Okay, but you call me when you need me."

He smiled. "Scout's honor."

Chapter 7

I emerged from the big stone Manzanita Congregational Church at eleven o'clock. The sermon, by a guest minister, had been a little heavily skewed toward the guilt and brimstone end of the spectrum for my taste. I never took any sermon as the absolute truth, though, and I bristled at anyone thinking they could tell me what to do.

I took in a deep breath of the morning air, now warming, and let it out, along with any negativity. My life was good, and I would hold on to that as long as I could. Yes, there were malicious and egotistical people out there, including some in positions of great power, but I had to believe the good ones outnumbered the bad.

Right now, I was headed for the farmers market, and I looked forward to joining Allie and her family later in the day for a cookout. I'd hoped Benjamin could join me, but he was away for the weekend and wouldn't be back until later tonight.

I'd worn a silk tee under a cardigan and a casual skirt for church, but it was already too warm out for the sweater, so I stashed it in my bike basket. I unlocked the cycle, clipped on my helmet, and pedaled the few blocks to the parking lot where the Sunday farmers market was held.

The market was in full fresh produce season. The gathering

of food producers ran weekly all year long, but winter markets featured mostly greens and nuts and products like olive oil, breads, and cheeses. Walking the bike with my helmet slung from a handlebar, I made one quick circuit of the stalls in the four aisles to see what was available. The variety and quantity of local grown vegetables and fruits was overwhelming. Many of the stands were from organic farms, always a bonus.

I retraced my steps to several of my favorite vendors. I bought three quarts of organic strawberries and nestled their green cardboard containers into my bike basket. I wouldn't get through more than two in a week, but I could take a quart to Richard to lift his spirits. Neither of us grew the fat, luscious berries.

At the PF Vineyards tent, I slowed to say hello to the owner. Paul Fenner operated the small-scale winery, although his main job was as Colinas police chief. I had no idea how he fit all that in, but he must have help with the grapes and wine production. I'd never seen anyone other than him at his market booth.

He had his back to the flow of shoppers, his cell phone pressed to his ear. I moseyed up to the table and picked up a bottle of merlot. He wasn't allowed to offer tasting at the market, but Benjamin was a fan of Paul's vintages, and I thought I'd take a couple of bottles home.

The chief spoke in short, terse phrases, his voice tense. "Yes. All hands on deck. I'll be there as soon as I can." He disconnected and turned. His eyes narrowed when he spotted me. "Cece?"

"Hi, Chief. Everything okay?"

"No. Not at all."

"Can I buy two bottles of the merlot?"

"No. I'm closed." He lifted a case from the ground and began loading display bottles into it.

"Please? I have cash."

"Take them." He ignored me, but I slid two twenties under his stack of business cards and grabbed the wine.

"Good luck." I stashed the bottles in one of my panniers and moved on. Clearly a crime had been committed that required his attention. But what?

Ten minutes later, my bags, basket, and panniers were full of creamy cheeses, crusty bread, crispy lettuce, and crunchy snap peas, plus the strawberries and the wine. A pound of slender cukes, a bundle of asparagus, and a selection of local mushrooms kept them company, but my stomach was growling. I walked the bike toward the last stand, the Tia Tamale food truck, run by Richard's great-nephew Pete. Nothing beat a warm blanket of masa rolled around a filling of beans and cheese. I always finished my marketing with a fat veggie tamale.

As I waited in line to order from the food truck's window, I considered pulling up Richard's exposé on my phone. I hadn't taken time to read it before leaving for church. As the line began moving forward, I decided to wait. I'd be home soon enough. At the window, a young woman took and delivered my order.

I'd settled onto a bench in the adjacent park when my phone rang. I forked in the first luscious bite instead of pulling out the device. The ringing stopped. I took another bite. The ringing began again. Sighing, I set down the paper boat on the bench and fished my phone out of my bag.

Oh. It was Allie. This call I would answer.

"What's up?" I asked.

"Big news, Cece."

"What? Did you win the lottery?" We all could use a windfall, although the odds of winning were miniscule.

"You've got to be kidding." The sound of bedlam came over the line. "Hang on, I have to get somewhere quiet." A door closed before she spoke again. "There's been another murder, sis."

My eyes widened. "Here in Colinas?"

"Yes. I heard about it a few minutes ago over the grapevine." Nobody was better connected locally than my twin.

"I'm at the farmers market," I said. "I just saw Paul Fenner on a call that sounded serious. He disconnected and began packing up his wine booth at double speed." I picked up my tamale and slid in a quick bite. It tasted much better warm.

"Figures. It's probably too soon to get the county sheriff up here."

"Do you know who the victim was?"

"Get this," Allie whispered. "It was Regan Greene."

"Whoa. The ambitious power grabber nobody liked."

"The same."

"Do you know how she died?" I asked.

"No."

In the background, the noise level rose and a boy's voice yelled, "Mom, we're waiting for you!"

"I gotta run, Cee. See you at four?"

"Yes. Thanks for the news."

She disconnected without saying goodbye. I kept eating my tamale as my brain buzzed. Judging from what I'd seen yesterday, there was no shortage of people who would rather the association director stop complicating their lives.

My breath rushed in. She'd threatened Richard with libel over his article. He would be, at the least, a person of interest in the homicide. No way could he have physically killed her. But death could come by means that didn't require brute strength, and the detective assigned to the case would be obliged to investigate even an elderly journalist.

I hurried through the rest of my lunch. I needed to get home and warn my dear friend of a storm that was likely about to descend on him.

Chapter 8

I was home by one o'clock. After I put away my market purchases in the kitchen, I unlocked the garden gate leading to Richard's side. I needed to tell him about Regan's murder.

The back door on the patio was closed, which was unusual on such a nice day. I knocked on the glass of the sliding door and got no response. When I peered inside, no lights were on, which could be ascribed to the early afternoon hour—except he usually had a lamp on all day long. I made my way around the far side of the house to the front. The driveway was empty of cars.

Richard's great-nephew Pete lived with him. He ran Tia Tamale, although today it had been Pete's employee, not him, who'd handed me my tamale less than an hour ago. Richard had said his great-nephew was coming by, so he must have another I hadn't met. I shrugged. Maybe my neighbor had gone out to lunch with friends, and his date to play board games was happening later. I turned to retrace my steps.

"Excuse me," a woman called from somewhere. "Ma'am?"

Uh-oh. This could be trouble. I made the mistake of turning back.

My hailer hurried up the driveway from the street. A dude carrying a big camera on his shoulder followed close behind.

In full makeup and perfectly coiffed shoulder-length hair, the woman wore a green dress under a cream-colored linen blazer.

"Hi." She smiled as she spoke, a particular skill of television broadcasters and politicians. "I'm Nan Tsujimoto with the local news."

As if I wouldn't recognize her. I waited without speaking.

"Do you live here?" She extended the microphone she held toward me.

"No." I wasn't about to tell her I lived next door.

"What do you think of Richard Flora's recent article exposing corruption in AVDA?"

"No comment."

"Are you a neighbor?"

"No comment."

"Have you heard that Regan Greene, your valley district association director, was discovered dead this morning under suspicious circumstances?"

"No comment. If you'll excuse me, I need to get going."

The cameraman murmured something to Tsujimoto.

"I understand you run a wine bar in town, Ms. Barton."

I swore under my breath. He must have been a Vino y Vida customer and recognized me, one of the perils of having a public-facing business.

"You're both on private property," I said. "You need to get back on the street before I call the authorities." I crossed my arms on my chest and watched as they retreated. Camera Dude walked backward, still filming. If I tried that, I'd trip and be flat on my keister in a New York minute.

"We've been speaking with Colinas wine bar proprietor Cece Barton about the horrific murder of the Alexander Valley District Association director Regan Greene," Tsujimoto said. "We'll bring you more breaking news, including our exclusive interview with elderly journalist and muckraker Richard Flora, at five."

She kept talking, but I didn't wait to hear more lies. I hurried to retrace my steps. I was quite sure Richard had not granted them an exclusive interview about anything. I didn't relax until I was safe in my own yard with the gate locked behind me.

Too late, I realized the reporter hadn't asked for my permission to be interviewed and filmed. Didn't she have to? Maybe news stations operated on the time-tested principle of "act first, ask for permission later—or never." I'd have been in the clear if Camera Dude hadn't recognized me. At least I was dressed in a decent outfit and had fluffed up my thick hair after I took off the bike helmet when I arrived home.

Still, I cringed at the thought of being in the public eye. Pouring wine and schmoozing with customers from behind a bar was plenty. I didn't need more.

And Richard needed it even less. I sat in one of the Adirondack chairs on my patio and texted him a heads-up. Not being a fan of texting, he probably wouldn't read it. But if his phone was on and if whoever he was with was a decade or more younger, they might prod him to see what the message was.

I laid the phone on the wide armrest and sat back. The real news was Regan Greene. She, the ambitious woman who rubbed everyone the wrong way, was dead, apparently by homicide. That meant that in the twenty-four hours between when I'd last seen her yesterday at the car show and now, someone had murdered her.

I didn't know a thing about Greene's personal life. I imagined she lived in the Alexander Valley, or the AVDA board wouldn't have made her director. Did she have a spouse? Children? A favorite charity or a place she volunteered, maybe. Perhaps she was a gardener or a devoted auntie. I firmly believed that nobody was all bad. Maybe she'd been bullied as a child, and her aggressive, entitled approach to life was a shield she'd created to protect herself.

My phone came to life with a video call on the app that provides free voice and video calls, including internationally. I smiled and quickly connected with my daughter, Zoe, who was finishing up a college semester abroad in Japan.

Gone were thoughts of murder. I had my beloved only child on the screen.

Chapter 9

I set down the salad I'd brought on Allie's kitchen table at about four fifteen. I'd combined sliced baby cucumbers, sweet, crunchy sticks of jicama, and slivered fresh apricots with cubes of feta cheese. Tossed with a vinaigrette featuring ribbons of fresh basil, the salad was both pretty and tasty. It wasn't themed for Memorial Day, but I figured other dishes might include a red, white, and blue motif.

Everyone was milling around the yard. Allie hadn't told me who else was on the invite list. I grabbed a plastic wine glass and the bottle of Viognier I'd brought and headed out. I set the bottle on the drinks table and glanced around.

"There she is!" Allie grinned and lifted her own outdoor wineglass. "My twinnie, the celebrity of the hour."

What? I froze. This was no casual family cookout. Twenty people sat or stood in various groupings. I spotted the mayor, a couple of people from Allie's real estate agency, my friends Ed and Henry, a local property developer named Gareth Rockwell, and others I didn't know. They were all looking at me.

I came close to turning around and speed-walking home. Instead, I mustered a wan smile and lifted my glass. I pretended to examine a pretend watch on my left wrist.

"Oh, look," I said. "That hour's over."

I let my shoulders relax when people laughed and returned to their conversations. Allie hurried toward me.

"Sorry, Cee," she said before I could speak.

"You should be. You know I hate being the center of attention."

"The video was posted online and everybody was talking about it."

I stared at her. "The reporter said it would air at five today. Last I checked, that was still in the future."

"No, sweetie." Ed Ramirez and Henry Cruvellier appeared at Allie's side. Ed gave me a sympathetic look. "Nan said the interview with Richard would be at five."

"You know her personally?" I asked.

"Sure." Ed beamed. "She eats at Edie's all the time. No idea where she puts the calories, but that girl can pack in a breakfast like you wouldn't believe."

"Some people are blessed with a high metabolism," Henry murmured. As the owner of the art gallery next to my wine bar, he had no trouble eating well and staying slim. His husband, Ed, a well-padded man who loved food with a passion, didn't try to restrict what he ate.

"Like you, Henry," I said. "Hey, it's good to see you both. But, Allie? Please don't spring something like that on me again."

"You're fine, sis." She elbowed me and moved back to her hosting tasks.

I rolled my eyes. "You guys caught the noninterview?"

"Allie told everybody to watch on their phones a half hour ago," Ed said.

"I thought she said this thing got under way at four." I wrinkled my nose.

"She told us three, and everybody else, apparently," Henry said. "We were beginning to wonder where you were."

"Frankly, I'm glad I missed the live showing." I gazed around the yard. Fuller sat in deep conversation with two men I didn't know. Arthur and a young woman who worked with Allie dribbled a soccer ball back and forth. His twin, Franklin, per usual sat at the picnic table lost in a book. Allie talked with Gareth, Malia, and a couple of other people. I lowered my voice. "Why is the mayor here?"

"Allie must be friendly with her." Ed gazed in the same direction.

"I didn't realize she knew her, I mean, well enough to invite to a social occasion."

"You know your sister loves to entertain," Henry said. "It's not that surprising."

"I guess not." I took a good swig of my wine.

"So, *mija*, give us the scoop on Richard."

"And on the murder," Henry said. "You must know something about that, too."

"While we can, let's sit and chat." Ed gestured at three chairs clustered near the house. "Somebody could interrupt us any minute."

"Okay." I blew out a breath as I let myself be led to a seat. "I basically don't know anything about Regan Greene except what I witnessed at the car show yesterday. But I talked with Richard this morning about how his article has gone viral. Have you read it?"

"We both have." Henry pursed his lips. "It's an unvarnished look at the sausage factory of the corrupt district association, and it's not pretty. I'm surprised he learned as much as he did without being discovered."

"I'm surprised he wasn't the homicide victim," Ed said.

I winced.

"Sorry, Cece, but he ruffled almost more feathers than Regan Greene's." Ed waggled his considerable eyebrows. "Richard should watch his back."

"He might already be doing that," I said. "He was supposed to be home hanging out with a twentysomething great-nephew, but nobody was around when I got back from church and the farmers market. I texted him about the reporter, but he might not have seen the message."

"My *madrecita* is younger than Richard," Ed said. "She has no idea how to text."

"Richard definitely knows how, but he doesn't like writing or reading anything other than fully formed sentences with appropriate punctuation." I smiled. "Can't blame him, really."

Henry glanced up from his phone. "Uh-oh. Fast moving wildfire near Cloverdale."

The sleepy town was over the hills about ten miles north of here.

"Which way is the wind blowing?" Ed asked.

"Not in our direction—yet." Henry slid the phone into his shirt pocket.

"May it stay that way and keep clear of the good people of Cloverdale," I said.

"We aren't Los Angeles, but nobody wants fire roaring into their town," Ed agreed.

"You're thinking of those horrible fires in the winter of 2025?" I asked.

He nodded. "They're still rebuilding down there."

"What a nightmare," Henry murmured.

"Hey, you didn't bring your Carrera to the car show yesterday." I knew Henry drove his primo-condition seventy-two Porsche sparingly.

"And have strangers' filthy hands pawing it?" He shuddered. "No thank you, Cece." He pulled out a folded handkerchief as pristine as his vintage auto and patted his forehead.

Ed gave him a fond smile. "My husband is rather protective of his sweet ride."

"I get it." I felt my shoulders relax. Between a quiet chat

with good friends and a nearly empty glass of wine, the tension I hadn't realized I was holding melted away.

My relaxed state didn't last long. Mayor Malia approached.

"Could I have a word with you, Cece?"

"Um, sure." I stayed seated.

She gave Henry and Ed a look. "Gentlemen?"

CHAPTER 10

Malia sat in the chair Ed had vacated. I sipped my wine and waited. She drummed her fingernails on the arm of the chair as she gazed around the yard. She finally looked over at me.

"Forgive me for interrupting your conversation with your friends, Cece, but I understand you are something of a private investigator."

"No." I shook my head. "I'm not."

"That's not what your sister and others say."

"Malia, I own a popular wine bar here in town. That's it."

"But you've looked into previous homicides in Colinas."

I lifted a shoulder and dropped it. "I've unavoidably been drawn into a couple of investigations, true. But I have no training, no expertise, no credentials. None. Zip."

She focused across the yard again. Arthur whooped as he kicked the soccer ball past Allie's colleague. Fuller turned on the gas grill and scrubbed the cooking grate with a wire brush. Gareth glanced over at us and gave me a little wave. I smiled at him. He'd managed to escape his money-grubbing family's possibly illegal clutches and now worked at building much-needed low-cost housing in the area.

"Very well," Malia said. "I'm the presiding mayor of our town. You must understand that I'm concerned about the criminal behind Regan's murder being apprehended with all due speed."

"Naturally," I said. "But that's the purview of Chief Fenner and the county sheriff's department. Not mine." I narrowed my eyes at her, remembering what she'd told me at the car show. "Are you worried because you have history with the victim?"

"What?" She blinked and gave her head a sharp little shake. "No, of course not. I'm not a murderer."

"Great. I should hope not."

"What about Richard Flora? You are friends with him as well as neighbors, I hear."

"I am." I drained my glass and desperately wished for an escape from this little mayoral grilling. "What about him?"

"Don't be cute, Cece. We all saw the TV bit. The association is already breathing down my neck to come out publicly and refute his accusations. It's not in my job description, but I'm getting a lot of pressure from the powers that be."

"Sorry to hear that," I said.

"So, where is he?"

I'd had enough. I stood. "I don't know. He's a well-respected private citizen, and he doesn't report to me. Have a nice afternoon, Malia." I refilled my wine at the drinks table and scooted onto the bench next to my studious nephew.

"Auntie Cee, were you arguing with the mayor?" Franklin asked.

"Not exactly."

"I bet she was asking you to solve the homicide Arthur and I aren't supposed to know about."

I smiled and ruffled his curly dark hair. "Yes, she was. I told her I had zero qualifications for that."

"And Chief Fenner and Deputy Sheriff Detective Sergeant Daniell are on the case, right?"

I stared at him. This kid was too smart. "Do you know that Kelly has been assigned to it?"

"Well, she called Mommy this morning." He tried not to smile but failed. "I have hyper-acute hearing, you know."

"I do know. Yes, I told the mayor that solving the case was the job of law enforcement officials."

"It looks like Ms. Gutierrez is leaving." He pointed.

Malia, purse slung over her shoulder, was speaking with Allie. As we watched, she first glanced in my direction but made her way toward the driveway.

"She doesn't look happy," Franklin said.

"She sure doesn't." I looked at his book. "What are you reading?"

"It's a history of the Great Migration, when Blacks moved north in great numbers."

"Good stuff."

"There are a few novels about it, but Daddy won't let me read them until I'm older, unless they're written for my age group."

"Let me guess," I said. "Novels for middle school kids are too easy and too lightweight for you."

"That's correct." Franklin let out the sigh of a much-older and much-burdened person. "It's really not fair."

"You'll get there, sweetie. You're lucky, you know. My dyslexia got in the way of my reading almost anything for years."

"But you read a lot." He looked up at me with big, curly lashed dark eyes. "You listen to books instead."

"I do. I'm always grateful for audiobooks."

"Hey, Cece, Franklin." Gareth strolled toward us. "How're you doing, kiddo?"

"I'm fine, thank you, Gareth." Franklin bent his head over his book again.

I slid off the bench. "How's the project going?" I asked Gareth.

"Pretty well." He gestured away from the tables, and I strolled with him to the edge of the yard.

"It looked like the mayor was grilling you about something." He lifted his Giants cap and rubbed his shaved head.

"She pretty much was. Trying to get me to say I'm a PI. She's the public servant. I run a business and own a house."

"You have to admit you and Allie caught the bad guy a few months ago, not the police."

"You helped a bit, as I recall." I smiled at him. "Anyway, I learned yesterday that Malia and Regan Greene shared a history. I don't know what, but the mayor seemed oddly interested in my neighbor's whereabouts."

"Mr. Flora?"

"Yes." I took a sip of wine. "So, tell me about the building project. Your response sounded qualified when I asked."

"Do you know the site?" he asked.

"On the outskirts of town, right?"

"Yeah, up against the hills. Permitting is hitting all kinds of snags. We'll have to do special fire-prevention clearing."

"That's got to be a good thing. A wildfire is raging near Cloverdale right now."

"I know. The state also has new requirements about drainage." Gareth let out a sigh. "I must say, Malia seems to be dragging her feet, and the city council is going along with her. I can't figure out why. But we'll get there."

"The need for affordable housing must be huge."

"It absolutely is. People who work at the lower-wage jobs need somewhere to live. Loads of vineyard workers fall into that category. You can't make the wine the valley is famous for if you can't house the people who make it."

The smell of meat grilling wafted over. I hadn't eaten any living-being flesh other than fish for over a decade, but the aroma of beef or chicken cooking over hot coals still made me drool.

"Everybody?" Allie called. "Food is ready."

"Shall we?" I asked Gareth.

"After you, ma'am."

Chapter 11

It was three weeks before the equinox, and the dusk was gathering but the sun hadn't quite set when I walked home a little after eight o'clock. I glanced at Richard's windows and didn't see any evidence he was home unless he was in his garden. In the back, I opened the gate from my own yard and peeked through. No neighbor in sight.

Maybe his great-nephew had driven him down to San Francisco to stay with his lady friend and get away from the pestering press. I locked my gate and headed inside. I had a tiny, nagging worry that Richard could be inside his house and not able to call for help. I tried to dismiss it. I didn't have a key to his door, and Pete should be home sooner or later. The next time I saw Pete, I was going to make a point of getting his cell number, just in case.

"Yes, kitties, you get your evening treat," I told Mittens and Martin, only one of which had complained about food not being forthcoming. I opened a chewy protein stick for each of them and dropped them into their respective treat bowls.

My human treat was a square of dark chocolate and a mug of apple-cinnamon tea spiked with a dash of cognac. Allie had offered a red, white, and blue cake for dessert, but after my grilled scallops and hefty portions of all the sides, I didn't have room for anything sweet. I took out my hair clip and settled in with my tablet on the couch. Maybe I could learn about Malia's history with Regan.

In my mind I rehashed the afternoon. Allie and I hadn't had a chance to catch up about anything, but we agreed to meet for breakfast at Edie's Diner tomorrow. Richard and his article had been the talk of the gathering for a little while, until nobody had any real news to add.

I hadn't heard any real news about Regan Greene's death, either. Why did the authorities believe it was a homicide? How had she died, and where? I might find developments about that online.

It was interesting that the county sheriff's detective I'd met last fall, Kelly Daniell, had called Allie about the case, according to Franklin. I was sure what he said was true. The kid recorded and valued facts way more than many adults. At least Kelly and I had come to a peaceful détente by the end of the previous investigation when I played a key role in nailing the villain. The county detective on last winter's murder had been Jim Quan, since Kelly had been out on maternity leave. He and I had ended the case on a friendly basis, too.

Malia pressuring me for information was what I found disturbing. She was the mayor of Colinas, for goodness' sake. I sipped my tea and nibbled at the chocolate. I popped the rest of the square in my mouth and fired up the internet.

I started by doing a simple search on Regan Greene. It seemed like an unusual enough name for the results to be about her and not a hundred others with the same name. I was wrong. Adding AVDA was the qualifier I needed.

First, not surprisingly, were a couple of articles about her death. I learned that she lived in a newish subdivision in Colinas, and that she'd been AVDA director for three years. Chief Fenner was quoted as saying the Colinas police were cooperating with the county sheriff's office, and anyone with information about the homicide should call the department.

What I did not learn was anything about where Regan's dead body was discovered, by whom, and how she lost her life. I knew it was too soon for all that to be made public, if it was even known, but looking was worth a try.

Next I paired Regan's name with Malia Gutierrez. Now we were getting somewhere. About ten years earlier, they had run against each other for state representative, one from each major party. The article I came across described the competition as an acrimonious race for a hotly contested seat. By the first Tuesday in November, a popular male candidate surged forward to capture the majority vote. He was a No Party Preference voter, not registered with either political party.

I wouldn't think running against each other for public office would be the source of a long-standing resentment, or whatever the hard feelings were. Both women had ended up in different kinds of public positions. I'd never run for any office, not even in elementary school. That kind of contest was for Allie, not me. She had been elected class president in sixth grade as well as in our senior year of high school.

Speaking of Allie, she said the two women had clashed over love, as well. That wasn't the kind of thing that made the news, though. I gave a quick glance at Malia's official web page on the town site. It didn't mention a spouse or children. I couldn't remember whether I'd noticed her wearing a wedding ring or not. I switched to Regan's AVDA page. Same lack of memory, same results.

I set down the tablet and yawned, cradling my mug in both hands. I'd decided to keep Vino y Vida closed tomorrow, Memorial Day, although we often opened on holidays. My employees and I all needed a day off. People had enough other places in town to sip wine.

I tapped in a message to Benjamin.

Miss you. Can't wait for tomorrow.

His reply came in almost immediately.

Same. About to board my flight home. XXOO.

That made me smile. I switched on the nonfiction book I was reading about young women cracking codes in World War II and resolved not to give homicide or missing neighbors another thought until the morning.

Chapter 12

Ed set down two heaping platters in front of Allie and me in an Edie's Diner booth the next morning at nine.

"One Memorial Day waffle with salmon bacon for Cece," Ed announced.

"Yum." I could always go for a plate-sized buckwheat waffle topped with cinnamon-spiced sour cream, blueberries, and strawberries. Thin strips of cured salmon were a perfect accompaniment.

"And one Butcher Shop Special for Allie," he added.

She rolled her eyes. "It's not called that. I ordered a ham-and-cheddar omelet with beef hash and chicken links."

Ed flipped his palms open. "I rest my case. Hey, thanks for a great party yesterday. Fabulous food."

"I'm glad you both could make it," Allie said. "Are you going to the town picnic this afternoon?"

"No," he said. "I'm open regular hours today, and two of my waitstaff asked for the day off weeks ago. A big town picnic isn't really Henry's thing. He's opening the gallery in an hour, anyway. Enjoy your meal, *queridas*."

I thanked him and cut into my waffle. Allie did the same with her meat-laden breakfast. We ate in silence for a moment. At home I normally began my day with granola over yogurt and cut-up fruit or berries. Sometimes I sipped a green smoothie on the side.

But breakfast at the diner was always a treat. I didn't care how decadent it was. I took a sip of my coffee.

"Where are your menfolk this morning?" I asked.

"They're making breakfast with Fuller and then going to fly kites. I mean, they're all going, but I'm sure Artie and Fuller will do the flying and Frankie will advise on the physics of it all."

I laughed. "Your twins are as different as you and I are."

"No kidding." She ate a bite of omelet. "So, did you ever find Richard?"

"No." I frowned. "He didn't seem to be home after I left your place last evening, and he hasn't replied to my text. That reminds me, I need to get Pete's number from Ed while I'm here."

"Because Pete used to cook for him."

"Exactly. Don't let me forget to ask. Richard might be fine, but I'm a little worried about him."

"I get it, believe me," Allie said.

"Did you ever have personal dealings with Regan Greene?"

"Not really. I met her at a mixer, but I never had to do anything official where she was involved." Her fork speared the taut casing of a sausage, making the juice spurt out toward me. "Oops, sorry."

"It's okay. You missed me." I kept my voice low. "I suppose you haven't heard anything about the investigation into Regan's death. You know, on the grapevine. You're nothing if not tied into all the local news."

She grinned. "Yes, and I love it, but so far, no news on that front. Today is a national holiday, remember. I bet we'll learn more tomorrow."

I glanced up when a woman in pants and a dark blazer approached our booth. I did a classic double take. "Kelly?"

"Good morning, ladies," the detective said. Kelly Daniell was looking vibrant and full of energy.

"Hello, Detective. Want to join us?" Allie scooted on the bench toward the wall.

"That'd be great, if you don't mind." Kelly sat next to my twin.

Ed appeared with a place setting, an empty mug, and a pot of coffee. "Would you like to order, Kelly?"

"Yes, please. A veggie omelet, no cheese, with fruit instead of toast." She eyed my small plate. "Is that salmon bacon?"

"Yes," I said. "It's delicious."

"And a side of that, Ed."

"Healthy special, coming right up." He held up the coffeepot. "Coffee all around?"

"Yes, please," Kelly said.

Allie nodded, but I held my hand over my mug. I was wired enough naturally, and I'd already had my two cups for the day.

"You're looking great," I said to Kelly after Ed left.

"Thanks."

"You had your second child, right?" Allie asked.

"Yes, and I decided it was time to pay attention to my well-being. Portion control and exercise combined with nursing can do wonders." She smiled, and the new definition in her face let the dimple in her cheek stand out.

"Congratulations on all of it." I raised my water glass. "Here's to health."

"Indeed, and thanks." The detective lifted her mug.

"I suppose you came looking to talk with us about Regan Greene," Allie murmured.

"I'd like to, yes," Kelly said. "It's my case, as I mentioned to you yesterday."

"Are there any developments?"

"Not as yet, no."

Ed delivered her low-carb breakfast. "Enjoy."

"*Gracias*, Eduardo." Kelly's accent in Spanish sounded nearly native.

"*No hay de qué*." He beamed.

"Ed," I began, "when you get a chance, will you please text me Pete Flora's number?"

"I'll do it right now, *mija*."

My phone dinged with the text. "Thanks."

"Let me know what else you need." He strolled back down the aisle, checking with customers as he went.

"Pete Flora, as in Richard Flora, yes?" Kelly frowned. "I haven't been able to reach Mr. Flora the elder."

"Nor I," I said. "I'm sure everything's fine, but Pete is his great-nephew who lives with him. I haven't seen him, either. He owns the Tia Tamale food truck, but he wasn't at the farmers market yesterday. I want to touch base with him about Richard."

"Please forward Pete's number to me." Kelly forked in a bite of omelet.

I obliged. "Done. Kelly, can you tell us anything about how Regan died and who found her?"

She held up a finger. I ate my last bite of waffle, scooting two berries onto my fork to go with it. My carnivorous twin finished her hash and half of the last sausage.

"The short answer to the first part of your question is no," Kelly said. "I'm not at liberty to share the second part."

"Was she at home?" Allie asked. "I know she lives in the subdivision where Cece and I ran into a murderer this winter."

"Allie, I can't talk about it, okay?" Kelly attacked her bowl of cut-up melon and pineapple.

She was running a classic one-way information street, as the police often do. Nothing much we could do about that, but what was important was finding the killer. I shared what I could.

"At the car show Saturday, Regan seemed to have run-ins with a couple of people," I offered.

"Yes?" Kelly's dark eyebrows shot up.

"With Greg Jardis, for one," Allie said. "She asked him why he moved to Colinas, as if he'd followed her here. She clearly wasn't happy about it."

"So noted," Kelly said. "Who else?"

"I saw her clash with Mayor Gutierrez," I said. "I did a little research yesterday. The two apparently had an acrimonious run for the same state office about a decade ago, and neither won."

"Yes, and there was a man they fought over, too," Allie added.

"Thank you both. Anything else?" Kelly popped in the last bite of her omelet.

Did I want to throw Dane under the bus? No. Her conflict with Regan might have been nothing. While my artist employee was a bit scatterbrained, she was generally a good worker, and I needed her.

"Not from me," Allie said.

I shook my head.

"All right. You both know the drill, right? You hear anything, learn anything, you let me know." She held thumb and pinkie to her ear to mimic a phone call. She patted her mouth with her napkin and stood, gesturing around the table. "Thanks for the tips. I've got your meals." She slung her bag over her shoulder and turned away.

"Thank you," Allie said.

"Good luck," I called after Kelly.

She was going to need it.

CHAPTER 13

Benjamin raised his cup that afternoon at one thirty. He was looking finc, as always. His dark hair was clean and smelled of rainwater, and the silver streaks at his temples gave him a handsome leading man vibe.

"Cheers, beautiful."

I reached across the picnic cloth where we sat and clinked my cup with his. I'd filled two insulated metal cups shaped like stemless wineglasses with a fine sauvignon blanc. The pint cups, which came with sipping lids, were from the Twomey winery, as was the vintage.

"Cheers. How was your trip?"

"All right. My parents are generally healthy, but they're talking about selling their house and buying into one of those full-service retirement communities." Benjamin had turned fifty in February, but his parents had him fairly late in life and were in their mid-eighties.

"A house in Brooklyn should be worth a hefty sum these days," I said. "I've heard Allie talk about the housing market on the East Coast. It's as out of control as it is around here."

"They'll be able to afford the move, for sure." He smiled at me. "I missed you."

"Likewise." I returned the smile. "This is a perfect spot."

The temperature had to be at least eighty, but he'd snagged a spot in the shade of a big tree. The bluegrass band playing in the gazebo wasn't overamplified, and all around us families and groups of young adults sat eating and talking, with kids running about and a rousing coed softball game happening on the nearby diamond.

"Hungry?" He flipped open the top of a small picnic basket and began drawing out containers.

A couple of minutes later, we each had a plate loaded with Greek eggplant salad, pasta salad with feta and olives, spicy, crunchy cornichons, and hunks of chewy bread we tore off a crusty baguette.

"This is wonderful," I said after tasting every dish. "Did you cook all morning?"

"As if." He laughed. "But Gourmet Provisions did, and I'm grateful."

"I am too."

We sat and ate and sipped. The music stopped. A few people clapped. The lead fiddler tapped the microphone.

"Thank you, everybody, and happy Memorial Day in Colinas!" He waited until cheers died down. "Now, please give our fine Mayor Gutierrez your ears for a few words."

Malia stepped forward. "Welcome, and thanks to everyone for coming out to honor our fallen heroes. Our honored veterans will present their program in a moment. But first, you may have heard of the untimely death of our esteemed district valley association director. We will now observe a moment of silence for Regan Greene, in thanks for her years of dedicated service. May she rest in peace."

I glanced at Benjamin's furrowed brow. As soon as Malia began speaking again, he turned to me.

"What happened to Greene?" he asked.

"I don't know, exactly, but they are investigating her death as a homicide."

He gave a low whistle. "Seriously?"

"Yes. I saw the woman in action at the car show Saturday. There didn't seem to be anyone she didn't come in conflict with. Me excluded, thank goodness."

"You're not exactly the type to provoke altercations." Benjamin, in green Bermuda shorts, leaned back against the tree trunk and stretched out his tanned runner's legs. Lean as well as muscled, I'd admired them from the beginning.

"Yeah. I'm about as averse to conflict as they come."

"So, who did the victim pick a fight with?" he asked.

I gestured toward the gazebo, where a uniformed veteran Richard's age leaned on a walker as he spoke in a quavering voice. Malia hovered nearby as if to rescue him if he needed it.

"Our esteemed mayor, for one." I added what I'd seen happen with Greg Jardis and with Dane. "Have you met Jardis?"

"The new hardware store owner?"

"Yes."

"Sure," Benjamin said. "I spoke with him when I was buying that new fencing a few weeks ago. Nice guy."

"He seems to be, although I doubt Regan would have agreed with you. But what really worries me is an article Richard wrote."

"I came across a link to that and read it on the plane to New York. Your sweet old neighbor is quite the muckraker."

"Yes, but now he's also missing in action."

"What?" Benjamin sat up straight. "He's not home and you can't reach him?"

"Both. I called his great-nephew and left a message, but I haven't heard back from him." I called Pete as soon as I left the diner this morning. "Reporters were apparently hounding Richard, and one accosted me yesterday when I was checking out his house. I wouldn't blame Richard for escaping elsewhere. I only wish he'd told me."

"Let me see what I can find out."

I gazed at him. I still wasn't quite sure what he did for work, other than it involved consulting on software issues, often including cybersecurity. He never wanted to go into detail with me about his various jobs, but he had his sources, which sometimes were people in various branches of law enforcement. I wasn't worried. I trusted him with my emotions, and I knew what he did wasn't illegal. That was all I needed.

Sitting with my favorite man as I sipped wine and nibbled little pickles was the extent of my ambition right now. People-watching was fun, too. And here came a person I knew or at least had met.

Greg Jardis strolled arm in arm with a somewhat younger woman in a sundress and sandals whose hair fell in waves on her shoulders. She wasn't the same person he was with Saturday night. Did I want to hail him to say hello? *Nah.*

She glanced over at me. "Hey, Cece."

I blinked. The woman was Dane Larsen, my part-time employee. I'd only ever seen her in practical clothes, hair in a messy knot on top of her head. She usually had paint on her hands or cheek, but not today.

"Um, hi, Dane." I laughed lightly. "I didn't recognize you for a second there. Hello, Greg." I pushed up to standing.

Benjamin followed suit and held out his hand to Greg. "Good to see you again, Jardis."

"Likewise." Greg shook his hand.

"Dane, you've met Benjamin?" I asked.

"Yes." She smiled.

"Are you two enjoying the afternoon?" Benjamin asked.

Dane shot Greg a smile. He blushed.

"We are," Dane said.

I was itching to ask her what she and Regan had a beef about. This didn't seem like one. I didn't know what Greg's marital status was, although he'd had a dinner date with a different woman Saturday night. Dane was happily divorced. If she'd found new happiness or at least an active dating life, more power to her.

Apparently Benjamin didn't share my opinion about not bothering them about the homicide. "I understand you both knew Regan Greene," Benjamin said. "Let me offer my condolences on her death."

Dane's jaw dropped. Greg's eyes narrowed for a brief moment.

"My sympathies, as well." I used the sweetest voice I had.

Greg recovered first. "That's very kind of you two. Well, we need to be getting along. We have early dinner reservations, isn't that right, Daney?"

"Yes." She gave a little smile as a frown wrinkled her forehead. "Enjoy the rest of your day." She nearly pulled Greg with her and didn't look back.

"Well, well," Benjamin said.

"You're a brave man. I considered asking at least her about her run-in with Regan but decided not to."

He turned to me and pulled me in close. "I hope you think brave is a good thing."

"Are you kidding?" I murmured into his chest. "Every time."

Chapter 14

Benjamin snored lightly next to me on the couch in his living room that evening. We came back and agreed to watch a movie. Benjamin slipped into dreamland after only ten minutes. The poor guy had a three-hour time difference to adjust to, and we both would be off to our respective jobs tomorrow. He deserved his beauty sleep.

I switched off the film and sat back to think. Dane plus Greg was an interesting pairing. He seemed to be a bit of a ladies' man, flirting with any woman in sight. Good heavens, even Allie had blushed when he'd greeted her.

But my impression of him could be wrong. He seemed sincere when he'd asked Regan to be friendly, and he'd used a nickname for her. Dane, whose her first marriage had ended at her own instigation, was honest and attractive. Who wouldn't want a romance with her? I hoped she knew he was also going out with other women.

Heck, my own first marriage hadn't been happy, either, except I didn't have the confidence to end it. My husband's sudden death had solved that problem. Coming back to a place of trusting men had taken me a decade, but I was there now, and grateful I'd met Benjamin last year when I was finally ready for romance and intimacy.

I was disturbed by the dual problems of not knowing how Regan had died along with not knowing where Richard was. I checked my phone, remembering I had muted it earlier in the afternoon. Nobody had tried to reach me. Why didn't Pete return at least a text? I kept the device set to Do Not Disturb so anything incoming wouldn't wake Benjamin.

Something else I didn't know was why both Dane and Greg had reacted the way they had when Benjamin brought up Regan's death. Had it been alarm? Shock, maybe, but for what reason? Each of them had interacted with the victim in public two days ago.

And then there was the conflict between Malia and Regan. Malia had mentioned something about . . . what? Jurisdiction, maybe, or power. She also said Richard's article addressed what was going on. Right now was a perfect time for me to finally give his exposé a careful read. I went in search of the link.

Before I could find it, an incoming text from Allie vibrated my phone.

Can you come over 7 AM Weds to see twins off to school? Fuller has early appt in SF, wants me with him.

I frowned at the message. What kind of appointment? If it was for his work as a financial adviser, why would he want Allie to go with him? I wrinkled my nose. Did they need to see a lawyer together? I'd never seen or heard about a speck of conflict in their marriage. They could be doing estate planning, but why go to San Francisco for that? Our area had plenty of good lawyers to choose from.

Maybe the reason was a doctor's visit, except nobody up here drove ninety miles into the big city unless they needed to see a high-power medical specialist. I didn't have a great feeling about this.

Regardless of the reason for the trip, I would always help them with my favorite kiddos when I could.

I'll be there. Can't do after school, tho.

It took her less than a minute to reply.

Thx. We'll be back in early PM.

K. What kind of appt?

I waited. She wouldn't tell me if she didn't want to. Or if Fuller didn't want her to, more likely.

Tell you later. XXOO

I pinged her in return.

OOXX

I almost never was up and presentable early in the morning. Wednesday, I'd have to be. I yawned. Maybe I'd read Richard's article tomorrow.

CHAPTER 15

I strode briskly home from Benjamin's at eight the next morning. He offered to give me a lift on his way to work, but my place was only two miles away, and I wanted the exercise.

Walking fast and breathing deeply made me cough. Smoke was in the air, with a haze overlaying the sunshine. If the wind had shifted, Cloverdale was in trouble. And if the fire kept coming south, we were, too.

Richard's driveway was empty of cars and reporters. Good on the second count, and possibly meaningless on the first. Richard still drove during daylight hours, and leaving his car in the attached garage for a week at a time wasn't a bit out of the ordinary for him.

Once inside, I changed into shorts and an old T-shirt. I didn't have to be at work until noonish to prepare for our one o'clock opening. The kitties got breakfast and either an extended jaw rub (Martin) or a session of ball play (Mittens). I let them out into the backyard with me and turned on the hose.

"*Ola*, Cecelia," Richard called from his side of the fence.

Awesome. "*Ola!*" I let the hose run into the nearest bed and hurried to unlock the gate. "You're back, Richard. I'm so glad." I pulled him into a hug.

"Well, land sakes, neighbor. Of course I'm back. I live here."

He stepped back, but he was smiling. "It isn't every morning I get a hug from a lovely young lady. Come sit with me, if you have time, and tell me what you've been up to."

If at all possible, I planned to flip that question straight back at him. I turned off the hose and followed him into his yard, shutting the gate before the cats could come with us. I perched on a chair facing him.

"Do you know why I hugged you?" I asked.

"Because I am a dapper, erudite, older gentleman?" He grinned. Richard was dapper when he dressed up. This morning, he was wearing his usual gardening pants and a misbuttoned and faded plaid shirt with holes in the elbows.

"Yeah, no. It's because you've been missing for forty-eight hours. You're back, and I'm beyond relieved. That's why I hugged you."

"Oh, that." He lifted his chin and gazed toward the grapevine trellised on the far wall, where pale green clusters of tiny infant grapes hung. Two California quail ran along the top of the wall, stopped to bob their topknots, then ran on.

"I mean," I began, "I understand you wanting to get away from the reporters and so on. One of them tried as hard as she could to question me Sunday afternoon. She also filmed me without my permission."

That got his attention. "I'm so sorry."

"Don't worry. I didn't reveal anything. But you could have let me know where you were, or at least that you were okay, especially in light of the news."

"I coerced my relative to drive me down to the city to see my sweetheart. When I wrote that article, I never for a moment suspected it would receive the kind of attention it has. I truly needed to get away for a bit."

"You didn't take your phone?" I asked.

"As a matter of fact, I forgot it. When I got in last night, it was on the dining table, where I'd left it. Pulling stunts like that comes with being more than nine decades old, I'm afraid." He cocked his head. "What's this news you mentioned?"

He didn't know about Regan. I wasn't sure how that was possible, but, whatever. He might not have turned on the news this morning or yesterday.

"Brace yourself," I said. "Regan Greene was murdered."

His breath rushed in. "My good heavens."

"As you can imagine, the police are wondering where you've been."

"But why? I had no wish to see her dead. For that matter, I wouldn't have the foggiest idea of how to commit homicide."

"Richard, you know that, and I know that. Except she was threatening you with libel and who knows what else. It would be reasonable for the authorities to wonder whether you figured out a way to poison her or hired someone to get rid of her."

"A hit man?" he asked. "Doesn't that happen only in books and movies?"

"I don't know." Was he being deliberately obtuse? "If you check your messages you might have one from Chief Fenner and another from Detective Daniell."

"I promise I'll check when I go indoors. Do you know how the poor woman died?"

"No. I spoke with Kelly Daniell yesterday, but she wouldn't tell me. I don't know who reported Regan's body, either."

"Interesting."

"I haven't had a chance yet to read your article," I said. "Did you get to know Regan personally?"

"I interviewed her, certainly, but we didn't become friendly. It's my job as a journalist, albeit an elderly one, to remain impartial."

I gazed at him. He seemed awfully calm. Maybe it came with the territory of having lived more than nine decades. I only hoped to be as alert and calm if I reached that age.

CHAPTER 16

I loved walking up to Vino y Vida. Colinas did an excellent job of preserving the four historic adobe buildings that were in a cluster at the end of Manzanita Avenue, the main shopping thoroughfare. The cluster was perched on a bank of the Russian River, which, due to the drought, right now was more of a streamlet.

After the public parking area, the first building was the historical museum just before my wine bar. A small riverside park area came next, including a bocce ball court. Acorn Fine Art and Sculpture, Henry's gallery, and Alexander Books were across the way. We all leased our buildings from the town, but interior improvements and paying utilities were up to each business owner.

And I was a business owner. When I'd first started working at Vino y Vida, I was the manager, but the business was owned by the town. I'd convinced them to change that status, and Allie used her considerable local influence to make sure I didn't have to pay for the ownership.

I often drove and parked Blue in a spot next to my building's back door that was reserved for wine bar staff, but today I had to leave early for a class at the Colinas Community Center, which wasn't far from my house. It would still be light out when I walked home after the class.

As I stepped in the door, I realized those cases of wine were still in Blue's trunk. I should have driven today. *Oh, well.* The car was in my cool, closed garage. The wine would keep until tomorrow.

Inside, I tied on one of our burgundy half aprons and set about preparing for the day and our opening time of one o'clock, a scant hour from now. As I brought out bottles and set up glasses, I thought about my conversation with Richard. He'd struck me as evasive, which wasn't like him, or maybe he was being avoidant. I hoped he wasn't losing his mental acuity. He was over ninety, and we all were lucky he was as sharp as he usually was.

I headed over to the patio door and unlocked it. Outside, a breeze rustled the leaves of the giant, ancient live oak tree that shaded the outdoor seating area. I wiped down the tops of the wine barrel tables and left the door propped open to the fresh air. The wind must have shifted, because it no longer smelled smoky.

I took a moment to lean my forearms on the iron railing and gaze down at the trickle of water in the middle of the streambed. We'd had more than the usual winter rains, but by now no precipitation had fallen since February. If we didn't get some soon, the grape harvest the valley depended on would be puny.

Mooncat arrived on time at twelve thirty clad in a black T-shirt tucked into a short denim skirt with black fishnet tights and red Doc Martens boots. I wore simple black capris and a pale pink top with three-quarter-length sleeves. I didn't ever opt for flamboyant. Mooncat had that covered for both of us.

Together we worked to set out crackers, both regular and gluten-free, and scribe the day's pourings onto the whiteboard. She wiped down all the inside tables and made sure we had lines of glasses ready, and I did all the other bits.

"Crazy about the murder, isn't it?" she asked along the way.

"Crazy scary, is what. Have you heard about Richard's article?"

"Kind of, but I haven't read it. Tell me more."

"Unfortunately, I haven't made time to go through it, either, but it sounds like he has a close focus on Regan's actions with the valley district association and how it's generally corrupt." I went on to tell her about my neighbor going missing and reappearing.

"Do you think he's losing it up here?" She tapped her head.

"Not really, but he has been acting a little off."

"The police must have their hands full, checking out people who had beefs with Regan Greene."

"Totally," I said. "Hey, remember I have my class tonight. Dane will be here at five."

"Got it."

"Speaking of beefs, at the town picnic yesterday, Benjamin and I saw Dane and Greg Jardis walking arm in arm. I told Benjamin about seeing each of them tangle—separately—with Regan at the car show. Benjamin offered his condolences to them on her death. Both Dane and Greg looked alarmed or shocked or something. I couldn't quite interpret their expressions, and then they hurried away."

"Maybe they killed her together." Mooncat's eyes sparkled at the thought.

"Or not, but if you get a chance to weasel anything out of Dane, let me know."

"You bet." She tilted her head. "He was with a different woman Saturday at Hoppy's. Playing the field, I guess."

"I hope for Dane's sake he's open about that." I glanced at the wall clock. "Time to unlock the door. Let's try to talk later. If you read the article, give me the Cliff Notes version, okay?"

"It's a deal."

I headed over to the front door and unlocked it without focusing on who was on the other side of the glass. When I saw Nan Tsujimoto trying to shove a fat microphone in my face, I almost slammed the door and relocked it. Instead, I took a step back but kept my hand on the door.

"Cece Barton, as Mr. Flora's next-door neighbor, have you seen him?" she asked.

The camera guy hovered behind her, device on his shoulder, lens aimed at me.

"I have nothing to say." I folded my arms on my chest. "I do not give my permission to be filmed or recorded."

Camera Dude nudged the reporter and gave his head a shake.

"Please, Ms. Barton," Nan said. "We only want an update."

I shook my head and turned away. Mooncat strode up and took my place. She was taller than either of them. She set her fists on her hips.

"You heard her," Mooncat said. "We need you both to turn around and leave. You're scaring the clientele." She gestured with her chin to the sidewalk, where several people milled around behind the news crew.

To my eye, they looked fascinated, not scared. I wasn't about to contradict my determined defender.

The man with the camera took it off his shoulder and sidled away.

"May I have your name?" Nan asked Mooncat.

"No." She took a step forward.

The reporter finally lowered the microphone and slipped through the growing crowd outside.

"Come on in, folks—as long as you aren't reporters." Mooncat laughed and ushered the would-be sippers inside.

I was content to focus on what I did best these days. I explained the wines and poured while I schmoozed with strangers from the other side of a wide slab of polished redwood, the beautiful bar that had come with the business. We served two couples visiting from Iowa, a class of five adult students studying to be restaurant sommeliers, a bride-to-be and her three sisters, and a group of Spanish tourists.

If work kept me distracted from worrying about Richard and considering who among the many of Regan's enemies had killed her, so much the better.

CHAPTER 17

Dane, her hair back up in its messy knot and a smudge of paint on her earlobe, arrived before her short shift at five. When she first started working for me, half the time she showed up late because she'd gotten lost in her painting. Without getting upset, I was firm and kept on her about how I needed her to be here on time or else employing her wasn't going to work out. She'd finally figured out how to accomplish that.

Today I didn't have to leave until 5:30 for my class. I'd learned a lot about vintages and grape varieties since I started managing Vino y Vida, but it had all been by the seat of my pants. I figured I could pick up knowledge useful to my job in a more structured setting from a teacher well versed in the wine industry.

After Dane was settled in with apron and clean hands behind the bar, I grabbed my dinner and perched on a stool next to her.

"Did you enjoy the festivities yesterday?" I took a bite of the sandwich I'd brought, a yummy combo of cheese, humus, and lettuce on whole-grain bread. "You and Greg looked happy together."

"It was fun." She straightened the baskets of crackers and the already straight row of glasses.

"Have you two been dating long?"

"No."

Mooncat came in from the patio carrying a tray full of dirty glasses. "Quite the party going on out there."

"As long as they're not tossing glasses into the riverbed, they are welcome to carouse." In here, only two tables were occupied, and all the glasses were still half full. Quiet was fine with me while it lasted.

"Hey, Dane," Mooncat said.

"How's it going, Martha?" Dane asked.

As a teenager, Dane's father had babysat Mooncat and her brother, at a time well before she'd officially changed her name. She allowed very few people to use her original name, and Dane was one of them.

"Life is good, you know?" Mooncat grinned. Her phone pinged and she pulled it out of the back pocket of her skirt. And frowned. "That woman wouldn't take no for an answer. Check this out, Cece." She tapped it and held up the device facing Dane and me.

Nan Tsujimoto spoke into the camera in the dramatic voice of a newscaster. "Colinas wine bar proprietor Cece Barton continues to refuse to talk about her neighbor Richard Flora's mysterious whereabouts and how his disappearance relates to the homicide of the Alexander Valley District Association director Regan Greene. What is Barton hiding? Stay tuned for news at five. For KSM News, this is Nan Tsujimoto." The camera backed up to show the front of Vino y Vida.

"Oh, for . . ." I kept myself from uttering the expletives I wanted to say. "I'm not hiding anything! Sheesh."

"At least they didn't sneak in a video you expressly didn't agree to," Mooncat said.

"Your phone dinged," I said. "How did you know that clip had aired?"

"I set a search alert for news about Regan Greene from that station."

"You can do that?" I was reasonably savvy when it came to the internet, but I had no idea one could set search alerts.

"Sure." Mooncat looked at Dane. "Speaking of Regan, Dane, a friend told me he saw you arguing with her on Saturday. How did you know her?"

Dane's eyes flew wide open. "What? Why do you want to know?"

"Just curious." Mooncat shrugged. "The woman was murdered, in case you haven't heard."

Dane winced. Mooncat folded her arms and waited. I ate the last bite of my sandwich.

"It was nothing, really," Dane finally said. "She had a complaint about one of my paintings. That's all it was."

"Did she commission something from you?" I asked.

"No, but the valley district association did as part of a campaign to support local art. My piece is pretty big, and it's hanging in the AVDA building over in Las Madres."

"How could she argue with a painting?" Mooncat asked. "It's not an Alexander Valley collage of green vineyards, restored Victorian homes, and rolling hills?"

"Not a bit. It depicts several of the many businesses that are part of AVDA along with the association's board. Let's just say I slid in a few subversive allusions, and the way I painted Regan wasn't that flattering to her." Dane rubbed at the bar with a rag. "Now I wish I hadn't done it that way, but it's too late."

The door opened to let in a half dozen customers.

"I'd love to know more." I stood and brushed a few crumbs into my sandwich container. I pressed on the lid. "But I have to get to class. Hold down the fort, ladies. I'll see you tomorrow, Mooncat, and thanks for coming in, Dane."

As I made my way the few blocks to the community center, I thought I might have to fit in a quick trip to Las Madres before work tomorrow.

Chapter 18

"Any questions on this section?" Zeke Cruz, our teacher, asked at the end of the first half of class. After the first hour, he always gave us a break. Many of the twenty students used the facilities or headed outdoors for a smoke or a breath of fresh air. Others munched on sandwiches, checked their phones, or got to know each other.

"No questions?" Zeke asked. "Then please be back in ten minutes. We have an exciting guest speaker joining us for the second hour."

Chairs scraped on the floor and a buzz of conversation rose up as most people stood and moved. This was only the second session of six, and I was surprised to see Greg Jardis at one of the desks when I came in earlier. He hadn't been in the first class last week.

"You sell wine, Cece." Greg approached my seat. "Don't you already know all this?" He gestured at the whiteboard, where Zeke had written the main varietals grown in the northern half of the state.

"Considering I knew nothing except the price of a box of chardonnay when I took on the job managing Vino y Vida last year?" I smiled as I stood. "I always have more to learn. What about you?"

"I confess I love to drink the stuff. Also, beyond your average homeowner, my store serves vineyard workers and owners alike. I want to be able to talk about their tools, equipment, and products."

"Sounds like a plan," I said. "If you'll excuse me, I have a question for the teacher."

Greg nodded and turned away. I made my way to the front desk, where Zeke sat jotting something down in his notes.

He glanced up. "How are you finding the class, Cece?" He looked to be in his early thirties.

"It's great, thanks. I'm learning a lot, but I have a question. Are you going to talk at some point about blends? I'm curious about why wineries make them, which varietals are good to combine, and so on. My customers sometimes ask, and I never have a good answer."

"I'm happy to cover that. Let me make a note to include that next week." He tapped a note into his phone and looked up at me again. "Didn't I hear you are something of a private investigator? I mean, you told me you own Vida y Vino, but you look into homicides as a sideline, don't you?"

"Not really, no." Did I want to go into the couple of cases I'd been unavoidably drawn into since I moved to Colinas? No.

"It's just that with Regan Greene's murder, everyone in town seems to be on edge." He kept his voice low, and his heavy dark eyebrows met in the middle as he spoke.

"Oh? I haven't noticed that."

"Yolanda sure is."

"Who's she?" I asked.

"Sorry. Yoli is my twin sister, and she worked for Ms. Greene."

"At AVDA?"

"Yes. She's the admin for the association, which means she mainly dealt with the director." He glanced at his phone. "Sorry. Break is almost over, and I have to go find our speaker. I told him which room, but he might be lost."

"I hear you. I'm also a twin, by the way."

"Cool," he said. "Maybe we can talk more later?"

"That would be great."

I'd like to hear more about Yolanda and how her experience of working for Regan was. But that was for another time. I was back in my seat by the time Zeke ushered in a man with salt-and-pepper hair who looked like he was in his sixties.

"Class, this is David Zelma," Zeke announced. "He owns and operates Zelma Vineyards and knows pretty much everything about the business."

"Thank you, Zeke." David smiled, revealing a mouth full of crooked teeth and ruddy cheeks that might have stemmed from overimbibing. Otherwise, he looked fit and neatly dressed in a pressed collared shirt with the cuffs turned up and khakis. "Yes, I came up in the industry and trained elsewhere before taking over my family's vineyards and winery. Who here has tasted a Zelma vintage?"

I raised my hand, as did Greg, along with most of the class. Zelma wines were one of the brands we served at Vino y Vida, although I hadn't met the owner personally.

"Excellent," David said. "Well, I understand you already had a speaker about the grape-growing side of the biz. I'm here to take it from there."

Our guest speaker last week was a woman from Alexander Valley Vineyards. We each left class with a wide illustrated poster labeled "Cycle of the Vine," which showed and described what was happening with a grapevine each month of the year. I planned to have mine framed so I could hang it on a wall at Vino y Vida.

"I'll go over the process from harvest through bottling," David continued. "I did part of my training at the Kendall Jackson production facility in Geyserville and worked my way up to plant manager. I know how the sausage is made, so to speak."

He clicked on the first slide of a presentation that was projected onto a big screen at the front of the room. Zeke dimmed the lights.

"Here you see the freshly picked grapes being dumped from the truck into a two-ton hopper. When it's very hot at *vendange*, we pick at night to keep the fruit cooler."

Greg raised his hand. "*Vendange?*"

"Sorry," David said. "It means harvest. Many of our wine words come from French, for obvious reasons. From the hopper the grapes run onto a kind of conveyor belt into a separator." David used a laser pointer to illustrate. "The separator mostly winnows out the stems and leaves from the grapes."

He continued showing slides and describing the process. We saw photos of huge, lethally sharp screws, enormous tanks three times the height of a tall man, and wooden barrels that had gas pumped into them.

"Do those giant tanks ever need cleaning?" a student asked.

"Certainly. They're on a rotation for that. When one is emptied, a person actually crawls inside and scrubs the walls."

He continued describing the process, right through bottling. "I'm happy to answer any questions you might have. What else would you like to know?"

"Are you hiring?" a woman with toned arms asked. "I want to learn the entire business."

David smiled at her. "We couldn't do any of it without our hardworking crew. I'll give everyone my card when we're done. Remind me, and I'll add the name of our recruiting manager to yours."

"I bet you use a bunch of pretty potent chemicals for cleaning." Greg leaned back and crossed his arms on his chest. "How do you ensure the safety of your workers?"

"Zelma as well as Kendall Jackson are OSHA-approved facilities." David frowned. "Yes, several of the steps can be seen as dangerous, but we take every measure to ensure the safety and well-being of our employees. There are trip wires, extensive checklists, buddy system safeguards in place, and much more."

Zeke stepped forward. "We're out of time, folks, but let's give David a big round of applause for taking time out of his busy schedule to give us an inside look at how the Alexander Valley's world-famed wines are made."

We all clapped. David held up his palm.

"Thanks so much, Zeke." He lifted a split out of a case on the floor. "I have a taste of last year's award-winning petite sirah for each of you, plus the promised card. If you bring it into our tasting room, you'll get a half-price session."

I waited until last to claim my half-size bottle. I introduced myself. "We pour Zelma wines at Vino y Vida, which I own."

"Of course, of course." David pumped my hand. "I'm happy to meet you, Cece. But don't you already know all about wine?"

I laughed. "Not exactly. Zeke is a great teacher, though, and I've already learned tons."

"I can arrange for you to tour our facility, if you'd like." David handed me his card. "Bring a friend."

"That would be great, thanks. I appreciate it." I said goodbye to both men and headed out.

But as I moseyed home in the twilight, I wondered why Greg was asking about the chemicals. Because he owned the hardware store? He must sell various potent chemicals himself.

Chapter 19

Fuller was already in the car when I biked over to Allie's the next morning at seven. I waved at him and hurried in the side door to the kitchen, where my twin was running a brush through her hair.

"Morning, gang." I smiled at the PJ-clad boys, one on the couch in the adjoined family room, one on the floor.

Franklin glanced up from his book and waved at me. Arthur was intent on the complex Lego construction he was building.

"Thank you for doing this, sis. Come say goodbye, kiddos." Allie leaned forward and held out her arms to the boys, who ran over to her.

"Be good for Auntie Cee, you two."

Franklin rolled his eyes. "We always are, Mama."

"Why are you and Daddy going to San Francisco?" Arthur asked.

"We have an appointment."

"Okay," Arthur said.

Franklin gave her a somber look but didn't press her for an explanation.

Allie squeezed them, an arm around each, and stood. "I'll be at the bus when you get off. Love you. Coffee's in the carafe, Cece."

I followed her to the door and murmured, "Tell me when you can."

She turned to look at me with full eyes. "I will."

I folded her into a hug and squeezed possibly tighter than she had squeezed her sons.

"Now go," I said. "I hope you don't get much traffic."

I busied myself by locking the door after her, blinking away my own tears. Something was seriously wrong, and I hated not knowing. Allie would fill me in when she could. I poured myself a cup of coffee.

"Okay, guysers, what are you making me for breakfast?" I asked.

Franklin giggled. Arthur abandoned his project and skipped over.

"Can we make banana pancakes?" Arthur, my light-haired nephew, asked.

"The bus is at eight thirty?" I asked.

"Eight thirty-six." Franklin, a small near-clone of his father, pushed his glasses back up the bridge of his dark nose.

"Plenty of time," I said.

With Arthur's assistance, the three of us feasted on buckwheat banana pancakes topped with maple syrup and yogurt. Unlike his brother, Franklin didn't care about cooking, but he set the table for breakfast.

"Auntie Cee," Franklin began, "why haven't they caught anybody for that lady's homicide?"

"I don't know, honey."

"What's homicide mean?" Arthur asked, his mouth full of pancake.

"Try not to talk with your mouth full, sweetheart," I admonished in a gentle tone.

"Homicide means when one person causes another person's death," Franklin said.

"Like murder?" Arthur looked at me.

"Yes." I wanted to change the subject, and fast. "So, when does school get out for the summer?"

We talked about their swimming lessons, a week at what they called Gramps camp, and a couple of sleepaway camps they were signed up for—soccer camp for Arthur, computer camp for Franklin.

"Will that be the first time you'll stay in separate places?" I asked.

"Yes." Franklin frowned.

"Looks like you're worried about that," I said.

"Arthur's going to miss me," he whispered.

"You'll miss each other." I smiled at him. "It's only for a week. I remember when your mommy and I slept apart for the first time. We were about your age. I was sad at first, but we both ended up having a good time."

"Okay."

"I learned a poem about twins," Arthur said. "Want to hear it?"

"Always." I smiled at him.

" 'Two-ones is the name for it, and that is what it ought to be, but when you say it very fast, it makes your lips say twins, you see. When I was just a little thing, about the year before the last, I called it two-ones all the time, but now I say it fast.' "

"Hey, that's good, Arturo." Franklin gave an appreciative nod.

"Thanks." Arthur gazed at me, swiping at a drop of syrup dribbling down his chin. "When will Zoe be home from Japan?" Despite my girl being a decade older than her cousins, they adored her, and it was mutual.

"At the end of June," I said. "Her boyfriend is going over to visit and they're going to travel together for a couple of weeks."

"Why aren't you going, too?" Franklin asked. "Don't you miss her?"

"I do, but I can't take that much time off work. I'll see her in a month."

Plus, I wasn't about to butt into the long-planned trip of two young lovers. I also had mixed feelings about seeing Japan again, which is where I'd lived with my late husband and Zoe when she was little. At an age when I should have been in college and not a new mother, I'd been happy with her. Not so much with her father and his serial infidelity. I was grateful she matured out of her anger at me after my husband died unexpectedly eleven years ago. She and I had finally grown close again in the last year.

"What are you thinking about, Auntie Cee?" Arthur asked.

I gave my head a little shake. "Was I woolgathering?"

"You mean, like a wool sweater?" Arthur frowned.

"It means daydreaming," Franklin said. "It comes from when sheep would rub up against fences and lose bits of their fleece. People went around and collected it. But I don't know why it ended up meaning daydreaming."

"I never knew that, Franklin," I said. "It's an expression my grandmother loves. I guess it's because when your mind wanders to unconnected thoughts, it's like plucking tufts of wool off fences."

"I want to visit Great-Granny Lila again," Arthur said. "She's fun. Do you think that's where Mommy and Daddy went today?"

"I'm not sure," I hedged. My maternal grandmother, Lila Flaherty, was a lively woman about Richard's age who lived near San Francisco in a retirement community in Marin County. "She is fun. Let's go together to see her this summer, shall we? Now, finish up. It's time to get dressed and brush your teeth. You don't want that bus to leave without you."

Chapter 20

With the boys safely on the bus, I pedaled home, resecured my hair in a tight ponytail, and threaded it through the green Colinas Cougars ball cap I wore when I put down Blue's convertible top. I changed into black pants and a new green top in case I didn't get back home before work. I added a light denim jacket for the cooler edges of the day.

I sniffed the air as I drove west to Las Madres. If there was a scent of smoke, it was a faint one. Just as well. Maybe the hotshots, those extra-brave specialty wildfire fighters, had been able to contain the blaze.

Holt Vineyards approached on the right. It looked like it was thriving, despite being under new ownership after what had happened this winter. When I spotted two vineyard workers who sometimes dropped into Vino y Vida, I beeped my horn. They glanced up from their work of tying vines to the supports and waved.

I previously had only been in Las Madres in the evening to go line dancing at the bar called the Rifle Club. Now in full daylight, I got a better picture of the town as I followed my GPS directions to the AVDA office. With its modest older homes and a slightly shabby downtown that included more than one empty storefront, it reminded me more of Cloverdale than Colinas.

My town wasn't fancy, but its residents were relatively comfortable financially, with housing costs to match. The town made an attractive and well-kept downtown a priority, and it was home to several affordable housing clusters, with one more coming if Gareth's project moved forward. At least Colinas wasn't Healdsburg, which was in a different league in terms of pricing out regular people. Sleepy Las Madres looked like a place where my vineyard worker friends and others with lower salaries could afford to live.

To my surprise, the AVDA office was on the main drag two doors down from the Rifle Club. I never noticed it when I came here to go dancing. Between the office and the bar was a hair salon, and beyond that was a hardware store, with bags of mulch, rakes, and beach chairs displayed on the sidewalk. I parallel parked and locked Blue, leaving the top down. I didn't expect to be here for long, and rain wasn't in the forecast.

Inside, a man in his twenties sat at a desk facing the door, his torso twisted so he could work on a laptop to the side. He seemed to perk up at seeing me.

"Welcome to AVDA." He smiled and tucked a lock of chin-length platinum hair behind his right ear, revealing three gold studs marching up the rim of his ear and a gold hoop threaded through the lobe. His head was shaved up the other side to two inches above his left ear. "I'm Jared. How can I help you?"

I stepped forward. "Nice to meet you, Jared. My name is Cece Barton, and I own a wine bar in Colinas." I'd decided on the drive over to tell the truth about everything—except my curiosity about Regan.

"Ooh, Vino y Vida? All my friends have been talking about that adorable place. I'll take them up on going next time."

"I hope you do," I said. "I thought maybe Yolanda Cruz would be working the front here. I heard she's the admin for AVDA."

"She's not in today. You can leave her a message if you'd like."

"Thanks, but that's not necessary." Especially since she had no idea who I was.

"Are you already a member of the association?" He stood and handed me a glossy brochure.

"I am, thanks." I accepted the leaflet and tucked it into my bag to study later. "I was in the area and thought I'd drop by and see headquarters. I've heard great things about all the projects and so on."

"Projects?" He wrinkled his nose.

Oops. "Or, you know, whatever the organization does. I joined last year, but I haven't gotten involved at all." The only artwork I saw was a large painting of gently rolling hills covered in verdant vines, with people sipping wine on the terrace of an unlabeled winery in the distance. It was signed YC in one lower corner and was lovely, but it wasn't Dane's. "I'd love a tour of the place while I'm here."

"You got it. Come with me." He wore a snug pink polo shirt tucked into even tighter jeans turned up at the cuff. His tennies matched his shirt, which also had a rainbow-flag pin on the lapel.

I followed him down a corridor. Doors to two offices on the left stood open but were empty. He stepped into a good-sized meeting room on the right with a long, wide table surrounded by cushioned black office chairs. A brass nameplate at the head of the table read "Director." On the near side of the room a large video monitor hung on the wall. Across from it was one of the reasons for my visit. Dane's artwork was bigger than the monitor.

The painting depicted five people standing like a group of investigators on a television show intro: not smiling, several with arms crossed, looking forward but bodies at an angle. Surrounding and behind them was a hodgepodge of local highlights, almost like a collage.

A field of grapevines morphed into the hilltop River Rock Casino, which had a dry riverbed below it. A Victorian cottage stood next to an old adobe like the one Vino y Vida occupied. Flames licked at a ridge, and the state highway 101 sign marked a four-lane freeway stretching into the distance. Dane, whose signature was in a bottom corner, had even included the Rifle Club.

I strolled up to the painting. "This is interesting." Regan Greene, in a collared shirt buttoned all the way to the top and a loose black jacket, was depicted in the middle of the group of people. Her eyes seemed to glitter in a threatening way, her expression was as severe as her collar, and the rattlesnake coiled at her feet made me shudder. No wonder Regan hadn't liked it.

"You could say that," Jared said. "It's been the subject of some controversy."

"Why? It seems to have all kinds of things typical of the valley."

He glanced down and cleared his throat. "I'm not actually supposed to talk about it. Let's just say one member of the board hated the piece, but the others overruled her."

I pointed to the director sign. "Who sits there?"

"It was Ms. Greene, but she is sadly no longer with us." His gaze strayed to her depiction in the painting.

"Did she get a better job?" I mustered my most innocent tone.

"No, not at all." He lowered his voice and widened his eyes at me. "I guess you didn't hear. She was murdered."

"My goodness, how awful. Come to think of it, I did hear that name. Regan Greene?"

"Yes." He pointed to the painting. "That's her in the middle, may she rest in peace."

"Do you know how she died?"

"We haven't heard."

"Well, I won't take up any more of your time," I said. "Thanks for showing me around. I hope I'll see you in Vino y Vida sometime soon."

He brightened. “You bet.” He ushered me back to the front.

“Do you ever go dancing next door?” I paused at the door.

“Are you kidding? It’s not my crowd.”

On the sidewalk, I unlocked Blue. I went to the club because I loved the music and the line dancing, but I needed to be more aware of places that weren’t inclusive to all. Our world needed more love, not less, more open arms, not arms closed to those who were different.

CHAPTER 21

Once home, I hoped to talk with Richard, but he didn't seem to be around. Today that didn't worry me, or not too much. I took a shower, played with my kitties, and headed out in the car.

By ten thirty, I was parked in front of Colinas Hardware. A little chat with Greg Jardis wouldn't hurt, plus I needed paint, and I didn't have to be at work until twelve thirty.

I'd decided to repaint Zoe's room to surprise her when she got back from Japan. The walls looked passable when I bought the house last year. At the time, I quickly ran out of money paying for other, more urgent improvements. She'd barely stayed at home since the move. But with our newish reconciliation, I wanted the room to be fresh and pretty for whenever she came to stay, whether that was for one night or the summer.

Greg was behind the three-sided counter when I entered the store. The store always had three or four employees ringing up sales, helping customers find what they needed, restocking shelves. I liked that the owner also chipped in on all those tasks.

He smiled at me. "If it isn't Cece Barton herself. How can we help you, darling?"

I sighed silently. I wasn't his darling, but I didn't need to engage in that fight at the moment.

"I need a can of paint," I said.

"Come with me." He led me back to the paint area, where a can was shaking back and forth on the mixing machine. "Interior or exterior, and do you have your color picked out?"

"Interior." I gave him the room dimensions and showed him the paint chip I'd selected, a pale, buttery yellow. "I'd also like the type of paint that doesn't off-gas."

"We do have the low VOC. It's from a different company than that exact color, but I should be able to match it."

"Thanks."

"Do you want to come back and pick it up?" Greg asked. "We can call when it's ready."

"No, I'll wait."

"Very well." His lips pursed as if he didn't like my answer, but he busied himself with the paint. After the mixer stopped shaking, he removed that can and fixed mine into the machine, then started it up.

"Did you enjoy the class last night?" I asked him.

"Learned a lot. You?"

"Absolutely. The slides of the facility were a little scary, frankly. I wouldn't want to get near that giant screw thing or crawl inside one of those tanks."

He laughed. "You'd better stick to pouring the wine instead of making it." He slid his hands into his jeans pockets.

"No kidding." I glanced at him. "You seemed curious about the chemicals they use and the safety of the plant's workers."

"And?" His smile vanished and he blinked.

"Is it because you sell some of the chemicals here?"

"Exactly." His shoulders relaxed. "I do."

"Have you heard when Regan Greene's funeral will be held?"

He tensed again. "No, why should I?"

"At the car show, you seemed to know her, maybe have some history with her. I thought . . ." I let my voice trail off.

Greg turned away as the machine slowed to a stop. He freed my can and picked up an opener and stirring stick. "I'll take this to the register for you." He strode away. At the counter, he set it down and murmured something to one of the guys, then disappeared into the back.

"Thank you," I called after Greg. He didn't turn around.

"Everything okay, my friend?" a voice asked from my other side.

I swiveled my head to see Henry standing next to me. He held a coil of thin wire and a package of picture hangers.

"Yes, thanks."

"Are you all set with brushes?" the man behind the counter asked.

"I am, thank you," I said.

He told me what I owed, and I handed him my credit card. They hadn't upgraded to self-tapping cards yet.

I faced Henry. "I seem to have asked the boss the wrong question," I whispered.

"As you are wont to do." Henry gave me a fond smile. "There's an investigation going on, I hear."

"Yes, as a matter of fact." I glanced at his purchases. "Did you run out at the gallery?"

He rolled his eyes. "My supply order is late. I have a new artist show opening tomorrow, and I can't wait. Come to the reception Friday if you want."

"Thanks. I'll try to stop by on my dinner break. Who is the artist?"

"Her name is Yolanda Cruz. Really innovative photographs, and she paints, too."

"That's interesting," I said. "I'm taking a class on wine from her brother."

"Zeke? He helped her bring in her stuff yesterday. Seems like a good guy."

"He's a good teacher." I thanked the employee who handed me my receipt, then faced Henry. "See you Friday, if not before."

"Sounds like a plan."

Paint can and supplies in hand, I headed out with yet more to think about.

CHAPTER 22

My breakfast of pancakes was a distant memory, and I'd forgotten to pack lunch or dinner. It was already eleven. A hearty lunch at Edie's Diner would fill my belly now and maybe provide some leftovers for dinner.

I slid onto a stool at the counter and greeted the older woman behind it.

"Coffee?" She slid a paper menu in front of me.

"No thanks, only water. Is Ed around?"

"He's running an errand. Should be back shortly. Are you ready to order?"

"I'll need a minute, thanks." I perused the sandwiches section and decided to go with one of my favorites. I looked up when the server returned. "I'd like a tuna melt on sourdough, please."

"Coming right up."

I glanced around the diner but didn't see anyone I knew. It was filling up fast with the early lunch crowd. I checked my phone. Allie hadn't written. It was probably too early to expect her to be back home.

By the time my lunch arrived, the only empty seat was the stool next to mine. Before I could take a bite, Ed came in from the back, tying a half-apron around his well-fed midsection.

"Cece, *querida.*" He slid onto the vacant stool. "Any news?"

"Not to speak of, unfortunately. You?"

"Maybe." He leaned an elbow on the counter and faced me as he spoke in a voice so soft I could barely hear him. "My cousin is pretty connected. She heard something on the police channels about Regan being poisoned."

My eyebrows went up. "Did she hear what the poison was?"

"No."

"That's the first concrete thing I've heard about her death," I said. "See if you can find out from her who reported finding Regan, okay?"

"I'll try."

He glanced over at the door when the bell on it jingled and rose. "Madam Mayor," he called to Malia, who stood backlit in the opening a few yards away. He pointed at the stool he'd vacated. "Come on over. I saved you the last seat."

Ooh. I wouldn't mind a little chat with Malia Guttierez at all, except the feeling might not be mutual. Her expression looked like she'd tasted a moldy tortilla. At least she didn't turn around and leave.

"Good morning, Malia," I said when she neared.

"Hi, Cece." She didn't return the smile as she slid onto the stool. "Thanks, Ed."

"Coffee?" he asked.

"Please." She folded her hands on the counter and looked straight ahead.

I took a bite of my sandwich, the creamy tuna salad tangy with capers and crunchy from bits of celery, the melted sharp cheddar exactly the right touch, the skillet-toasted bread crisp and buttery. I was happy to eat while she decided whether she wanted to speak to me.

Ed set down a mug of coffee in front of her.

"I'd like the turkey burger with avocado and caramelized onions, please," she told him.

"Coming right up." Ed turned away.

"No hamburger for you?" I asked her.

"I'm allergic to beef. My family doesn't believe me, but I get the worst rash from consuming it. Too bad. Our family eats lots of it."

"That must get tricky at family gatherings. Do you have relatives nearby?"

"My father lives with me as well as my kids, who are in high school." She added cream and sugar to her coffee and stirred. "I'm your classic sandwich generation. Padrito, my dad, is getting more frail, and teenage boys a year apart? I can't wait for them to graduate from Colinas High and head out to college."

"I hear you. My daughter is a junior at Davis, and our relationship has improved a lot in the last year."

"Your only child?"

I only nodded, having a good-sized bite of food in my mouth.

"I have an older daughter, as well. Listen, I apologize for coming down hard on you at your sister's cookout."

"Thank you." I left it at that.

"The city council is doing the same to me. Four days after a homicide with no arrests doesn't look reassuring to the public."

"I expect not," I said.

The server who'd taken my order delivered Malia's plate. "Something else, ma'am?" she asked the mayor.

"No, this looks good. Thanks." To me, Malia said, "*Buen provecho*."

"Likewise." Her burger looked delicious. I could eat avocado at every meal and never tire of it. I made a note to ask Ed if he could make the burger with a fishcake instead of turkey. "Sounds like you live here in Colinas."

"It's a requirement of the job for all town employees."

"I didn't know that. Colinas has quite a few great neighborhoods. I have a cottage on Rivera. What part do you live in?"

She held her hand in front of her mouth and waited until she finished chewing. “I’m at the other end of the block where Allie lives. My great-grandfather built the house. *Abuelito* worked for the Italian Swiss Colony winery after they bought up his orange grove.” She smiled. “Yes, like the little old winemaker, except he was neither Swiss nor Italian. We’re Californios all the way.” She took another bite.

I’d read about Californios, who were settlers of Mexican origin. They predated most of the gringos who moved in after them over a hundred years ago. Many of the Californios later had their land stolen from them.

“Cool.” Could I keep asking her questions? No harm in trying. “At the car show, as you know, I heard you and Regan arguing, and later you told me she was trying to take over powers reserved for the town. I’m fairly new to this area, and I don’t really know what AVDA’s scope or mission is.”

Malia swallowed. “It was formed about a decade ago when the county supervisors seemed like they were growing too corrupt to function well. Certain people in Sonoma County got together to form district associations under one umbrella. Part of their mission is to support valley businesses but also to monitor county functions. These days, the supervisors have cleaned up their act, and the district organizations are a bit redundant.”

“Regan was the director of AVDA. Isn’t there a board to oversee what she did? Otherwise it could be as corrupt as the reason the associations were formed.”

“Yes, but the Alexander Valley board has always rubberstamped her decisions and actions.” She popped in the last bite of her burger and chased it with half a pickle spear.

“What kinds of powers was she trying to usurp from you? Are they functions that should be part of Colinas government? She said something about it being in her job description.” I wondered if Malia thought I was grilling her. “I’m sorry, I’m simply trying to understand how things operate around here.”

"Well, it wasn't departments like fire or policing or education, thank goodness." Her phone rang from the counter where she'd set it next to her coffee. "Excuse me, Cece." She connected the call, frowning. "Yes, Paul?"

Chief Paul Fenner? Possibly. I listened to her side of a terse conversation that lasted less than a minute.

She disconnected, drained her coffee, and stood. When she began rummaging in her bag, I held up a hand.

"I can get your lunch," I said.

"Can't accept gifts, but thanks." She laid a twenty on the counter. "Gotta run. Catch you later." Near the door she waved to Ed and rattled off her farewell in Spanish, the only word of which I caught was "*gracias.*"

I finished my lunch. I'd been so close to learning more about Malia's current conflict with Regan. I could only hope I'd learn about it in another way. I'd also wanted to ask about the past, but that hadn't gone well a couple of days ago. This was the end of May, not Groundhog Day. I didn't need to repeat what hadn't worked before.

CHAPTER 23

I arrived at Vino y Vida before noon. On my way here, I considered stopping at the police station to see if Kelly Daniell was there. Instead, I kept on driving. I had nothing specific to tell the detective, and she wouldn't appreciate a nosy civilian asking her questions in front of law enforcement professionals.

After I put a history podcast on the speakers, I moved around the wine bar, setting up to open. I filled a half dozen baskets with crackers and selected several vintages for today's pours. Dishwasher emptied and glasses wiped and set out, I sat with my phone at one of the tables.

My heart sank when I still didn't have a message from Allie. I sent her a quick text, asking her to let me know when she was home. I added heart and flower emojis and threw in a unicorn and a cookie for good measure.

Next I called Richard, but he didn't pick up. Unlike my generation and everyone younger, his age group listened to voice mail. I left him a quick spoken message saying that I hoped he was okay and that I looked forward to seeing him in the garden tomorrow morning.

I moved on to news sites. It was going on four days since Regan's death. Why wasn't anything being reported? Reporters like Nan were usually able to dig up what the official investigation had uncovered to date, and sometimes things the police hadn't. Malia should have called a press conference by now, asking the county detective and the police chief to present their findings. The absence of that might mean they knew nothing. Except, at a minimum, they should have been checking alibis for anyone who'd been in public conflict with Regan. Or maybe the mayor stayed quiet because she herself was a person of interest.

The news was apparently a dead end for now, so my thoughts turned to poison, something about which I knew next to nothing. Ed's cousin told him that was how Regan died, however, and it made my curiosity dial up to maximum. How did one administer a poison without the victim knowing? By mouth, perhaps, or via injection. Through the skin was another avenue, as was airborne.

I shuddered to remember when a murderer nearly sprayed me with the powder of a botanical toxin last year in the wine bar's back room. I managed to disable the villain first, and with Allie's help, we secured the person well enough to make our escape and call the authorities.

The list of locals who had run-ins with Regan wasn't extensive, and now I had to include notations about poisons. Greg certainly knew about poisons ranging from cleaning solutions to garden chemicals, and probably many more. Dane, as an artist, must have paint fixatives and additives that were surely toxic, not to mention solutions to clean oil paint off brushes and hands. Henry would have information on that, for sure.

Who else? Malia made jewelry as a hobby. Toxic chemicals might be involved in that. Zeke had said his sister worked for Regan and had issues with her, but would Yolanda know anything about poisons? *Wait.* Henry had told me she was an artist like Dane. And then we had Richard, who must be on Kelly's radar. He gardened organically, and I refused to think of him as a suspect, regardless. Just . . . no.

I was about to jot down a list of the connections I'd run through when Mooncat breezed in. She stopped and stared at me.

"What's going on, boss?" she asked. "Usually you're bustling around in here like the proverbial Energizer rabbit. You do know it's twelve forty-five, right?"

"Sheesh." I jumped to my feet. "I was sitting here playing amateur sleuth, but this isn't the place and it definitely isn't the time." I grabbed an apron and tossed one to her.

As I went over the reds, whites, and a rosé we'd be pouring, she scribed them on the whiteboard behind the bar. She had a clear, artistic hand that was way beyond my limited abilities. She added touches of color and sometimes a fanciful drawing of a smiling wine bottle.

"What's the Melon?" She tilted her head, marker in hand.

"It's a rare white grape from the Burgundy region. Alexander Valley Vineyards makes the wine using the cold settling technique, and it's super refreshing. But it's pronounced meh-LOH, kind of."

"Those French." She laughed. "Any news, quick before we open?" she asked as she wrote.

"Just a hint. Ed's cousin has a connection with the police."

"A hint is good." Mooncat stashed the markers and washed her hands. "Dish."

"The cousin heard Regan was poisoned, but Ed didn't know what kind of poison."

"We have poison in our own back room in the form of the gas we pump into the bottles we save over for the next day."

"So we do." We had a practice of pumping argon gas into open bottles a half or more full that we'd poured from. After we added the gas and a Haley's cork, the wine was preserved for the next day. Bottles that were less than half full I corked and sent home with an employee or took it myself. If nobody wanted it, a vinegar maker was happy to pick up a bucket of accumulated lees whenever we let him know it was full.

"Not that you or any of your staff would use the gas for nefarious purposes," she added.

"Let's hope not. But when you came in, I was thinking about poisons the various persons of interest might keep handy or have knowledge of."

"I'll keep that in mind. Right now?" She pointed at the people peering through the front window. "We have customers."

Chapter 24

By four o'clock we'd had a steady stream of happy sippers and were running low on crackers. I headed into the storeroom in the back to grab another large bag. I pushed open the back door to check the air for the odor of wildfire smoke.

Instead of smoke, all I detected was a gorgeous last day of May. The sun was warm but not too hot. A mild breeze rustled the leaves on the big oak, and two couples were enjoying a game of bocce in the court beyond Vino y Vivo. The heavy balls thudded into the sand or made a thwacking sound when one ball hit another.

A slim woman with spiky blond hair opened the door of Acorn Fine Art and Sculpture. She held it for a dark-haired man about the same height and build. I took a closer look. It was Zeke Cruz. The woman might be his sister, Yolanda, who had worked for Regan Greene.

I hurried back inside. Business looked settled, with everyone served. I plunked down the bag of crackers behind the bar next to Mooncat. "I have to run over to the gallery. Back in ten minutes, okay?"

"Sure," she said. "We're good here. You have your phone, yeah?"

I felt my back pocket. "I do."

"I'll call if a tour bus arrives."

"Thanks. I won't be long." I hurried back out through the storeroom, mostly so nobody wanting wine would waylay me.

I made my way along the path and into Henry's gallery, where Henry, Zeke, and the woman stood gazing at a wall full of paintings.

Henry glanced my way. "Cece, darling. Perfect timing. Come in and tell us what you think of the placement."

I moved toward them. Zeke cocked his head.

"Cece Barton from my class?" He smiled. "What a coincidence."

Henry laughed. "Not really. You passed her wine bar on your way here. It's in the second adobe."

"Vino y Vida is only yards away, and Henry here is a good friend," I said to Zeke. I smiled at the woman and held out my hand. "Hi, I'm Cece."

"Yolanda Cruz." She shook with the strong grip of someone who has worked with her hands. Up close her resemblance to Zeke was unmistakable. The long-lashed brown eyes, the wiry build and athletic stance, the slight overbite. After that, her thinned eyebrows, makeup, lipstick, and bleached hair set them apart, along with her form-fitting hot pink top and equally tight calf-length leggings. "I've been meaning to check out your wine bar."

"I hope you do." I gestured toward the pictures. "These are lovely. Your paintings, I gather?"

"They are. It's my first gallery show, and I'm not ashamed to admit that I'm nervous." Her smile wobbled.

"Yoli, they're each gorgeous. Together it makes for a stunning show," Zeke said.

"What he said." Henry wasn't given to beaming, but he looked pleased.

I glanced at each of the paintings. They mostly depicted outdoor, realistic scenes. Colorful bicycles lined up in a stand.

Bunches of cut flowers in metal buckets on the ground, perhaps at a farmers market. Beach peas sprouting out of a dune, their tiny purple flowers the foreground for the Pacific Ocean sparkling in the background. The one that especially captured my attention was of rolling hills covered with trellised grapevines and the patio of a winery with customers sipping wine under umbrellas in bright primary colors.

"Yolanda, I was in the AVDA office in Las Madres this morning. I saw a painting a lot like this one. Is it yours?" I realized I'd seen the initials YC in the corner and hadn't thought about them.

"It is," she said. "Thanks for noticing."

"It's lovely, as are all of these." I smiled. "The young man who showed me around the place said you worked as the admin for Regan Greene. I'm sorry for your loss."

She stared at me. "Um, thanks?"

"Regan was a difficult person to get along with under the best of circumstances," Henry said. "I can't imagine working for her was easy."

"It wasn't." Yolanda shook her head. "Not a bit. I know this isn't a popular thing to say, but I'm not sorry she's gone."

Zeke's breath rushed in. "Yoli." He spoke softly, but the urgency was unmistakable.

"I don't care what anyone thinks, Zeke," his twin replied. "You can't even believe how many people she made miserable, how many lives she ruined. She was a despicable human being."

"Have the police been at the office as part of their investigation?" I asked.

Zeke studied me. *Oops*. He'd asked me last night about my sleuthing experience and I'd denied it.

"I don't know," Yolanda said. "I haven't been in since Friday. I'd already arranged to take this week as vacation so I could set up the show and stuff."

And maybe she hadn't answered their calls, either. My phone

vibrated in my pocket, probably Mooncat telling me the wine bar was busy.

"I have to get back to work," I said. "Good to meet you, Yolanda."

She didn't reply, having turned away to whisper something to Zeke.

"Remember the reception Friday, Cece," Henry said.

"I'll try to stop by."

In fact, I would make a point of it. Yolanda Cruz's animosity toward Regan was deep and sharp. I wanted to know more. A lot more.

Chapter 25

Oy. Sure enough, Mooncat was swamped when I hurried back into Vino y Vida. I hadn't looked at the text that had come in while I was in the gallery, and now I didn't have time to. If it wasn't a tour bus, then certainly a flood of customers had arrived.

"Sorry," I said, tying my apron on again. "Where do you want me?"

"Can you do a sweep through the patio and come back inside?"

"I'm on it." I grabbed an empty tray, a clean cloth, and a spray bottle filled with the vinegar-based solution we used on the tables.

Outside was a veritable bar scene. Every stool was filled, but so was every inch along the railing, and a couple of sippers sat cross-legged on the decking with their faces to the sun, which was still high in the sky. Even the top of our service stand in the corner was being used as a table. All the sippers appeared younger than me, and I assumed Mooncat had checked IDs.

I moved among the customers, collecting empty glasses, inquiring about refills. Soon enough, I needed to set my tray on the service stand.

"Excuse me, folks, but I need that surface." I smiled at the three women clustered around the stand. "Pick up your glasses for just a minute. You can use it again when I go back inside."

"No prob," a redhead said. Her pale cheeks were sprinkled with freckles, and her hair was as full and luxuriant as my honey-colored mane, except curlier.

"Thanks." I set down my tray and pulled out my notepad and pen. One of these days I'd move to ordering and paying on a handheld device, but I hadn't yet. I began taking orders around the patio, noting the name each patron's open tab was under. We required anyone drinking out here to leave their credit card at the bar. Otherwise, it was too hard to keep track of payment. Nearly everyone wanted a second or third glass.

I picked up my tray and thanked the women whose surface I'd usurped. "It's all yours."

"Pardon me, ma'am," Redhead said.

I no longer winced when someone addressed me as "ma'am." It came with the territory of being over forty.

"You're the private detective, right?" she asked, hazel eyes wide. "My friend Jared said you're investigating that lady's murder."

"Jared who works at AVDA?" I asked.

"Yeah. He said he was going to join us out here when he got off. He told me you were in there this morning asking all kinds of questions."

"I did stop by the office because I was in the area and curious about the organization, but I'm not a detective of any kind. I own this wine bar and, if you'll excuse me, I have orders to fill." I headed inside through the propped-open door.

It was similarly busy in here, if not busier. I tried to pull off the waitperson's classic make-no-eye-contact trick, but still several people hailed me.

"I'll be right with you," I repeated more than once. Behind the bar, I set down the tray and quickly loaded the glassware into the dishwasher.

"It's a madhouse out there," I muttered to Mooncat, who seemed to be pouring as fast as she could.

"In here, too. Want to see if Dane can come in and lend a hand?"

"I'll try." I dug up her number and called. It rang forever and never went to voice mail. "No luck."

"Back in a jiff." She carried a loaded tray and delivered glasses to two tables, then cleared three more.

I set to work filling the patio orders I'd taken, hoping I was keeping them straight. I would research portable ordering stations on my next day off.

Mooncat came back. "I'm sorry, but if I don't take a fluids break right this second—"

I cut her off. "Go."

She stripped off her apron and fled into the back to our tiny staff restroom.

Two young men sauntered in. I hated to feel discouraged about additional paying customers, but we were slammed right now. I blinked when I realized who one of them was. Jared lifted a hand in a wave to me and followed his buddy onto the patio.

Why had he told the redhead that story about me being an investigator? I was quite sure my visit had appeared innocent, merely a drop-in from a curious valley resident. Apparently not.

It didn't matter. I was way too busy to think about it. Mooncat hurried back in.

"Can we swap in and out?" I pointed at the full tray. "These groupings are all labeled with the name on the tab. Two new men came in a minute ago but headed straight out to the patio. They probably joined the women using the service stand as a table. The dudes need carding first, and the one named Jared worked for Regan at AVDA." I really didn't want to be grilled again about investigating Regan's death.

"That's a lot to take in, but sure."

"Thanks."

Mooncat relayed info about the tables in here and headed out. Two older men, one with a full head of silver hair and the other with a high forehead and a thin white ponytail, stood at the end of the bar conversing in low voices. When the one with the ponytail gestured to me, I slid down there.

"I'd like a refill on the chardonnay, please, and my old friend wants to try the pinot noir."

"Coming right up, gentlemen." Out of the corner of my eye I noticed another man come in, but I focused on my work.

I delivered the glasses and glanced around to find the newcomer. I broke into a wide smile. Benjamin stood at the other end of the bar and returned my smile. That was great news if I ever saw some. I nearly skipped down there to give him a kiss. My heart did skip, and in a good way.

"I was thirsty after my trail run," he began. "Where better to get a cool adult beverage than my favorite wine bar?"

"Where indeed?" I grabbed a glass for him. "It might have to be self-serve, though. We're slammed right now."

He glanced around. "Can I help? I can pour wine as good as the next guy."

"Seriously?"

"Sure." He looked down at his T-shirt and trail shorts. "You want me like this or should I run home and change?"

If he'd been sweaty from his run, it had dried. Customers might appreciate a handsome guy serving their wine, especially the women. I knew I would follow those legs anywhere.

"You're fine, and the apron will look cute on you." I poured a glass of the Melon and handed it to him. "Thank you."

He took a hearty sip and set the glass behind the bar. "Let me go wash my face and hands. Back in a flash."

I set a clean half apron next to his drink as Mooncat strode up. "Benjamin's here, and he's going to help out."

"Way to scramble, boss." She held up her palm for a high five.

"He showed up like a rescuing angel and offered." I slapped her hand. "The only part I'm responsible for is saying yes. It's a win all the way around."

CHAPTER 26

By six o'clock, business in Vino y Viva was back to a dull roar. A few sippers still occupied the patio on this mild early evening. Inside, we had empty tables along with a half dozen relaxed customers content to drink leisurely as they talked.

Behind the bar, Benjamin unloaded clean glasses from the dishwasher, while Mooncat swiped at the few remaining drops of water with a dish towel before lining them up open side down.

"Thank you, my dear." I smiled at him.

"You totally saved our, um, bacon," Mooncat added.

"It was my pleasure." Benjamin straightened.

I hadn't had a minute to think about how Yolanda had spoken about Regan, but now it popped back into my brain.

"I heard something pretty shocking when I stopped into the gallery a couple of hours ago," I began in a low voice.

"Do tell," Mooncat said. "What's Henry been up to?"

"Not Henry. An artist named Yolanda Cruz is setting up a new show. She and her brother, who happens to teach the wine class I'm taking, were in there."

"Zeke Cruz?" Benjamin frowned.

"Yes," I said. "Do you know him?"

"I might." He folded his arms. "Please go on."

"Well, Yolanda works at AVDA, the district organization Regan Greene led. Yolanda basically said she was glad Regan was dead."

"Ouch." Mooncat grimaced. "People think things like that, but to say it out loud among people you don't know? That's the definition of poor taste."

"And dangerous when the death is due to a homicide," Benjamin murmured.

"Zeke looked alarmed that she'd voiced her feelings," I added.

Benjamin blew out a breath. "Listen, can I order take-out dinner for you hardworking ladies? I'm starving."

"That sounds great," I said. "I ate lunch at the diner before noon, and I'm hungry, too." I'd gobbled down every bite of my lunchtime tuna melt, leaving nothing for dinner.

"If you're serious, I'll also take you up on it," Mooncat said.

"Chinese, pizza, Greek?" he asked.

"I like everything." I gazed at Mooncat, who shrugged.

"So do I," she said, "but pizza is probably easiest to grab bites of if we get busy again."

"Right," I said. "And we can fold pieces over to keep it neater to eat."

"Sounds like a plan," Benjamin said. "Anything you don't want on it, Mooncat?"

"No raw onions, and I'd prefer no olives, but those are easy to pick out."

"Anchovies?" Benjamin queried.

I personally loved the salty little fish, but I waited to see her reaction.

"Why not?" Mooncat grinned. "Bring 'em on."

"Will do." He pulled out his phone and headed into the back room to order.

"You and I are a rare breed, Mooncat," I said. "Anchovy lovers are underrepresented in the general populace."

"All the more for us."

Benjamin stuck his head through the door to the back. "They don't deliver, so I have to pick it up. I'll be back in ten."

I blew him a kiss before he disappeared.

Mooncat lifted her chin toward the front door. "We have customers."

We did, and there went our chance to eat without interruptions. The only food we served were the complimentary crackers. I never liked for us to eat openly in front of the clientele. After Benjamin returned, we would take turns eating in the back.

Young people, older people, and people in between streamed in, ten or twelve in all. I blinked at the last two and nudged Mooncat with my elbow.

"That's Zeke and his sister."

"Interesting."

They snagged a small table near the patio door. Most of the other newcomers headed outside, with two men about my age sidling up to the bar.

"I'll do table orders, okay?" I asked Mooncat.

"Sure." She smiled at the men. "Welcome to Vino y Vida. What can I pour for you this evening?"

I grabbed a fresh basket of crackers and headed over to the Cruz siblings. "Hey, guys. Glad you could stop in." I smiled.

"I figured it was about time I checked this place out," Zeke said. "I had to twist Yoli's arm, but she finally agreed to come with me."

"I'm glad you did," I said. "What we're pouring is on the board there. Do you want a minute to decide?"

Zeke twisted to look behind him, but Yolanda shook her head.

"After the week I've had," she began, "I want a full glass of the biggest red you've got."

"I'll let your brother be the judge of that."

"She'd like the cab sauv, and I'll try the Melon."

"You got it." I checked with the few other occupied tables on my way to the bar, but everyone was still content with what they had. After I poured both glasses, I turned to find Zeke standing in front of me.

"I can take those." He held out both hands.

"Here you go." I told him which glass held which wine. "Thanks."

He lowered his voice. "I'm sorry about what my sister said earlier, Cece. She's been super stressed about this gallery show."

"I understand. How long had she worked for Regan?"

"A year, year and a half."

"She must have gotten to know her pretty well."

"Yes." He stared down at the wine for a moment, then lifted his gaze again. "You have to believe me that she never in the world would have acted on her dislike of the woman."

"I'm happy to hear that." I wasn't sure I believed him. "Excuse me, but I have to help customers outside. I hope you enjoy the wine."

"Thanks."

When I returned inside holding half a dozen orders, Benjamin was behind the bar tying on his apron and chewing. I didn't see Mooncat anywhere.

"Pizza's here?" I asked.

He nodded, swallowing. "In the back. You were outside, so Mooncat's grabbing a slice now." He washed his hands at the sink behind the bar.

"Awesome. Thanks so much for getting that." I turned my back to the room. "Zeke came in with Yolanda. They're at the small table near the patio door. He came to the bar without her and apologized that she'd badmouthed a dead woman."

Benjamin let his gaze wander around the room, passing over where the siblings sat. "I'm pretty sure I met him on a job last year. And she looks like someone who ran the same road race I did recently. Let me wait on their table? I might be able to squeeze in a little chat with them."

"Whatever you'd like, except you don't have to keep working if you need to get going."

"I like to help out, but I do have a couple of things to do at home. I'll stay maybe another half hour."

Mooncat came out and pointed her thumb over her shoulder toward the back room. "Your turn, Cece. That's a very fine pizza your man ordered."

Benjamin laughed. "I didn't make it myself, you know."

"I bet you could if you wanted to." She washed her hands. "Go, Cece, while you can."

Without hesitating, I went to down a quick slice of pizza.

Chapter 27

Benjamin left before seven after whispering that he'd tell me later what he knew. Zeke and Yolanda departed without me getting another chance to speak at length with either of them.

A few minutes later, Ed Ramirez held the front door open. A man in a wheelchair without armrests wheeled himself through, followed by Henry. They made their way to an open table. As Mooncat was helping a couple at the bar, I headed over to greet the newcomers and meet the third person in the party.

"Good evening, friends." I pulled out an unoccupied chair and sat facing the stranger so I could be on the same level. I held out my hand. "I'm Cece Barton. Welcome to Vino y Vida."

"Thanks, Cece. My name is Tino Ribeiro." He shook my hand with a strong, smooth grip. Wavy, dark hair curled over his ears, and a dimple split his cheek when he smiled.

"I'm glad to meet you, Tino." I pegged him as being maybe five years younger than me.

"Tino is the director of the Colinas Library," Henry said. "We ran into him at dinner, and he said he'd never been in here. We insisted he join us. Guess where he's from."

"I have no idea. Somewhere Spanish speaking?"

"Portuguese." Tino's dark eyes, set off by his green shirt,

sparkled from behind wire-rim glasses. "My parents are from Brazil."

"I've always wanted to visit Brazil." I heard my wistful tone. "I've lived in Japan, but that's the only other country I've been to." I hadn't even traveled to Baja California, and I'd only been north to Washington once. I was also a no-show in the Midwest and back east, and Europe remained a bucket-list item.

"You'll get there, hon," Ed said.

"Maybe. Anyway, you run a great library, Tino," I said. "I don't go in that often, because I mostly listen to books, which I check out online. I'm a charter member of the dyslexia club."

"As am I," Tino said. "We can't let it stop us. By the way, I appreciate the flat entrance out front."

"Thanks. I happened to inherit the threshold from the previous owner, but accessibility is important for everybody. I would have added a ramp if the place had come with a step up or down to get in." I stood. "What can I pour for you all tonight?"

"Do you have a dessert wine?" Tino asked.

"Yes, a smooth muscat."

"I'd like to try that, please."

I took Ed's and Henry's orders and made my way to the bar. My phone vibrated with an incoming call before I could pour, and the ID was Allie. Things were still pretty quiet in here, and I connected the call.

"Hey, Al. How . . ." I wasn't sure which question to ask first. How was the appointment? How was the drive? How was Fuller?

"I'm coming over for breakfast tomorrow, okay?" she asked. "I'll be there before nine."

"Sounds good." I waited for more, for news, for idle chat.

"Love you." She disconnected.

Wow. Zero information provided. At least I'd have her captive in the morning. I slipped the phone back into my pocket and poured three glasses of wine for my friends and their friend, apparently a fellow traveler on the dyslexia journey. I couldn't imagine attempting a career in books, but Tino had clearly made it work for him. I carried the tray of drinks over to their table and passed them out.

"Thanks, Cece," Henry said. "Did Zeke and his sister come in earlier? He said they might."

"They did."

"I bet you were as shocked as I was by what she said."

"For sure." I slid the small tray under one arm. "Zeke got me alone at the bar and apologized for what she said. He wanted to be sure I knew she would never act on her feelings."

Tino was following our conversation closely, which Henry also seemed to notice.

"A local artist worked for the recent homicide victim," Henry said.

"Regan Greene," Tino murmured.

"Yes. In my gallery this afternoon, Yolanda Cruz was vehement about her hatred for Ms. Greene. Her brother and I were standing right there along with Cece and heard it all. She went so far as to say she wasn't sorry Regan was gone."

Tino gave a slow bob of his head. "It's been quite some time since the body was discovered. I read a lot of crime novels and listen to true crime podcasts. From what I understand, the longer the authorities go without making an arrest, the chances of ever doing so dwindle rapidly."

"Cece," Ed began, "are they still thinking Richard might have been involved?"

"I sure hope not, but I have no idea what they're thinking," I said. "Kelly Daniell is the detective on the case. So far, she's not telling me anything."

Tino frowned. "Why would she?"

Ed beamed. "Cece has tracked down murderers before. She's not a professional but has quite the talent for it."

"Not really," I protested.

"Amateur sleuths are quite popular in certain subgenres of mystery fiction." Tino tapped the table. "Let me put my librarian superpowers to work, and I'll get back to you, Cece, all right?"

"That'd be great. These two know how to find me." I smiled at the trio. "Enjoy your wine."

As I made my way back to the bar, I mused on Tino Ribeiro. The dude was cute, smart, and helpful, and he understood dyslexia on a personal level. If I weren't already in love with Benjamin, I might have considered trying to get to know the librarian better.

CHAPTER 28

By nine thirty, Mooncat and I had cleaned up Vino y Vivo and locked the door.

"Remember Dane is subbing in for me tomorrow afternoon," Mooncat said. "I have that physics seminar I signed up for. It might seem silly at my age, but I like to keep my knowledge current."

"It's not silly, and thanks for the reminder."

"I should be in by five thirty."

"Great." I said goodbye, wrinkling my nose after I turned away. I could manage with Dane, but she was less reliable than Mooncat. The brilliant and quirky former hippie was my right-hand helper, plus she hadn't been associated with Regan at all.

I'd had a full day. I was bushed and looked forward to relaxing at home with nothing but kitties to think about. Speaking of cats, they were going to be miffed at such a late dinner. I drove home along Manzanita, wincing at all the bright headlights. Blue was low slung and couldn't compete with the big SUVs and trucks that sat higher off the pavement. Even the lower-profile models blinded me.

The downtown bustled with people out enjoying the evening, probably a combination of tourists and locals. Who knew a Wednesday night could be this busy? Granted, the wine bar had been packed earlier, both inside and out.

I frowned at my rearview mirror. Whoever was behind me had been driving too close for comfort all the way down the boulevard. It was a car with the newer horizontal bands of headlights instead of two discrete beams. I'd been followed, harassed, and attacked during past investigations. May this merely be a driver in a hurry, not someone malicious.

I neared the Hoppy Hills brewpub, which sat on the corner of Orange Grove where I turned off Manzanita to go home. If this person was tailing me, I didn't want to telegraph my destination. On the other hand, I had no desire for my precious antique auto—with me in it—to be rear-ended. My heart thudding, I tapped the turn signal lever. If the car behind me also turned, I could zip into the well-lit bar parking lot.

After the oncoming cars cleared, I swung right but immediately jammed on the Mustang's brakes to avoid hitting a car already halfway out of the Hoppy Hills lot. My breath rushed in, and I braced myself to be hit from the back.

But nothing happened. No crash sounded, no bright lights shone into my mirrors. *Whew.* The thought I was being pursued was a false alarm, a figment of my worried imagination. An imagined attack that never happened was far preferable to a real person intent on harming me. The person tailgating me must have been one of those impatient drivers who thinks arriving at their destination thirty seconds faster was more important than safety. Anyway, I'd be home in a quarter mile from here.

Chapter 29

Two minutes later my automatic garage door creaked shut behind Blue, and I headed through the connecting door into the kitchen. Sure enough, I was greeted by one gray cat and one black and white version who wove noisily around their food dishes and my ankles.

"Give me a second, guys." I locked the door behind me. When I was looking to buy a place in Colinas, one of the draws of this house for me as a single woman owning a vintage car was the garage and that it was attached to the house. After both Blue and I were safely inside with doors closed behind us, I could breathe easy.

I dished up a small half can for each cat. After that it was Cece time. I freshened up and slipped into loose pants and a light sweatshirt. With my thick hair loose from its clip and a little cognac poured into a glass, I settled onto the couch with my phone. I savored a lovely taste of the fine liquor, which warmed all the way down.

I first checked my texts and frowned. *Huh*. That message I hadn't checked when I got back to Vino y Vida earlier was from a number and an area code I didn't recognize. All it said was, "Lay Off," words that made me queasy. If it had been an anonymous "Hi," I would have tagged it as spam, blocked the sender, and not thought any more about it. But "lay off" sounded like a warning, although it was missing the "or else" part of a real threat. It felt too late to forward it to Kelly tonight, but I'd try to remember to pass it along tomorrow.

Benjamin had texted to say he hadn't learned anything useful from Zeke or Yolanda. Too bad.

Martin sat on the rug washing. Mittens jumped up next to me and circled twice before she curled up touching my thigh. I began to mentally run through my very long day. The worry about the reason for Fuller's appointment in San Francisco. My visit to AVDA and Jared's comments about Regan. Greg's turning cold at the hardware store. Ed saying he'd heard Regan was poisoned, and all my thoughts about which of the people of interest might have access to poisons. It turned out to be all of them, including my employee Dane.

And that was only the morning before lunch. At the diner, Malia had outlined the AVDA history but received an urgent call from someone named Paul. At the gallery later, Yolanda had made her shocking statement, and Zeke tried to backpedal it out of earshot from her at the bar.

The only person I hadn't had contact with during the day was Richard. I would try to speak with him tomorrow morning. I sipped my drink, thinking about my neighbor who'd lived a long and productive life. What must it be like to have spouse, friends, and even younger family members die and have your own mortality in sight?

My mother's mother was still relatively hearty at eighty-five, but she had slowed down in recent years and had seen her husband die twenty years earlier. My Van Ness grandparents, *Opa* and *Oma,* were both gone, as was my own father.

But thinking of Richard reminded me I still hadn't read his article. I scooted sideways away from Mittens so I didn't disturb her and got up to fetch my tablet. Yes, I could read it on my phone, but I prefer a larger surface.

It was way past time for me to finally read Richard's article. Maybe he had uncovered additional information about her background. I decided to listen rather than read and set the device to read the article aloud at a slightly faster-than-normal speed. I sat back to listen. By the end, I was no wiser. What he'd written clarified how Regan had used her position with AVDA to mount a power grab, especially at the municipal level. Malia being upset with her made sense.

My focus shifted to Yolanda Cruz, and I thought I'd see what I could learn about her online. Zeke and Yolanda looked a few years older than thirty. An internet search didn't get me far, since there was a well-known film producer by the same name, as well as a singer. Social media didn't help, either. I added Sonoma County to the search bar with no results. Had she gone to college? Were she and Zeke from Colinas or nearby, or had they moved here more recently? Yolanda either wasn't married or hadn't taken her spouse's last name, which wasn't that unusual. At least I didn't see her mentioned on a police blotter list of arrests.

I drained the last sip of my drink. Maybe I should search for Zeke. I rose and added another splash to my glass and grabbed a couple of oatmeal cookies while I was up.

When I curled up on the couch again, I heard a noise that didn't belong. I stopped chewing, stilled my movements, and quieted my breath to listen. It wasn't the gentle snoring of the cats nor the weird clunking noises my refrigerator sometimes emitted. I had a few windows open at the top, but they were locked to no more than three inches. The sound wasn't a night owl or a distant truck downshifting on the highway.

From the front of the house came an irregular tapping noise that turned into a scratch. My blinds were closed everywhere, thank goodness. If someone was outside and determined to get in, no way did I want them watching my actions. My throat was thick as I tried to swallow my nerves. I set down my glass and cookies with a clammy hand and rose, switching off the lamp as I did, in case there was a crack in the blinds. The sound continued.

I considered calling Benjamin, but first I tiptoed toward the front door to listen. It was late, and maybe the noise was nothing. I'd thought of adding a security camera but had never gotten around to it.

The scratching went quiet. My eyebrows flew up when it was replaced by a shout from the street, followed by silence. I waited but didn't hear any more noises or voices. I took a deep, trembling breath. It was time for me to crawl into bed and pull the covers over my head.

Chapter 30

My sleep was restless, plagued by dreams ranging from weird to terrifying. I usually found sleep restorative and a comfort. Not this time. I was relieved to open my eyes to see sunshine pouring into my bedroom window at seven thirty. The images from the dreams were already slipping away. The memories of someone trying to get into my front door, not so much.

At least the sound last night hadn't come from the rear of the house, which was visible to no one. Someone attempted to break into my house through the back door last year. The motion-detector light I'd installed out there after the incident was responsive and bright. I didn't have one on the front porch, but the streetlight wasn't far, and neighbors were all around.

I gave my head a shake and slid out of bed. Twenty minutes later, lidded coffee mug in hand and minimally presentable, I turned the deadbolt on the front door and stepped out onto the porch. *Ugh*. Smoke was in the air again. I should check the news about that wildfire.

Right now, I wanted to see the evidence if someone had actually been trying to tamper with the door. A piece of paper fluttered down to the flagstone. Where had that come from? It looked like one of the cheap paper napkins that gets tucked into a bag of take-out food except it had handwriting on it.

I picked up the napkin and smoothed it out. Scrawled in blue ink was a message. "Somebody with a crowbar tried to break into your house. I scared them off." The note was signed "Just Driving By." The napkin was likely the only scrap of paper the driver could find in their car.

So, the yell I heard had been a Good Samaritan telling my intruder to beat it. Which was awesome, but I wished the driver had identified themselves. I wanted to thank them, and I was also dying for more information. Had the crowbar wielder been a man or a woman? How tall were they, and how old? Now I'd never know.

I slid the note into the pocket of the shorts I'd pulled on and turned to examine the door. Sure enough, scratches marred the jamb and the metal door latch strike plate. Could they have gotten in with a crowbar? I didn't think a deadbolt would yield to that kind of forcing, but it was time for me to add a porch or doorbell camera and change the light to one triggered by motion.

Glancing around, I didn't spot a crowbar nearby. The would-be intruder might have been scared off, but they'd kept their grip on their weapon.

I went inside and made sure my trusty deadbolt was engaged, then ventured into my garden and unlocked the gate in the fence. I called through before opening it.

"Richard? Good morning."

He didn't reply.

I tried again. "Knock-knock." I got only silence in return. I opened the gate anyway.

He wasn't in his chair on his patio. I didn't see him bent over weeding or standing with hose in hand to make sure his prized Meyer lemon tree had water. I knocked on the sliding glass patio door. He didn't come to answer.

My breath raced in at what I saw in the reflection. I dropped the travel mug as I whirled and rushed toward Richard. He lay on his side nearly hidden between two of his raised beds. I knelt next to his head and laid my hand on his cheek.

"Richard."

His skin was warm, possibly too warm, and his chest moved slightly with his breath, thank goodness.

"My friend." I shook his shoulder gently. "What happened?"

His eyes fluttered open. "Cecelia, dear. What are you doing here?"

"The question is, what are you doing lying on the ground? Did you fall?"

He gave a soft chuckle. "Why, I can't rightly say. I will say, the dirt is a heck of a hard mattress."

I pressed two fingers against his neck. Without actually keeping a count, I could tell his pulse was racing. Should I see if he could sit up? If he couldn't remember what happened, he probably had no idea if his head had crashed into the wooden side of the garden bed.

"I'm going to feel your head to see if it has a lump on it," I said. "Is that all right?"

"Of course, my dear, but you can just call my wife, you know. She's in the house somewhere. As a matter of fact, I'm surprised she hasn't already come out looking for me."

Uh-oh. His wife had passed away over a decade earlier. My normally clear-minded neighbor no longer was, at least not right now. He could have simply tripped and hit his head. But he might have had a stroke or a cardiac incident. And what if he'd been attacked?

I sat back on my heels. "I'm going to call an ambulance." Where was Pete? Didn't he live here anymore?

I hit 911 and described Richard's condition and age. I answered a couple of questions from the dispatcher, including Richard's address. "He's in the garden out back. They can come in around the right side of the house," I added. "There's no gate or anything."

"Please try to keep him awake," the dispatcher said.

"I will."

As soon as I disconnected, a siren started up in the distance, but Richard's eyes had closed.

"Richard, listen."

"What?" He blinked. "Oh, hello, neighbor."

"Hi. Nice to see you." I smiled through my concern. "Did you enjoy the town picnic?"

"The Memorial Day festivities? I chose not to go this year, my dear. Even though we did lose our beloved Charlie in the war, I simply had too much on my plate."

At least he knew what week it was.

"Did you enjoy it?" He hadn't tried to sit up and was asking me about the picnic as if it were perfectly normal to lie on his side in the path between garden beds and have a conversation.

"It was lovely."

"I expect you went with that good-looking beau of yours."

"I did." I smiled at him, at the same time wondering if I should run and grab a blanket to cover him. The day hadn't begun to warm, and the ground was cool. I didn't want to leave him, though, and the EMTs should be here soon enough.

"Richard, does Pete still live here?"

"My great-nephew?"

"Yes."

"Well, I think so, although I haven't seen him in quite a long time." He frowned. "I'm sorry. My mind seems a bit foggy at the moment."

"It's okay. I have his number. I'll call him later."

"Good. Would you tell him we're out of celery, please? He does my marketing for me from time to time, you see."

"Sure," I lied. Adding celery to a shopping list wasn't my highest priority right now.

The siren grew ever louder, then stopped. A moment later, two EMTs in dark short-sleeved shirts and Bermuda shorts hurried in from around the house.

I waved them over. "Help is here, Richard."

"That's lovely, dear." He raised a quavering hand. "You're a good friend."

I squeezed it gently and laid it down, then stood and stepped out of the way. Richard had come to feel like family to me. My eyes welled up. He was old, and I knew he'd go one day, perhaps soon. I wasn't ready for that day. Not now, and probably not ever.

Chapter 31

I poured Allie a fresh cup of dark roast and topped off my own at a little after nine. I portioned out scrambled eggs to which I'd added grated sharp cheddar and slivered fresh basil and set the plates on the kitchen table next to the chocolate croissants she'd brought from the bakery.

"Thanks, Cee," she said.

"Bon appetit." I smiled at her.

A makeup-free Allie, wearing jeans and a T-shirt, had been quiet since arriving a few minutes ago. I was letting her set the conversational pace, at least about her trip to the city with Fuller yesterday.

I bit into the flaky, buttery, crisp pastry, savoring the narrow bar of dark chocolate that ran through the middle.

"Did you hear the sirens earlier?" she asked.

"I summoned them."

"What?" Her blue eyes, bigger than my gray-green ones, flew open.

I nodded and told her about finding Richard on the ground in his garden. "You can't believe how glad I was to find him alive and conscious."

"How did he seem?"

"Kind of cheery and also kind of out of it. He thought his

wife was in the house, and he didn't try to sit up. The EMTs took him to the hospital. I'm going to go by later if I can."

"The poor thing. His wife has been gone for a while. Do you know what happened to him?"

"No idea. He didn't seem to have any awareness of how he ended up on the ground." I took a bite of egg.

"The uproar about his article hasn't died down," Allie said. "I wonder if someone attacked him."

"It's possible. He really needs to block off his side yard. But who would assault an old man?"

"I know. He's such a nice person, plus experienced and wise." She pushed around her eggs, the portion of which had hardly diminished, and stared at her plate. "Should we all live that long."

"What, you don't like my cooking?" I used a gentle tone. "The eggs are from a little farm in Cloverdale, and they're super tasty. I bought them at the farmers market."

"The eggs are great." She set down her fork and her shoulders slumped as if the weight of the world was draped over them. She lifted her face. "Cece, Fuller has cancer. That's why we went to San Francisco yesterday."

No. I jumped up and wrapped my arms around her.

"Oh, sweetie," I murmured into her hair, which smelled as always of eucalyptus and vanilla. I held her as she sobbed. She and Fuller were still deeply in love after fifteen years of marriage. When her crying ebbed, I sat again but kept hold of her hand.

"Tell me everything," I murmured.

"Well, he started feeling off a couple of months ago. I had to kind of prod him to go to the doctor. I knew it was a problem when she referred him right away to a specialist." Her posture slid lower. "It's colon cancer, Cee. They apparently caught it fairly early, but he's going to need treatment several times a week at least at the beginning."

"Can he be treated up here?" I asked.

"He can. There's a great center in Healdsburg. But what if it doesn't work? I can't lose him. The boys need him."

"We all need him, sweetie." I squeezed her hand. "He's a hearty man in his forties who is otherwise healthy, and you said they caught it earlyish. Medicine has come a long way. He'll make it."

She mindlessly tore off a piece of croissant and popped it in. She covered her mouth with her hand as she laughed. "This is really good."

"Uh, yeah. Finish it. You're going to need your strength. Want me to heat up your eggs?"

"No. All of a sudden I'm famished. I don't think I ate anything yesterday." She dug into her breakfast.

"Atta girl!" I also resumed eating.

When both our plates were clean, she sat back. "I know we're going to be okay. It was just such a shock yesterday."

"I hear you. Do you want to tell me anything else?"

"Let's talk about homicide, instead."

I barely swallowed my mouthful of coffee. "Hey, you almost made me spit my drink with that U-turn."

"Sorry. It's that I heard something about Malia Guttierez you might be interested in. I figure you've probably picked up new info, as well, and frankly, I've been thinking a little too much about illness the last few days."

"For sure. Let's see. I talked with Malia at the diner yesterday at lunchtime. She told me about her family and their roots here."

"She has taproots in the area," Allie said. "Did you learn anything relevant to the murder?"

"Unfortunately, she was starting to talk about Regan when she got a call and had to leave. It might have been from Chief Fenner."

Allie nodded. "I can check my inside sources when I get home."

"Your connections never cease to amaze me."

"It's part of the job, plus I love knowing what's going on in town. I've lived here a lot longer than you, sis. Anyway, I learned Malia was accused of assault some years ago."

"Really?"

"Yes, but the case was dropped," she said. "Thing is, I can't find out who brought the charges."

"She and Regan ran against each other for that state seat. Maybe Regan was goading her and Malia lost it. Did the incident happen about a decade ago?"

"Possibly. So, what else happened yesterday?"

"Well," I began, "I met Yolanda Cruz."

"Who's that?"

"She worked for Regan." I ticked off what I knew about her on my fingers. "Her twin brother, Zeke, teaches that wine class I'm taking. Yolanda is also an artist, with a new show going up at Henry's gallery."

"And you think she might have murdered Regan?"

"I don't know. If she did, she's not good at hiding her hatred for the victim. Get a load of what she said about Regan." I quoted Yolanda.

"Ouch. Talk about poor taste."

"No kidding." I shifted in my chair and felt the note from my guardian angel in my pocket. I pulled it out and laid it on the table. "Somebody tried to tamper with my front door last night."

"Seriously?" Allie's voice rose in alarm.

"I was sitting on the couch after work at, like, ten thirty. I heard a noise at the front door followed by a shout outside. The noises stopped, so I went and hid in bed."

My twin read the note. "A brave stranger driving by told the would-be intruder to get lost. Wow."

"Isn't that amazing? But also, what kind of idiot uses a crowbar to attack a door near a streetlight?"

"True words, Cece. True words. Do you think they were trying to scare you off investigating?"

"Maybe. Good luck with that."

We resumed eating, agreeing to split one more croissant.

"What are next steps for Fuller?" I asked.

"We have to line up appointments for the treatment, but around his work and mine. Or maybe the reverse."

"You know I'm here for both of you." I leaned toward her. "Taking the boys, giving Fuller rides, meals, whatever you need."

"I know." She grabbed my hand. "I'm super happy you agreed to move to Colinas last year. I needed you nearby, Cece."

"I needed to be here, too, except I didn't realize it." I smiled as I squeezed her hand. "Thanks to you, I'm close, and I landed a great job and a boyfriend in the bargain."

Allie's phone dinged. She glanced at it and swore. "I have to get home and get dressed. I have a showing in an hour."

"Go, then."

We both stood and hugged, murmuring our goodbyes.

"Give Fuller my love," I said.

"You bet." She hurried toward the door. "Call me with a Richard update."

"I promise," I called after her.

I doubted the hospital would give me information over the phone. Pete hadn't picked up my call earlier. It was time for me to get ready for my own day. Stopping in to see Richard was top on the list of places to go before work.

CHAPTER 32

I slowed as I approached the sprawling single-floor campus of Healdsburg Hospital. The hospital had nearly closed a number of times in the last fifty years but ended up being a public-supported health care facility for all of northern Sonoma County. Urgent care sites served certain needs, but any population also needed an ER, surgery rooms, neonatal and adult intensive care departments, rooms for overnight stays, and so much more.

I noticed a sign on one wing reading, "Providence Cancer Center." That must be where Fuller would go for his treatments. Poor Allie. Her husband having a life-threatening illness was going to be hard on her. She'd want to shower him with love and support while shielding the twins from worry. She knew I would be there for her, for all of them, but it was my sister's and Fuller's burden to bear.

I parked Blue and headed inside the main entrance to an information desk. I still hadn't heard back from Pete and didn't know if Richard was languishing in the emergency department or if he'd been checked into a room for observation.

He'd been given a room, I was told, and the gray-haired volunteer provided directions to it. It was a regular room, not in the ICU, which I thought was a good sign.

A couple of minutes later I hesitated at the door of my neighbor's room. Richard, a bandage covering the right side of his head, lay in bed with the head of it halfway raised and the side rails up. An IV tube led to the back of his hand. Green lines traced up and down in a blessedly regular rhythm across a heart monitor next to the bed. His eyes were closed, and I didn't want to disturb his rest.

When an announcement came over the speakers in the hall, his lids flickered open. "Cecelia, dear. Come in, come in."

I sanitized my hands at the dispenser near the door and moved next to the bed.

"How are you feeling, my friend?"

"They've certainly made a fuss over me. My head is sore, but otherwise I'm as tough an old coot as they come." He smiled. "I keep asking to go home, but they want to keep an eye on me until tomorrow."

"I think that's a sensible plan, don't you?"

"I suppose. I'm terribly hungry, though."

"Did you eat breakfast this morning?" I asked.

"Why, I don't recall." He eyed up a pink plastic water pitcher on the movable table next to the bed. "Could you please pour me a cup of that, dear?"

I filled the plastic cup, which already had a bendy straw in it, and handed it to him.

"Thank you." He sucked down half the water. "That's better. Now, before you ask, I still don't remember what happened this morning. It's the oddest thing. I do recall dreaming about my dear late wife, as if she was in the house, but that was only a dream."

At least now he realized thinking his wife was in the house was a dream, even if it had been a hallucination, and he was cognizant that she was no longer with the living.

"Why do you have a bandage on your head?" I asked.

He touched the bandage gingerly. "I apparently suffered a contusion. I'm sure I simply tripped over my own elderly feet and hit my noggin on the side of the raised bed."

The light at the entrance to the room dimmed with the appearance of a backlit person. I had a flash of panic. If Richard had been attacked, the assailant could have come here to finish him off. I hadn't seen a police guard at the door. I jumped to my feet, ready to fight for my friend.

My tense shoulders relaxed. The figure in the doorway *was* the police. Kelly Daniell sauntered in. A nurse in purple scrubs followed close behind.

"Ah, Deputy Sheriff Detective Sergeant Daniell," Richard said. "Do join us, ma'am."

"Five minutes, max," the nurse cautioned. "Then I need both of you out of here." His name tag read Chris, and his trim, athletic build hinted at an ongoing devotion to fitness.

Kelly gave the young man a mock salute. "Yes, Chris. We promise."

"Richard says he's hungry," I told the nurse. "Will you be bringing him a meal soon?"

"We need to be sure he's stable first, ma'am. After that, we will."

"Thank you."

The nurse turned and left. Kelly moved to the other side of the bed from where I stood.

"Before you ask, Detective, I don't remember a thing from this morning," Richard said. "I wish I did. I expect you're here because you suspect malfeasance."

"I am certainly wondering," she said. "Have you had communication with anyone unexpected, other than the press? Anyone angry or aggressive?"

My hand flew to my mouth as my breath rushed in. What if the person who'd tried to get into my house escaped to Richard's backyard? They could have hidden there and attacked him this morning. Maybe it was his house all along they wanted to invade.

Kelly gave me a sharp look, but Richard didn't seem to notice.

"No, ma'am," Richard answered. "Not that I've noticed."

"I understand your great-nephew lives with you," Kelly said. "A Peter Flora. We haven't been able to reach him."

"Why, yes, Pete does, and he's a grand help to me. Except he's out of town for a week at a culinary event. I believe it's in San Diego."

That explained his absence, but not why he was unresponsive to calls and messages.

"If you'll excuse me, ladies, I am rather fatigued." His eyes began to close.

"Richard." I touched his shoulder gently. "Does your brother know you're here, or any other family member?"

"I quite doubt that, Cecelia."

"Remind me of your brother's name," I said.

"It's Victor."

"I'll get in touch with him or Pete," I murmured. "Rest well. I'll check in with you later."

He gave me a sweet smile with his eyes closed. Kelly and I headed for the hall.

"Something happened outside my house last night you should know about." I kept my voice low.

"Okay. Let me have a quick word with Chris. I'll meet you outside."

The air was less smoky here a little farther south of Colinas, but the sky was hazy. We sometimes got valley fog in the mornings. This seemed different, a high layer of pale gray that dimmed the sun. I sank onto a bench facing the parking lot, but I didn't have to wait long.

"I'm here." Kelly appeared through the automatic door and stood in front of me.

I rose and told her about the noise, the shout, and the note.

"Why didn't you call it in?" she asked.

"I don't know. Whoever it was had apparently left. It was late, and I was tired. This morning I did find scratches around the lock on the outside of the door, but no other evidence that I could see."

"All right." She tucked her hair behind her ear. "In Mr. Flora's room, you realized something. What was it?"

"I suddenly thought that maybe the person at my door had the wrong house. That they were after Richard, instead. When the passing driver chased them off, they might have escaped around the side of Richard's house and hidden in the garden until morning."

"His garden has open access to the street?" She frowned.

"It does, on the other side of his house from mine. I've hinted he should add a fence and a gate, but he never seems to care."

"Highly unsecure. We don't recommend such practices." She checked her watch. "I have to get a move on. Anything else new from you?"

"Kind of." I related the scene at the gallery and what Yolanda had said. "She worked for Regan. Yolanda knew her well, at least in that context. Her brother, Zeke, later assured me she would never have acted on her dislike."

"So noted. Is that it?"

"Apparently the mayor was accused of assault years ago."

"Guttierez?"

"Yes," I said. "But the charges were dropped."

"And you're thinking she might have tangled with Greene."

I nodded.

"I'll check into it," she said. "Now I really do have to go."

"Wait. Last evening someone texted me from a number I don't know. The only message was, 'Lay off.' "

"I don't like the sound of that. Forward it to me, okay?"

"Will do. And I'll let you know if I find Richard's brother," I called after her.

She raised a hand in acknowledgment without looking back. I forwarded the text, then headed for Blue and the rest of my day.

CHAPTER 33

As I drove back to Colinas through emerald vineyards in full leaf, a rasping sound came from the right front of the car. I couldn't identify it, except that the noise was new. It was only eleven o'clock. I had time to stop by Jo's garage and see if she had time to check out the cause.

The irrigated green scenery turned to scrubby hills, already parched and prone to going up in flames. Fire was an ever-present danger here, as it was in most of the state. When I lived in Pasadena, we'd thought an urban area was immune, but several nearby communities that abutted the foothills turned out not to be. The Eaton fire had been terribly destructive. It happened in Altadena only a few miles from my house. Zoe and I had hiked in Eaton Canyon when she was younger, but a friend's home had burned to the ground in that wildfire, leaving only the arched entryway standing vigil over a quarter acre filled with ash-coated rubble.

I'd heard of a group of volunteer artists painting house portraits from photographs of the destroyed residences and presenting them as gifts to the now unhoused families. A donation to the group had secured my friend that small physical memory of the home she'd lost.

I pulled into the lot at JJ's Automotive next to a silver sixties Porsche as Ouro, Jo's golden retriever, napped in the sun next to the building. I was pretty sure this car was Greg Jardis's Pamela. I wouldn't mind another chance to speak with him. I had no idea whether he'd been involved in Regan's death, but he'd certainly gotten his back up when I tried to talk with him about her yesterday.

First I texted Pete Flora.

Richard took a fall, is in Healdsburg Hosp. Need to contact your grandfather, father, or brother. Pls send number.

Maybe that would get a response out of Pete. Except . . . he would have no idea who the message was from, since we'd never texted each other before. We'd only met in person. I tapped out another note.

The prev was from Richard's neighbor, Cecc Barton.

There. In this era of spam and phishing popping up everywhere, I was sure others were as hesitant as I was about opening anything from a number not in their list of contacts. I left my bag on the front seat and climbed out.

The wide bay door was open and an old Saab was perched on the raised lift, but I didn't see Jo anywhere. I pulled open the door to the office. The mechanic stood behind the counter talking to Greg. He swiveled his head toward me.

"Hey, Cece," Jo began. "Got a problem with the Mustang?"

"Maybe," I said. "She has a new noise. Hi, Greg. I thought that was Pamela out there."

"It is." He folded his arms over his chest, unsmiling. "How's your investigation going?"

"Excuse me?" I asked. "What investigation?"

"Everyone knows you fancy yourself a sleuth." He cocked one hip. "Frankly, it's not very attractive."

As if I cared about his standard for what was attractive.

Jo cleared her throat. "Greg, I think we're all set. I'll give the Porsche a full service, including a tune-up, and check out the vibration you mentioned. Like I said, she probably won't be ready to pick up until tomorrow."

"Fine. Thank you. I'll wait for your call." His phone buzzed and he glanced down at it at the same time as a car horn beeped outside. "My ride is here. Have a nice day, ladies." He looked only at Jo before turning toward the door.

I was blocking the exit and stepped to the side to let him leave. The ride awaiting him was a battered Volkswagen bus from the seventies. I knew that vehicle. When I checked who was driving the VW, sure enough, Dane sat behind the wheel. I didn't think she'd seen me before the door closed behind Greg. *Whatever*. She was entitled to a personal life, and she wasn't due at work until one o'clock to fill in for Mooncat.

"Geez, Cece." Jo came out from behind the counter. "What have you been getting into? Jardis had his back up, for sure."

"He seems to have a habit of doing that." I flipped my palms open. "What can I say? I asked him a couple of questions at the hardware store yesterday. I guess he didn't like being grilled, not that it was a grilling, *per se*."

"I'm sure it was most unattractive." She snorted.

"There's no accounting for taste, right?"

"Exactly." She grinned. "Anyway, what's up with Blue?"

I described the noise and followed her outside. Jo first squatted, then lay on her back to peer up into the wheel well. She reached, grabbed something, and sat up, flourishing a branch.

"You were holding a branch captive and it was rubbing." She pushed up to standing.

"Amazing." I shook my head. "Thank you. I hadn't thought to look for something like that."

"Got a minute?" Jo drew her arm back and threw the stick into the brush at the edge of the parking lot. "I need to finish up with the Saab."

"Nice arm, and sure." I followed her into the bay.

"Good thing I have a set of metric tools." She tightened the plug on the oil pan. Then she moved the oil catch basin on its adjustable pole out from underneath and headed over to the lever that controlled the hydraulic lift. The car slowly descended to the floor, finally landing with a clunk as the tires took over from the lift arms.

"Doesn't it freak you out to use that, given what happened in the winter?" I asked.

"A tiny bit, but I wouldn't have an automotive repair business if I couldn't use the lift, Cece. What happened, happened, you know? Nobody can change the past."

"True enough."

"Excuse me for one minute. Don't go anywhere." She wiped her hands on a rag and slid in behind the steering wheel. She switched on the Saab, revved the engine and let it run for a few moments before she backed it out. Soon the Porsche glided in. Jo parked it over the lift arms and climbed out. She popped the hood and lifted it.

I joined her in gazing at the engine. "Another use for your metric wrenches?"

"Yep." She glanced over at me. "Cece, I heard something odd. You know, about the Greene homicide."

"Dish, please."

"Regan was a piece of work, as you're aware." She stepped back and leaned against the workbench, shoving her hands in the pockets of her dark blue cargo pants. "Everybody was aware of that."

"Did you know her personally?"

"I did, unfortunately." She pressed her lips into a line, and a furrow formed between her eyebrows.

Ouro moseyed inside and came over to sniff at me first.

"Hey, buddy." I scratched his ears and gave his back a couple of pats.

The dog headed for Jo. She bent over and rubbed his head with both hands. Having made the rounds, he wandered back out to the sunshine.

"Anyway," Jo continued, "I tangled with Regan more than once in regard to that stupid district association."

"Tangled how?"

"First it was about my yurt, how it was violating this or that regulation. She had the nerve to come onto my property. It was none of her business, and Ouro wasn't happy to see her."

"He's such an easygoing animal," I said.

"Yes, when he's with well-behaved people. Dogs can sense when somebody's up to no good. I kept him away from her and showed her my permit of occupancy from the town, which is all I needed, legally."

"Wow."

"And she was on my case about how I dispose of used motor oil, which was none of her business, and I told her so."

"Sounds like she was hungry for power," I said.

"Ya think? She would have been czar if she could, or the queen of all she surveyed."

"You also said you heard something odd?"

"Yeah." Jose nodded. "My aunt heard that the mayor has a background in chemicals, and the poison Greene died from was a chemical."

"Malia knows about chemicals?"

"She has an undergrad degree in industrial chemistry or something like that. Maybe it was agricultural chem. UC Davis has both."

"Interesting," I said. It was, in the extreme. "You know my mom teaches there."

"Yes, but I'd forgotten. Zoe's a student at Davis, right?"

"She is."

Jo glanced at the wall clock. "Sorry, Cece. I have to get to work on this. A Porsche engine isn't an easy tune-up."

"And I need to truck my little rear end over to the wine bar. It's not going to open itself." I thanked her again for finding the source of my noise. "I appreciate the intel. Everything helps."

Outside, I gave the snoozing dog another stroke. Malia knew about chemicals, did she? That was one more factoid to add to the growing murder list.

I hoped the authorities weren't aware of Jo's past clash with the victim. I wouldn't want her to be on the suspect list. She'd been there before, and I'd had to exert all my powers to figure out how to clear my friend's name.

Chapter 34

Even though Dane and I were working together at Vino y Vida that afternoon, she seemed to be ignoring me. There was no congenial chitchat like Mooncat and I always exchanged. If I asked Dane a question, she answered it with the minimum of words. She avoided eye contact. Had her budding romance with Greg turned her against me? I didn't know, but I hoped I'd have a chance to ask her what was up. I also hoped this cold shoulder didn't last.

That said, the artist was polite and welcoming to our customers, which really was all that mattered. Her hair was neatly tied back and her hands were free of paint.

As I wiped water drops off a clean glass, I thought about Dane having unpleasant history with Regan. The two had argued fiercely on Saturday. What if Dane and Greg had worked together to kill Regan? I couldn't allow a murderer to work for me. But that was a decision for later.

We weren't slammed with people. Instead, a steady stream stopped in for a glass or two. During a fairly quiet time at around two thirty, I thought about Regan showing up on Jo's property and harassing her about oil disposal at the shop. Surely the dead woman knew where the boundaries of her job were. Maybe she'd been greedy for workplace power because her personal life was a shambles.

I poured a glass of a new red blend and two of a smooth sauvignon blanc for three women about fifty perched on stools at the bar.

"We're from Seattle on a girls' getaway," a raven-haired one said. "After we got here, we heard your cute little town has a murderer at large."

"Are we safe?" her bottle-blond friend asked. "I mean, do you even have a police department in your town? It's terribly small."

I kept my groan silent. "We do, and it's an excellent department. The Colinas police are assisting the county homicide detective, and last I heard they're getting close to making an arrest. You have nothing to worry about." I mentally crossed my fingers. May all that actually be true.

"Let's hope so," the dark-haired woman said.

It was time to change the topic. "I guess Colinas does seem small compared to Seattle. What a great city that is. Do you know the spice shop in the Pike Place Market?" I'd taken Zoe to Seattle for her birthday one year, and we'd had great fun one morning poking around the market.

The third woman beamed. "It's fabulous. Did you know the owner's name is Pepper? What a hoot."

The trio began comparing notes on their favorite shops in the iconic market area. I slid down to the other end of the bar. I understood why visitors would be worried about an unsolved homicide in the area, and I didn't blame the women for asking about it. I was worried, too.

I loaded a half dozen glasses into the dishwasher and wiped down the counter. When I looked up, tall, lean Paul Fenner stood glancing around near the front door. The chief held his uniform hat at his side. Dane backed in from the patio, a tray full of empty glasses in her hands.

As she turned toward the bar and saw him, her cheeks went pale and the tray tipped. Glasses crashed to the floor. Every customer in the room whipped their gaze in her direction. Luckily nobody was seated near enough to be at risk of a cut.

I let out a deep sigh, then hurried toward Dane. Chief Fenner's long strides beat me to her.

"Is something wrong, Ms. Larsen?" His tone was as steely as his expression.

"No, not at all." Dane lifted her chin. "Just clumsy. Excuse me while I get the broom."

I approached.

"Sorry, Cece," she said.

"Accidents happen."

She made a beeline to the back room. I met Paul's gaze.

"Can we help you, sir? I assume you aren't here to taste wine."

"No, I'm not. I wanted a word with your employee." He kept his voice low.

"It's not really a good time. We only have the two of us here." How did he know Dane would be working today? She wasn't normally in Vino y Vida on Thursdays. More important, why had seeing him made her drop the tray? I supposed she could have a criminal background I wasn't aware of, whether in the distant past or, more disturbingly, the recent past.

He sat at the nearest vacant two-top. "I can wait."

Great. "Would you like a glass of water?"

"Please." He drew out his phone and ignored everything around him, including Dane sweeping up the glass shards.

She ignored him in turn. But, by three o'clock, the patio was empty and only three couples sipped inside, all seated together. Dane and I both stood behind the bar.

"Things are under control here," I told her. "You need to speak with Chief Fenner."

Her shoulders sagged. "I know." She trudged over to his table and sat across from him.

I grabbed a rag and wandered around, wiping down empty

tables, eavesdropping to the best of my ability. While my back was turned, I heard Paul ask her where she had been last Saturday night and early Sunday. He wanted to know if she had an alibi for the time Regan was killed.

I couldn't make out her muttered response. He pressed her about whether anyone could vouch for her whereabouts. Again, I missed her answer.

Had I thought about alibis? I had not. Saturday night was when Mooncat and I had seen Greg out to dinner at Hoppy's with a different woman than Dane. That probably nixed the possibility that she'd killed Regan in collaboration with him. Or maybe his date was a smoke screen. He and Dane could have planned the murder for later in the evening.

It was frustrating not knowing more about Regan's death. She'd died from a toxin, but what kind? Who reported her dead? Paul or Kelly or someone on one of their teams must have asked the various persons of interest about their alibis for the period around the time of death. The authorities couldn't have learned much or the chief of the department wouldn't be in my wine bar grilling my employee.

Maybe I should look at why I cared so much about this case. In the past, I'd been drawn into investigations because someone I was close to—or I, myself—was a person of interest. That ramped up one's motivation to find the real killer.

I supposed that was still true. I thought it ludicrous that anyone might suspect Richard of murder. I cared deeply for him, and the sooner this was solved, the better. Even if it meant one of my employees was guilty.

CHAPTER 35

As soon as Paul left, we had a flood of thirsty customers. Being crowded was good for the bottom line but bad for me getting a chance to sit down with Dane and find out what was going on.

Now at around five-fifteen, she'd been constantly checking either her phone or the wall clock for an hour. A few tables were full in here, and two sippers sat at the other end of the bar from where I stood. Dane poured five glasses and took them out to the patio. She hurried back in and glared at me.

"I thought Mooncat would be in by now," she said.

"No, I told you five thirty." I peered at her. "What's going on, Dane? You've seemed bothered by something all afternoon."

She looked away, at the front door, down at her hands, at the patio door, and, finally, at me.

She turned her back to the room and spoke in a hoarse whisper, "Do you think I like being suspected of murder, Cece?"

"Of course not. Is that what Chief Fenner said?"

"He as good as did."

"I thought I overheard him asking you about an alibi," I murmured.

"I live alone. I got nothing." Dane glanced over my shoulder and her expression lightened. "Man, it's about time." She reached back with both hands to untie her apron.

Mooncat strode up to us. "Sheesh, you wouldn't believe the traffic on the 101. What do people think this is, summer vacation? It's a Thursday afternoon and it's only June first." She set down a brown paper bag stapled at the top. "Thanks for subbing in for me, Dane."

"Sure. See you guys." Dane headed into the back room. A moment later, I heard the rear door thud closed.

"It smells like smoke outside, but who in heck lit a fire under her?" Mooncat stared at the swinging door to the workroom.

"She's kind of been like that all afternoon."

"Go figure. Anyway, I picked up dinner for us." Mooncat tucked her embroidered purse under the counter, washed her hands, and tied on an apron.

"You did?" Once again, I'd forgotten to bring anything. "Thanks."

"No prob. This thing I went to was interesting, but they barely fed us. I mean, look at me." She brushed her hands with a flourish down her statuesque figure. "I didn't get these curves by subsisting on crackers and cheese, you know, with a few meager cookies midafternoon."

I laughed.

"Anyway," she went on, "I got you a bean and cheese burrito, and mine is Cuban pulled pork. Which is to die for, in case you were wondering."

I winced at the words. "I wasn't, but thanks."

"That was a cringe at me saying 'to die for.' "

"Yes, but don't worry about it."

"You're right," Mooncat said. "Sorry about the phrase. It doesn't bring up a positive image. Anyway, what do we have for clientele?"

"The customers you see in here plus a smattering on the

patio. Dane took new pours out to them a minute ago. They should be set for a bit."

"Got it." She leaned toward me. "Listen, I learned something this morning."

"About the—?" The rest of my question was cut off by a noisy group of twentysomethings pushing in through the front door. Men and women alike wore well-cut business casual and looked relaxed and ready to party. I let out a breath. "Rain check on info?"

"Yeah, although it might not be until we close. Wanna bet these are financial types from the city on a team-building field trip?"

I smiled. "Good call. I hope they have a designated van and driver parked out front."

"Safe assumption. I'll make sure we have space on the patio. I'd say these folks are going for the whole NorCal wine experience." She headed outside.

"Welcome to Vino y Vida." I came out from behind the bar. "Have you visited us before?"

Chapter 36

The team builders lingered on the patio until almost dark. Luckily their hired driver and vehicle stayed, as well. By eight o'clock I was cashing out a considerable tab on the corporate credit card one of them proffered for the group when Gareth Rockwell sauntered in. At first I thought he'd come alone—until I spotted the mayor behind him. Or maybe the timing was coincidence.

I thought back to Allie's cookout. Gareth had thought Malia was slowing down the permitting process for his low-cost housing development. Maybe she had a conflict of interest with the project? One would think supporting affordable apartments would be a popular move for an elected mayor, but maybe the more-well-off Colinas residents thought such a project would bring so-called less desirable elements to town, a classic NIMBY—not in my backyard—attitude.

Gareth motioned to Malia to precede him to the bar. "Hey, Cece. I twisted the mayor's arm to come out for a glass of wine with me."

"Welcome, both of you." I gestured at the board behind me. "Our pours for the evening are there. What can I get you?"

"I'd like the Madeira, please," Malia said.

"I'll take a glass of the Petrolo." Gareth pointed at the board.

"I finished an Italian dinner a little while ago. I might as well continue the theme. Do you have water, too?"

"Sure." I kept a big glass water dispenser with a spigot and a tray of small glasses next to it. No way was I providing plastic cups. I could have offered paper cups, but washing the glasses with our super-efficient dishwasher powered by the rooftop solar panels seemed like a better environmental decision. "It's on the table over near the patio door."

"Thanks." He turned away toward the water.

"Malia, have you been to Vino y Vida before?" I asked as I poured their drinks.

"No. I've been meaning to, though."

"We have a lovely patio overlooking the river," I said.

The corporate group trouped in from outside. Most of them headed for the front door, while the credit card owner split off. She added a hefty tip, signed, and thanked me, then joined her coworkers. Mooncat returned from the back room.

"A patio that is now empty," I added.

"I'll go clear it," Mooncat said. "Evening, Malia."

Malia nodded at her before Mooncat headed outside. I wasn't surprised she knew the mayor. She knew everyone. Gareth set two glasses of water on the bar and slid onto a stool.

"Cheers." He lifted his glass of red.

Malia frowned. "Don't we want to sit at a table?" she asked him while giving me a sideways glance.

"You can sit wherever you'd like," I told them both.

"This is fine," Gareth said. "Come on, Mayor, pull up a stool."

She sat, but the lines between her eyebrows remained.

"Enjoy your wine." I slid down to the other end of the bar to give them space. Whatever they planned to talk about, I wasn't welcome to hear, at least in her eyes. I moseyed over to one of the occupied inside tables.

"Another pour, folks?" I asked a threesome of older men.

"No thanks," the man closest to me said. "We're all set."

My phone vibrated in my pocket. I moved back to the other end of the bar and checked it. *Ooh*. It was a text from David Zelma saying he'd be happy to give me a tour of their production facility at nine the next morning, if I was free.

I quickly wrote back and said I'd love to.

He returned with the address and offered that I could bring someone, if I wanted.

I thanked him and pocketed my phone. Maybe Allie would like to come. It might be a welcome respite from worrying about Fuller. I'd ask her after we closed. At the very least, the tour would be a fascinating peek into the sausage factory, so to speak. And I might learn more about those chemicals Greg Jardis had been asking about.

As I loaded glasses into the dishwasher, I tried to keep the noise to a minimum. I really wanted to hear what Gareth and Malia were talking about.

"The thing is, the need is great." Gareth rubbed a hand over his shaved head. "I've run other projects, and it never takes this long to get to the point of breaking ground. I'm sure you could expedite the permits if you wanted."

"It's nice of you to buy me a glass of wine," Malia said. "But I will never be bribed."

"What?" He reared back and spoke more loudly. "This isn't a bribe. I merely want to have a conversation about the project."

Malia raised and dropped a shoulder, looking away from him. "The applications have to make their way through the channels, Gareth. I really can't do anything about it."

He drained his glass and stood. He fished out a couple of twenties and laid them on the bar. "Thanks, Cece," he called down to me. "You have a good evening, Madam Mayor." He strode with a brisk step toward the door and out into the twilight.

Malia picked up her glass and moved down to my end of the

bar. "Our young friend wasn't happy with me. More accurately, he's dissatisfied with the slow pace of government. What can you do?"

"From what I've heard about his new development, it's something the area really needs."

"Certainly. But these things can't be rushed. I don't know if you're aware, but he comes from a family that often uses their influence to get what they want. I'm sure they have different ways of achieving their goals, and not necessarily legal or ethical ones."

I kept my mouth shut. I knew exactly what Gareth's family was like. I also knew he'd extricated himself from them. It was entirely inappropriate for an elected official to be badmouthing a local businessperson like Gareth, and I wasn't about to engage in that kind of discussion with her.

Mooncat came in from the patio and set down a tray full of glasses and empty cracker baskets.

"Is anyone still out there?" I asked.

"One couple swooning over each other." Mooncat grinned. "They might be on their honeymoon, and since a blood orange moon is rising, they're even more gaga."

"Colored from the smoke, I'd guess."

"Unfortunately, yes, but you wouldn't convince them of that." She glanced at Malia. "Another glass?"

"I don't mind if I do. I'm not driving, since I walked over."

"Is Gareth in the head?" Mooncat asked. "I can pour his refill, too."

"No," Malia said. "He decided to leave."

Mooncat turned and squinted at me. I made sure my back was to the mayor. "Tell you later," I mouthed.

She gave me a slight nod.

I wondered if I could find Gareth tomorrow morning for a private chat. He hadn't expected Malia's reaction tonight, that was certain, and he definitely didn't like it.

CHAPTER 37

Vino y Vida was empty of customers both inside and out by ten after nine.

"Let's close early, yeah?" I asked Mooncat. "I've had a long day."

"No argument here. I can always use an extra twenty minutes at night."

I headed over to lock the reinforced glass front door. After I did, I paused for a moment to appreciate the moonlight illuminating the walkways leading to the various buildings in the cluster. We had solar-powered lamps on posts here and there, but dark corners often remained. Now the full moon cast a welcome light on the area and added new shadows.

Gazing at Henry's gallery reminded me of that interaction with Yolanda yesterday. I didn't know if Kelly had followed up on what I'd told her. Who was I kidding? I basically didn't know anything about this case, including how Richard was doing. I'd meant to call the hospital this afternoon and never got to it. Pete hadn't gotten back to me, either. I'd at least left a message for Richard's brother, as promised.

I was about to turn away when I caught sight of movement in the shadows. Was it a person skulking about? The motion stopped. I flipped off the switch that lit the main part of the table area in here, including near the door. I stepped away but crouched under the window near the door, poking my head up to do my best periscope imitation.

The figure I'd seen had been too tall to be an animal. I shivered as I searched, realizing it could have been a murderer intent on removing a snoopy wine bar owner. I had a security camera over the back door because the small employee parking lot could be dark and was out of sight of the main areas. But I didn't have a camera in front here, although the historical museum to our right did.

"What's going on, Cece?" Mooncat asked from the bar.

"Shh." I waved my hand in a backward motion, hoping to signal for her not to approach. "Stay where you are and act normal." I moved my gaze slowly around the area but didn't see any more skulking. *Darn*.

I moved to the side of the window and pushed up to standing before joining Mooncat.

"I thought I saw someone out there," I said. "Something moving, anyway."

"Not a coyote or a deer?"

"I don't think it was a deer. The profile was wrong, and it was way too tall to be a coyote." I stared at the windows on the front.

"You turned off the lights because you felt it was suspicious movement."

"Yeah. I didn't want to be seen watching to see what happened next."

"You think it might have been whoever killed Regan?" she asked.

"Maybe? But it could have been anybody. You know what happens when there's a full moon."

"It makes us all a little nuts," she said. "I know all about it. Better watch out or I'll be running out to howl at that pretty orb."

"Be my guest." I relaxed at her humor. "I guess I was wrong

about the skulker, but if I wasn't, your howling will make them run."

"Or jump into the Russian Trickle, more likely."

I laughed at her reference to the nearly dry river as I picked up an open bottle of unoaked chardonnay and held it up to the light. Its fullness was on the border between saving for tomorrow or consuming tonight. "A glass while we clean?"

"You bet."

I poured. We clinked glasses and I took a sip. She resumed loading the dishwasher. I opened the cash drawer and sorted the bills in the till.

An incoming text distracted me. I smiled to see Benjamin's name on it. Even though I'd seen him yesterday, I missed the guy. I opened his message.

I get you all to myself on Saturday, yes?

You bet. Miss you. XXOO

Miss you more. OOXX

I stashed the phone and got back to the various jobs at hand.

Mooncat turned on the dishwasher. "You were going to tell me what went down between Gareth and our illustrious mayor."

"Right. And you were going to tell me what you learned this morning."

"You go first."

I related what Gareth had said at Allie's cookout, followed by the bit I'd overheard tonight before things grew heated.

"She claimed these processes took time and there was nothing she could do," I went on. "You weren't there when she essentially accused him of trying to bribe her with a glass of wine."

"Right. He'd left when I came back inside."

"She got kind of ugly after that. She said she knew all about his crime family and their shady real estate dealings."

"Did you debunk her idea?" Mooncat asked.

"I didn't. I know he's escaped from their grasp and has worked super hard to start over. I thought I'd be stooping to Malia's level to get into an argument with her about it during business hours."

"Good move. Makes you wonder how she got to be mayor, though."

"For sure." I pointed at her. "Your turn."

"It was actually in the seminar I attended. Over the pitiful spread they called lunch, I was chatting with a scientist who lives in Sonoma. When he heard that I live and work here, he got all excited. Well, not excited, but he said he had information you might be interested in."

"He knew who I was?" I gaped. "How in the world would somebody down there ever have heard of me?"

"I might have done a little bragging about my PI boss."

"You didn't."

"I sure did." She tossed her braid behind her, grinning. "At any rate, don't you want to hear what he said?"

I folded my arms. "Yes. Out with it."

"He was Greg Jardis's neighbor when he lived there. Did you know Greg used to run a vintage car show in Sebastopol?"

"Like we had here on Saturday."

"Exactly. One year he apparently met Regan Greene and the two became regular sleepover buddies at Greg's house, according to this guy. Maybe she had incriminating information about him, and after he moved up here she was using it to get money or influence, or to threaten him."

"The neighbor didn't have that kind of detail, I gather."

"Unfortunately, no." Mooncat took a sip of her wine.

"If he'd been unfaithful to Regan, maybe she was threatening to tell his new dates up here."

"Possible." She emptied her glass. "Let's finish up and get out of here."

"Sounds like a plan."

After we locked up, together Mooncat and I made our way the short distance out back to our cars in the illumination triggered by the motion detector light. Had I imagined the figure skulking in the dark earlier? Maybe. Maybe not. It could be my door attacker from last night. I shivered at the thought.

Chapter 38

Allie picked me up at eight thirty the next morning. I arranged the outing with her after I got home last night. She was mostly silent on the drive to what was technically the next valley, although I thought of Dry Creek Valley as part of the Alexander Valley.

As we crested a hill, I gasped. Dry Creek was definitely separate. Fog rose up toward us filling everything below. The skies had been clear on the other side of this range of low hills. In a moment we were enveloped in the mist as we descended. Allie flipped on her lights and slowed.

"Classic valley fog," she said. "It'll burn off by eleven."

"How do you know?"

She shrugged. "It always does. I've lived here a long time, sis. We get it on the Colinas side, too."

"True." I clutched my travel mug of dark coffee with both hands, but Allie seemed confident to drive with only a dozen yards of pavement visible in front of us at any given time, and fewer on the curves. I'd experienced the valley fog a couple of times in the last year, but it hadn't been while I was driving on a twisting road.

"In Pasadena, people called it June gloom," I said. "We had days the fog never lifted around this time of year. Plenty of tourists were disappointed, expecting a classic, always sunny California."

"The Golden State isn't all the movies make us out to be."

"No. At least they've considerably cleaned up the smog in the San Gabriel Valley. My eightysomething neighbor had lived there all her life. She said in the sixties there were days the smog was so bad you could barely see the San Gabriel Mountains, which are only a few miles away."

"Mount Wilson is like six thousand feet high, isn't it?" Allie asked.

"Nearly, yes."

Once we got to the flat valley bottom, the sky seemed to lighten a little. I spotted the Zelma Vineyards sign and pointed. Allie turned in where it said, "Visitor Parking." She pulled into a spot and turned off the car.

"That didn't take long," I said. "We're about ten minutes early. Are you okay to talk a little?"

"I guess."

"How are you and Fuller doing with his news?"

Her shoulders sagged. "He seems fine. He's getting organized in case he can't work as much after his treatment starts. He also has an amazing attitude. It's not like he loves his diagnosis, but he's level about it all. He says this is his life, and whichever way it goes, it's still his life. Something like that."

"And you?" I spoke softly and reached my hand out to grasp hers.

"I'm a total wreck. You know me, I like to control my life and make everything go well. This? I can't control one bit of it." She looked straight ahead, but from the side her expression was stricken. Her eyes dragged down at the corners, as did her mouth, and her forehead was wrinkled in anguish.

"Um, Al." I cleared my throat. "You know exactly what you can offer. Your support for Fuller and for the boys. Logistical everything, which you excel at. And maybe try to take a lesson from the man himself. Your husband is a wise person."

She nodded.

"Try to soak up a bit of his equanimity, yeah? You guys will get through this. We'll all get through it."

She let out a shaky breath but squared her shoulders and twisted to gaze at me. "Thanks, Cee. You're right. We will."

I smiled, squeezed her hand, and relinquished it.

"Hey, any word on how Richard is?" she asked.

"Not really. I saw him yesterday in the hospital. He still hadn't remembered what happened to him. I'll go by again on my way to work."

"We can go together after we're done here, if you want."

"Thanks. That's a thought," I said. "It's almost nine, but I have one more thing I wanted to ask you. Has Gareth talked with you about the permitting for his new development?"

"Ugh. Yes."

I told her about the interaction between Gareth and Malia last night. "After he left, she basically insulted him, implying he's still under his uncle's control. Do you think she's trying to block the development?"

"I wouldn't put it past Malia, but it's a mean thing to do." She shook her head. "He's totally free of that wretched family. Still, I wonder if the more affluent Colinas residents have been influencing her."

"People who claim to support low-cost housing but don't actually want it in their backyard. I thought the same thing."

"Right, because they don't want the 'riff raff' polluting their pretty little town. I'd be happy to tell them exactly where they can shove that kind of view." She flipped open her palms. "You know the deep-pockets folks are among my real estate clients, but that doesn't mean I agree with them. Let me see what I can find out about our not-so-esteemed mayor."

"Perfect."

She gazed at me. "You know, sis, can I say something?"

"What are you talking about? You can say anything."

"You have such a self-confidence about you these days. You had too long a run of not believing in yourself, and I love seeing the change. You're good at your job, you have Zoe back in your life, and you absolutely glow when you talk about Benjamin. Turning into a crack amateur sleuth is the cherry on top."

My cheeks warmed. "Thank you. Life does seem to be going my way recently, doesn't it?"

"You bet, and rightly so."

"I don't want to jinx it, though." I crossed my fingers on both hands. "Shall we go in now?"

"Let's do it."

I loved how quickly Allie was able to pivot away from her worries. She would be fine, as would Fuller. In the past, my twin had assisted me more often than the reverse. Today I'd been able to help her, and that felt good.

Chapter 39

David Zelma met us at the front door to the building after I texted him that we'd arrived. My sister and I put on the white hard hats and orange reflective vests he handed to us.

"They're required for all visitors. To be sure, I'll keep you well away from anything dangerous." He led us through a series of cavernous rooms filled with tables and chairs, closed cardboard cases, wooden barrels, and more. One had tubing, machinery, and conveyor belts holding glass bottles. "This is your tour in reverse, but don't worry. We'll come back through all of it." He led us outside and up a set of metal steps.

In his presentation to my class, I'd already seen the slide of the truck full of freshly picked grapes, dumping them into a giant hopper, but Allie's jaw dropped at the sight of that process happening in front of us.

"That's a lot of grapes," she murmured.

David laughed. "We make a lot of wine."

While she was marveling at the volume of the fruit, my own thoughts flashed on how that seven-foot-long hopper could easily accommodate a dead body or, worse, an unconscious person, who would be crushed and suffocated by the weight of the grapes. *Yikes.* Was I thinking about murder too much? Possibly.

David talked us through the process as he had in the class. This time I smelled the pungent ripe . . . *wait*.

"David, how can you have ripe grapes at this time of year?" I asked. "The harvest around here happens in September and October, doesn't it?"

"Good catch, Cece," he said. "These were picked in Mexico and driven up overnight in a refrigerated truck. Their juice will become part of a less expensive blend."

Allie and I watched as the contents of the hopper slowly fed into a channel that carried the fruit into the first of many machines. This one separated stems and leaves from the berries. The output spilled down another channel, one with rubbery robot fingers that further selected out the unwanted plant parts.

The huge stainless steel screw was next, grinding the grapes as they passed through. I shuddered at the razor-sharp edges of the helical device. David described the next steps in the process, including how they filled smaller tanks and pumped air into bladder membranes, which pressed out the juice.

Taking the tour as a slide show in class had been one thing. Being here in person was another experience entirely. He led us along a catwalk and asked us to wait there. It overlooked a row of the enormous tanks I'd seen on the screen. We both promised not to stray, but a young worker in a matching vest joined us to be sure.

"How long have you worked here?" Allie asked her.

"A year." She smiled and flipped her long braid back over her back.

"Do you like the work?" I asked.

"You bet," she said. "I want to be a winemaker, and this is a great place to start out. I'm going to work the *vendange* in the fall. I want to learn every aspect of the business."

"Good luck." I smiled at her.

After a minute, David appeared on the pavement below. He

called up to us about the tanks. These were the ones he'd described in class, the containers that needed to be cleaned by a person crawling inside once they were empty of wine.

The tour continued, with the young worker bringing us down to ground level to join David. I thanked her.

"If you're ever in Colinas, stop by Vino y Vida and have a glass on the house. If I'm not there, tell them Cece sent you."

"Wow, thanks, Cece." She shook hands with Allie and me, then headed back to whatever her regular job was.

I leaned back to take in the size of the tank up close. "That's enormous."

"It holds over sixty-two thousand gallons."

"Wow." Allie pointed to an oval hatch in the side near the bottom of the tank. It looked about eighteen inches by two feet and was latched by a rod that turned. "What's that for?"

"The tanks need to be cleaned when they're empty. One of our smaller employees crawls in there with a scrub brush and cleaning solution."

"You're kidding." Allie stared at David, at the hatch, and back at him. "Somebody slides in that small opening and scrubs the walls?"

"I'm not kidding," he said.

"Is there ventilation?" I asked. "Fumes could really build up."

"Absolutely. There's a vent on top we open, and trip wires inside in case of emergency. We also have a CO_2 meter and use a buddy system."

"What's the cleaning solution?" I asked.

"We can't use bleach, but getting rid of bacteria is a must. We clean with a mix of sulfur dioxide, water, and citric acid." He pointed to a yellow hose coiled up between this tank and the one next to it. "The tanks are thoroughly flushed with water from the top after the cleaning."

"Sulfur dioxide," Allie said. "Isn't that also the gas that gets pumped in to replace oxygen?"

"Indeed, it is. Let's move on to the barreling stage."

David seemed to want to get off the topic of sulfites, which was the common way to refer to SO_2 when it was added to wine. Some of my customers at Vino y Vida insisted they could only drink sulfite-free wines. What they didn't realize was that the gas was super important to prevent the spoilage and discoloration that contact with oxygen could cause.

Come to think of it, Regan Greene asked if I had any sulfite-free options at the car show. Maybe she was prone to allergies. Some people did have a specific allergy to sulfites, and I'd seen her use an inhaler on Saturday.

We finished our tour, and David handed each of us a bottle from a limited-release petite sirah.

"This is lovely, David." Allie beamed. "Thank you so much for the bottle and the tour. Where do you grow your grapes, and do you have a tasting room? I'm in real estate, and I'd love to hold a meeting there."

"We can certainly work with you on that. The vineyard abuts this facility, and the tasting room has a beautiful view of the fields, with outdoor serving capacity." He handed her his card.

"That sounds great." Allie reciprocated with a card of her own.

"Thank you from me, as well," I said. "What I learned today will help me be more informed for my customers. Even though all we do is pour wine, I sometimes get questions about the winemaking process"

"I'm glad your visit here will be useful," David said. "I'll stop into Vino y Vida next time I'm in the area." He showed us out.

Allie and I made our way to the car. The fog had burned off early. It was now a classic sunny California morning.

"I bet your sleuthing mind was working overtime on a few of the things he said." She winked at me.

"I confess it was. Did you have fun?"

"Yes." She pulled me into a hug. "It was a perfect distraction. Thanks, Cee."

Chapter 40

Allie opted out of coming with me to see Richard after the visit to the Zelma facility and dropped me at home so I could get my car.

"I have work to do, and I really want to check out the Zelma tasting room sometime soon," she said. "My agency is hosting the valley's real estate social next month, and that might be a perfect spot."

I loved that she had rediscovered her usual energy and drive. She was going to need it going forward. I started up the Mustang and headed over to Healdsburg, but my visit didn't last long.

I was able to pop in and say hello to Richard, but a different nurse was busy with him doing final stuff prior to discharging him, and then the doctor came in. I wasn't invited to stay.

When I asked Richard if he needed a ride, he said his nephew and his wife were on their way to Healdsburg to drive him back to their house in Cloverdale for a few days. It was good for him not to be alone, although he'd griped about how nobody trusted him to be in his own house. When you're over ninety and having both balance and memory issues, maybe that came with the territory.

As I climbed into Blue in the hospital parking lot, a text came into my phone.

"Huh," I said out loud after I read it. Librarian Tino Ribeiro said he had information I might want to see. He invited me to stop by the library any time today. I liked the sound of that.

I drove slowly back to Colinas, thinking about Richard. While it was great that my friend was going to get out of the hospital today, he still didn't seem to know how he'd hit his head.

I parked in the library's lot and made my way inside. A person at the main desk pointed me to Tino's office across the way. The door stood open, and he glanced up from his monitor as I approached.

"Cece, good." He smiled and waved me in. "You got my text."

"Yes, thanks."

"Could you pull the door shut, please?" he asked.

I obliged, then sat in the chair across from his desk.

"How's your investigation going?" he asked.

"Slowly." I gave my head a little shake. "As you know, I'm strictly an amateur, and the police and sheriff's detective have no obligation to share information with me. Unfortunately, I also haven't heard that they're making any progress."

"Maybe this will help." He turned toward the nearest of his two monitors. "I was able to dig into a few special-access databases. The Sonoma County Sheriff's Department has learned that the late Regan Greene was poisoned by a toxin contained in a bottle of red wine. Wine made in this area."

"Whoa. That's a lot to take in." I tilted my head, regarding him. "Did you hack into those restricted databases?"

"It wasn't hacking, exactly." He sat back in his wheelchair, tenting his fingers, a sly smile on his face. "But we have our methods," he said with a fake German accent.

"More power to you." I began thinking out loud. "Regan

was alive and well Saturday afternoon. She was reported dead Sunday morning, although I still don't know by whom. That must have been a fast-acting poison."

"True. Many toxins take time to finish off a victim. The exceptions can be because of an allergic reaction or an underlying health issue."

I peered at him.

He chuckled. "I mean, or so I understand from the novels and podcasts I listen to."

"But you didn't find out what the poison was?" I asked.

"Alas, no."

"How about who reported her dead?"

"Sorry. Even librarians have their limits."

"That's hard to believe." I smiled. "It's an interesting puzzle to consider that bottle of wine. The killer could have pierced the cork with a syringe and injected the poison. Or maybe they uncorked it, added the poison, and recorked the bottle in a way that made it look unopened, which would be less detectable. That makes it a carefully planned murder, not anything spontaneous."

"It does. Amateur winemakers around here must have corking devices."

"I suppose." I'd never heard Dane talk about making her own wine, and Richard certainly didn't. "Huh . . ." My voice trailed off.

"Yes?"

"I wonder if Greg Jardis sells winemaking equipment at Colinas Hardware."

"Good thought. It should be easy to find out."

"It should," I said. "Although I shouldn't be snooping around there, at least not if Greg is working. I think he already has his back up about my questions."

"I'll give them a call after we're done here."

"You will?"

He nodded.

"Thanks," I said. "But once the bottle was ready, whoever dosed it had to have given it to Regan."

"But perhaps not personally. They could have dropped off a gift basket on her porch or had someone deliver it."

"Good thought, Tino. The gourmet market makes wine-adjacent picnic baskets."

"Exchange Bakery and Gourmet Provisions. 'Everything for wine tasting except the wine.' Isn't that their motto?" he asked.

"Something like that, yes," I said. "I'd think the police or the county would have checked her neighborhood for door cams, but even if there aren't any, somebody dropping by with a gift basket wouldn't look suspicious."

"True. I doubt Greene would have opened it without a note, but the killer could have left a false name or made it seem like a thank-you gift from an organization. The Colinas chamber of commerce, say, or the county board of supervisors."

"And if the card was typed, it'd be hard to trace it back."

"Indeed." Tino leaned back and interlaced his fingers behind his head. "We make a pretty good team, Ms. Barton." His eyes sparkled.

"I really appreciate your help."

"You know, I was wondering—"

A knock came at his door, which swung open a few inches. "Are you coming to the meeting?" a woman's voice asked.

"Is it that time already? I'll be right there," he replied.

"I have to go, anyway." I stood and extended my hand. "Let's be in touch."

"Please." His handshake was firm and smooth. "I'll let you know what I find out about the hardware store." He wheeled out from behind the desk.

I made my way to my car. It had felt good, talking through

the logistics of the wine bottle with him. He was curious and knowledgeable and interested in solving the case.

I had the sneaking suspicion that right when he was called to his meeting, he'd been wondering if he could ask me out. I would have told him no, of course, but I was flattered to think I still had game. It's always nice to be liked.

Chapter 41

The gourmet market was on my way from the library to work, and once again I hadn't brought lunch or dinner. I pulled into a space in front of the store and headed inside.

As always, it smelled divine. Between the aroma of scones baking, the tangy local olive oil, and meatballs cooking, I felt like I'd eaten a full meal from the smells alone. Or rather, when my stomach growled, like I hadn't eaten in days.

I spotted a rack of preassembled picnic baskets and wandered over to check them out. They were filled with things like rosemary olive-oil crackers, hard sausage, aged chevre and little red disks of Babybel cheese, containers of multicolored olives, tiny jars of cornichons, fancy potato chips, and chocolate biscotti. One had preserved salmon instead of the sausage and gluten-free rice crackers, and the vegetarian version included neither salmon nor sausage. A sign above the baskets read, "Just Add Wine!" In fact, one could easily slide a bottle of wine in alongside the food items.

A staff person approached me. "Can I help you with a basket?" they asked.

"I'm glad to see one with salmon rather than sausage. These baskets must be pretty popular. Do you sell a lot of them?"

"They do move, especially on weekends and during the holidays. Besides wine, you can add your own grapes or a container of our pasta salad. The baskets also make great consumable gifts."

How much more could I ask? Surely I couldn't run through the list of suspects and inquire if any of them had bought a basket last Friday or Saturday.

"Thank you," I said. "I'll remember that."

"Let me know if there's anything else I can help you with." The employee moved on to straighten boxes of cookies in the next aisle.

I headed over to the deli counter and joined the line. I studied the list of sandwiches, wraps, and salads they offered. I didn't see any new options, but the one I usually ordered was always yummy. The man in front of me stepped forward.

"I'd like a meatball sub, please, with everything."

My eyes flew open. I hadn't really looked at him, but that voice belonged to Zeke Cruz.

"Toasted roll?" the deli worker asked.

"Yes."

"That'll be twelve-fifty. Number forty-eight."

Zeke pulled out a credit card and tapped it on the card reader on the counter. The skin around his fingernails was stained a dark color. He moved to the side.

"Hi, Zeke," I said.

He turned, but he didn't smile when he saw who I was. "How's it going, Cece?"

"Good."

"Next please," the counter worker said.

"The goat gouda sandwich, please, with avocado, on sourdough." It came with avocado mayo and grainy Dijon mustard, and their house dill pickles were to die for. *Ugh.* There was that phrase again. I selected a bag of home-style potato chips from the basket. "And these."

The man at the counter gave me my total. "You're number forty-nine."

I thanked him and tapped my card, then added several bills to the tips jar next to the reader. I moved out of the way of the person behind me and joined Zeke. "They make great sandwiches here."

"They do."

"The smell of meatballs cooking might make me abandon being a vegetarian." I laughed.

"They're delicious." Still no smile.

"Are you helping out with Yolanda's opening tonight?"

"I am."

He didn't seem to want to talk, but I wasn't ready to give up.

"I can't remember what time it begins," I said.

He stared at me. "You plan to be there?"

"Sure. I like to support local artists and my friend's gallery, and I work a few yards away."

"So you do. Well, the reception is from seven to nine."

"Cool. Are there going to be refreshments?"

"Wine and cheese." His shoulders relaxed. "In fact, one reason I'm here is to pick up the platter. You know, cheese, crackers, grapes, and so on. They arrange it all balanced and attractive."

"Good choice." I was about to ask which wines he and Yolanda would be serving when a multipierced, multi-inked woman at the end of the counter called out number forty-eight.

"Excuse me, Cece." Zeke stepped toward her. "That's me."

"Zee, my man," she exclaimed. "Yo, how's the winemaking going?"

Winemaking? That might explain the dark stains on his fingers. It might also mean Zeke had a corking device at home. Zeke, whose twin sister had hated the now-dead Regan Greene.

"Well, I'm a rank amateur," he told the woman. "But I enjoy

it." He accepted his paper-wrapped bundle of meat on a roll and hurried out, not making eye contact with me.

"Forty-nine," the woman called.

I took my sandwich, thanking her. I had much to think about, but right now I had a workplace to prep and open.

CHAPTER 42

I moved around Vino y Vida with the lights off. I propped open the door to the patio and wiped down the tabletops of any leaves, pollen, or ash that had descended since last evening. I found a bit of each. At least the air didn't currently smell of smoke.

When I grew too hungry to wait, I sat at the counter behind the bar and opened my sandwich, then rewrapped half to eat for supper. It was only twelve fifteen. I had plenty of time to prep before our one o'clock opening.

I was chewing my second bite when Tino called. "Hey," I said.

"Guess what?" he asked.

"What?"

"Colinas Hardware stocks a full section of winemaking equipment. Carboys, tubing, sterilizing solution, corks and corking equipment, hydrometers. You name it, they have it."

"Wow," I said. "Thanks for checking." I told him about Zeke Cruz making his own wine. "Yolanda Cruz is his twin, and you remember what Henry said about her feelings about Regan. Maybe Zeke got the equipment at Greg's store."

"Interesting. You think they might have worked together to poison the wine that killed Greene?"

"No idea, but it's a thought."

Tino cleared his throat. "Do you work on the weekend?"

There it was. "I don't, and my boyfriend has something planned for us. It'll be nice to have a couple of days off."

He didn't speak for a telltale moment. "Well, have fun."

"Thanks. Hey, I enjoyed talking about the case with you earlier. I appreciate you sharing your expertise and brainstorming with me."

"Sure, no problem." His voice was flat.

"Maybe once this is solved, we can record a true crime podcast episode about it."

He laughed, but I was glad I couldn't see his face.

"Maybe. Catch you later, Cece." He disconnected the call.

C'est la vie. I hated to dash anyone's hopes, but I wasn't interested in dating anyone except Benjamin. We'd both agreed to be exclusive.

I swiped through my phone with my left hand while eating with my right, but I was disappointed. In particular, I couldn't find a speck of news about Regan Greene's murder, no matter how I mixed up and recombined the search terms. Murder, homicide, poisoning, AVDA, Colinas, Regan Greene. Nada. Zip. Zilch.

Sitting back, I tried to put my brain to work. Yolanda probably had a key to her twin's apartment or house. She might have borrowed his wine corker without him knowing. Alternatively, Zeke could have aided and abetted his sister. I flashed on their names, wondering if Yolanda was older, with her name preceding his in the alphabet. Did they have a brother called Xavier and an oldest sibling named Wanda?

Back to corking wine bottles. Greg Jardis stocked the devices in his store. Maybe he liberated one for his own nefarious purposes and then cleaned and returned it to the shelf.

Another possibility was Dane, my own trusted employee, working together with Greg to poison Regan or perhaps acting on her own. I hated the thought of a murderer right here in my wine bar, but she certainly had been acting strange this week. And then there was Malia, our town's mayor, who knew chemicals. She might have access to winemaking equipment somewhere, whether in her own home or elsewhere. She said she had a family member who worked in the industry.

Or maybe I was making too much of the wine bottle thing.

I ate the last bite of my lunch and chased it with a pickle. I would crack open the chips with dinner. It was time for this business owner to switch gears and get serious. Fridays were always busy, and I was sure today would be no exception.

With clean hands, a half sandwich in the minifridge in the back room, and a Vino y Vida apron tied on, I began setting out glasses, opening bottles, and filling cracker baskets. Mooncat bustled in after a couple of minutes.

"What in the world is going on out there?" she asked. "Traffic is nuts again. This time a bunch of pickup trucks are in a caravan that also included a couple of big tractors."

"Is it a farmers' event?"

"Could be, or maybe an action, like a protest. You weren't alive at that time, Cece, but I remember my parents talking about the United Farm Workers' boycott against nonunion grapes. Nobody ate California grapes in the late sixties. I was little and loved them, but my parents supported the boycott, led in part by Cesar Chavez. The whole country did, and the UFW got their demands met."

"The power of spending, right?" I glanced at the clock. "We're going to have thirsty customers lining up to spend money on us in about ten minutes. I already wiped down outside. Can you write the pours on the board, please? We have a Zelma petite sirah, a Twomey pinot noir, and a Pedroncelli chardonnay."

"I'm on it, boss lady." Mooncat whistled a tune as she tied an apron over today's hot pink denim miniskirt and peasant blouse that she'd paired with colorful striped tights and combat boots.

How strange it was that I, who hadn't finished college and

had barely accomplished anything in my life until last year, now owned a successful business and had an accomplished woman twenty-five years my senior cheerfully calling me "boss lady."

I shook my head at the unlikeliness of it all. If Allie hadn't urged me to move to Colinas, I'd still be in Pasadena feeling like a lonely failure. But I wasn't, and now was now.

CHAPTER 43

Sure enough, we were busy. Customers kept Mooncat and me on our toes from when we opened to now at a little after three o'clock. A group filed in from the patio and left.

"They were the last ones out there," Mooncat said.

A couple hailed her from a two-top in the corner.

"I'll go make sure it's ready for the next wave," I said. I grabbed a rag and a tray.

Before I could reach the patio, Kelly Daniell came through the front door. I waited for her to approach.

"Can we talk?" she asked.

"Come outside with me." I exchanged a glance with Mooncat, who nodded. I unpropped the patio door and let it swing shut after the detective. "Go ahead and talk, but I need to do a bit of work."

She sank onto a stool with a heavy exhale.

"Tough case?" I started on the farthest table, clearing glasses onto the tray and spraying and wiping down the surface.

"I'll say. We can't seem to pin anything down."

"Want a glass of wine? No charge."

"I'd love to have one, but I can't. I'm on duty twenty-four seven until I've made an arrest that can stick, but I'll take a rain check." She watched me clean the next table. "What have you heard?"

"In the last twenty-four hours?" She and I had caught up only yesterday at the hospital.

"It's worth asking."

I nodded. "I did hear that Regan might have been poisoned, and that the toxin was in a bottle of wine."

Kelly's jaw dropped. "You're kidding."

"Nope."

"Who did you learn that from?"

"Um, a friend." *Ugh.* Maybe I shouldn't have blown Tino's cover. Was his access to wherever he'd been digging entirely legal?

"I need to know this friend's name." Her expression was steelier than those giant tanks at the production facility, and her posture made her backbone look like it was an iron rod instead of a spine. "We have not released that information to the public."

"It's a librarian with excellent searching skills and resources."

"Oh! Do you mean Tino?"

It was my turn to gape. "Yes. You know him?"

"I do." Her shoulders relaxed. "He's amazing. We keep trying to hire him into the department, but he loves his position at the library. Instead, he's on speed dial as an occasional information consultant."

"Was he not supposed to tell me?"

"Actually, he wasn't. And if he'd told anyone else, I'd never talk to him again. But you?" She barked out a laugh. "It's okay."

Whew. I was glad Tino wasn't in trouble.

"Have you thought about how the poison got into the wine in a way that didn't make Regan suspicious?" I asked.

"Cece." She looked down her nose at me. "Of course we have."

"Sorry. But if the bottle was dosed up and recorked, I was thinking about who among those who hated Regan would have had access to a corking device."

She tilted her head. "Interesting. So have I. What are your thoughts?"

I ticked them off on my fingers. "Greg Jardis. Zeke Cruz and therefore Yolanda. Maybe Malia, and maybe Dane."

"Yep."

I waited, but she didn't add anything else. "I'm interested in what kind of poison Regan died from." I left it at that. She would tell me or she wouldn't.

Kelly drummed her fingers on the table, gazing at the big tree. "Unfortunately, the lab is backed up. They can't run tests for all extant toxins in the world. I mean, they can, but it takes way too long. We might have an idea, but the logjam is what's messing with the results at the moment. Investigations are never as fast and tidy as they appear on TV."

"I suppose not." I wiped down the last table in need of it.

"Anything else you happened to learn?" she asked.

"Let's see. Jo Jarvin said Malia Gutierrez has a background in chemicals. And Mooncat learned that Greg Jardis and Regan were lovers in Sebastopol."

"Interesting, and duly noted. That's it?"

"I think so. Did Regan live alone? Because there're also the questions of how the wine got to her and why she was willing to open the bottle and drink enough to kill her."

"Important questions. Yes, she lived alone. I have people canvassing and looking at door cam footage. So far, nothing."

Mooncat poked her head out the door. "David Zelma is here to see you."

"Thanks," I said. "Please ask David to come out."

Kelly stood. "I have to get going, anyway. Thanks, Cece. You can believe I'll take you up on that glass the minute I can."

"Good." I smiled.

At the door, David appeared and motioned for Kelly to come through.

"Good luck, Detective," I called to her.

David twisted his head to watch her go, then joined me on the patio. "She's a detective?"

"She is, a deputy sheriff with Sonoma County."

He frowned. "And she needs good luck why?" He sat on one of the stools.

"Haven't you heard about the most recent Colinas homicide?" He must have been living under a rock not to have heard. Either that, or I was way too close to it. Regan's murder was almost all I'd thought about since Sunday.

"I guess I did. Work has been busy, and I don't live in Colinas." A cloud passed over his face. A cloud of emotions, not one in the sky. "My father's ill, too. We're not sure he'll make it."

"I'm really sorry."

"I appreciate that, Cece. It's a tough time for my family."

Mooncat returned carrying a stemless glass with a hefty pour of red. "Your pinot, sir."

"Sampling the competition?" I asked.

"Why not?" He smiled up at my employee as he accepted the glass. "Thank you, Mooncat."

"You know each other?" I asked.

She blushed, something I'd never seen her do before. "We're starting to."

I glanced at his left hand, which was bare of a wedding band. I was pretty sure Mooncat was single. She sashayed back inside, swinging her impressive hips. His cheeks also pinked up as his gaze followed her. Well, well. More power to them.

Chapter 44

"This is an attractive patio, Cece," David said.

"Thanks, it is. I mean, I can't take credit for it existing, but I've done a few improvements in the last year, and it's a popular place for people to enjoy their wine." I had the wrought iron metal fencing sanded and repainted and the floor resurfaced with polished concrete. I thought up the tables made of half wine barrels, as well. "The tree and the river are God's handiwork, not mine."

"It's a welcoming space." He swirled the wine in his mouth. "This is good. They make a fine product over at Twomey."

"I have to agree. How's your grape crop doing?"

"The bloom is complete and the berries are forming. So far my vineyard manager is saying it looks like we have a good fruit set. But from now until the fall, our harvest will depend a lot on the weather."

"Enough rain, but not too much. Enough sun, but not too much."

"Exactly." He sipped again. "The *véraison* isn't until late July."

"That means the ripening, right?"

"It does. It's when the berries plump up and sweeten and when we get a sense of this year's crop quality, at least as far as making wine goes."

"It must be tough to be a farmer," I said.

"The business can be unpredictable, for sure. We control all we can, but as you say, the weather is largely God's handiwork, not ours. Anyone who grows food for a living has to factor in losses, sometimes steep ones."

A text beeped at me. I gave my phone a quick glance, but when I saw it was from Kelly Daniell, I excused myself and turned away from David.

"I know you're busy," he said. "I'll take my glass inside."

"Thanks. I'll be right in."

Kelly's message made me frown. She said she forgot to tell me that the open bottle of wine she suspected was poisoned bore a Zelma Vineyards label. Zelma wines were available for sale everywhere in the county. It didn't implicate David in the crime—did it?

It had better not, not if Mooncat was interested in him. David claimed to barely know about Regan's murder. I wanted to believe him. But . . . I frowned. As a valley winemaker, he had to be part of her district. Strictly speaking, the winery wasn't in the Alexander Valley, but I believed AVDA covered the entire Alexander Valley region, which would include Dry Creek.

I propped open the door to the patio and headed inside, where business was picking up again. I spent a few minutes taking orders and delivering glasses to tables. David was perched on a stool at the bar, chatting with Mooncat when she was free, making her laugh.

A group of women in their fifties came in, their heels clicking on the floor. One with dyed and streaked hair wearing a well-tossed scarf approached me.

"We can sit outside?" Her voice was French accented, her makeup perfect.

"Please." I gestured toward the patio. "I'll be out in a minute to talk about what wines we have today. They're also written on the board out there."

"*Merci.*" She led her friends out.

Whether French or from Quebec, they were all equally chic in clothing and coiffures. We served only local wines, and I hoped terroir snobbery wasn't part of their approach to sipping.

I moseyed over to the bar, order slip in hand for the four-top, and selected four glasses.

"David, this morning you were talking about sulfur dioxide and sulfites in wine. Does Zelma make any with less than ten percent? I had a customer asking." I poured as I spoke and didn't make eye contact with him. Wines containing under 10 percent sulfites weren't required to list the substance on the label.

"We have only one. I'm sure you know how important sulfites are for preservation."

"I do." I loaded the glasses onto a tray. "Thanks." I headed across the room to deliver the drinks, but my thoughts traveled back to Regan asking about sulfites at the car show. If she had a severe allergy to them, maybe more of the preservative didn't have to be added to the Zelma wine. My meanderings about who had access to a corking device could be moot. Except she wouldn't drink a wine not labeled as sulfite-free, would she? She must have been given the single vintage Zelma sold without the preservative.

I hoped I hadn't burned my bridges with Tino by telling him I had a boyfriend. He could be a good source of information about allergic reactions to sulfite.

Who could I ask about Regan's allergies? I planned to stop by Yolanda's art opening, but I doubted she would take kindly to being questioned about her late boss. Maybe young Jared would know, except today was Friday. I doubted the office would be open on a Saturday, and I didn't have his contact information. On the other hand, he might show up at the reception to support his coworker.

Kelly had said Regan lived alone. Everybody had family somewhere, didn't they? She could have had deceased parents and been an only child. I hadn't seen an obituary or notice of a funeral or memorial service. Still, nobody to mourn for her seemed harsh, or sad, more correctly.

I gave myself a little shake. I'd promised the French speakers on the patio that I'd be out to take their orders. Time for idle speculation was over.

Chapter 45

Business stayed steady but not crazy busy for the next couple of hours.

"I'm putting in a dinner order." Mooncat held up her phone at five thirty. "I can also get something for you, if you want."

"Thanks, but I have supper."

A few minutes later, she left to pick up her food. I puttered around, clearing tables, talking to a couple about their vacation drive here from Montana, and settling the tab for the women on the patio, who'd said they were from Quebec City.

By six o'clock Mooncat was back and had nearly inhaled her falafel sandwich.

"I'm going to pop over to the gallery at seven for the opening reception Henry's hosting, if you don't mind," I said.

"Not a bit. You won't be far away if we get a Friday night rush."

"True. Right now I'll be in the back room for a few." I headed through the swinging door and grabbed my half sandwich from the employee fridge back room. A corked half-full bottle of sauvignon blanc was in the door. Why not? I poured a glassful into a mug and sat at the work table with my supper and my phone.

I had run an internet search for Regan Greene at the beginning of the week. Could I glean any more information about her with what I knew now? It was worth a try.

I tried to dig up her birthplace or age. An obituary or a death notice would include that information, but I still couldn't locate one. I wished I had a better contact in the Colinas PD. I'd like to ask if anyone had come forward to claim her for whenever the authorities were done with her remains.

Next I checked the AVDA website. At least there someone had expressed condolences. A black-rimmed box on the home page stated that the director, Regan Greene, had passed away. The statement was followed by a plain vanilla message that the organization would miss her service and dedication to the district and that it sent their condolences to her family and the community. Whether they actually knew anything about her family was unclear.

I sat back, popped in the last bite of my sandwich, and washed it down with a sip of wine.

I decided I would ask Yolanda tonight about Regan's family, after all. If Regan's administrative assistant didn't know about her next of kin, who would? Unless maybe cheerful, friendly Jared. I would certainly question him next time I saw him.

Mooncat appeared in the doorway to the front. "Ed Ramirez is here. Want me to send him back?"

"No, I'm all done. Be there in a sec." I stood and crumpled my sandwich paper into a ball and tossed it in the trash, then washed my hands and headed back to the bar.

Ed, a glass of red in hand, stood at the bar. "*Ola, mija.*" He beamed at me.

"*Ola*, yourself. Looks like Mooncat already poured for you."

"She did, and an excellent pinot it is."

"You're looking fancy tonight. Isn't that called a wedding shirt?"

He wore a black short-sleeved Mexican shirt. Square cut, it had vertical strips of black embroidery sewn on both sides of the chest. His gray linen trousers were neatly pressed, and his black shoes shone with polish. Ed usually dressed in a more casual style.

"It is, or more accurately, a Guayabera shirt. We wear them in all colors."

"It suits you." I glanced around but then slapped my forehead. "I was looking for Henry. But he must be getting ready for the reception."

"He is, and I'm going over there after I enjoy this. Thus the getup."

"I plan to go, as well, if I can get away. Let's walk together." Except I was way underdressed if Ed had put on his best going-out clothes. At least I'd donned a black-and-white-patterned skirt this morning, but the black tee I wore with it was nothing special, and my feet were in comfortable sports sandals. The outfit would have to do. If I brushed out my hair and threw on lip gloss, that might help dress up my appearance.

Ed sipped from the glass, then leaned toward me, speaking in a low voice. "I might have something to whisper in your ear when you have a moment."

"Ooh." I gave Mooncat a quick look. She stood holding a full tray of empties near the patio door, and beckoned to me. "I think it's going to have to wait for a bit. Sorry."

"No worries, *querida*. I have a whole glass to enjoy."

"So you do." I joined Mooncat.

"Can you service the patio?" She spoke fast, sounding as frazzled as she looked. "A big group just came in and made a beeline out there."

"Sure."

"The mayor is part of the crowd," she murmured.

"Got it." Outside, I recognized a couple of familiar faces from the town offices, including the clerk, the home inspector, and a woman from the office where I paid the property tax on my house. Malia stood at the farthest table schmoozing with the others.

"Hello, everybody," I said, raising my voice to get their attention. I smiled and added, "Welcome to Vino y Vida. This looks like a town government Friday happy hour."

"You got that right," the building inspector said. "In addition, we're taking the mayor out for her birthday."

I knew him from the changes I'd made here as well as a project at my house that had also required him signing off on a permit. He seemed like a decent guy who never put me down for asking new-homeowner questions or for being a female business owner. I'd certainly run into other officials in my past—including in Colinas—who were not as equitable.

"Excellent," I said. "Happy birthday, Madam Mayor." Having an early June birthday made her a Gemini. Interesting, except I couldn't remember the characteristics of that astrological sign, only that it included today's date.

"Thank you." She didn't return my smile.

"What can I get you all to sip?" I asked. "Offerings are on the whiteboard there. I'll bring out fresh crackers when I bring your drinks." I took their orders and made my way inside.

Other new customers had joined the crowd in here. Getting a quiet moment with Ed was looking less and less likely. Maybe we could accomplish that if we headed over to the gallery together at seven.

"Sorry, my friend," I said to Ed as I approached the bar. "It's madhouse city right now. Rain check?"

"Of course."

I poured the patio drinks and set them on a big tray along with fresh baskets of wheat and rice crackers. I made my way carefully outside, gripping the tray with both hands. I'd never worked as waitstaff before I began here and didn't have the knack for carrying a tray of full glasses one-handed up above the heads of those seated around me.

On the patio, I set the tray on an empty table and dispensed the glasses and baskets.

"Can I get you all anything else right now?"

The inspector lifted his glass. "Join us in song?" He began singing the birthday song. Everyone else but the mayor joined him.

Ugh. Nobody wanted to hear me sing in public. I didn't even like it when people sang that song to me. Not wanting to appear unfriendly, I stood and mouthed the familiar words until the tune was over. But when someone else in the group segued into, "For she's a jolly good fellow," I gave a little wave and left the scene.

How jolly would they think she was if she were arrested for murder?

CHAPTER 46

Despite my comfortable footwear, my feet were killing me by six thirty. The stream of customers had been relentless for the last hour or two, and both Mooncat and I were working as fast as we could. I was at the bar for the moment, pouring and tallying and trying to smile at bar sippers who wanted to schmooze.

Ed, bless his heart, still sat on the stool, still nursing his wine. We'd agreed to walk over to the reception together. Now I worried I might not be able to go at all.

When two more people made their way through the door, I kept my groan silent. Not a single seat was open in here or on the patio, not even the barstools. My entirely unbusinesslike dismay morphed into interest when I saw that the newcomers were Greg Jardis and Dane. They approached the end of the bar, Dane with a tentative step, her date urging her along.

"Is there room outside?" Greg tilted his head toward the patio.

"No, I'm afraid we're at capacity on the patio. It's a safety thing." What with the riverbed nearly twenty feet below, I never wanted to have too many people crowding the railing out there, even though I'd had the platform inspected. It was structurally well supported, for which I was grateful. "You can stand at the bar here and have a glass of wine if you'd like."

"Very well." He glanced at Dane. "What would you like, babe?"

Babe. I cringed inwardly at the endearment. I really should examine why the word bugged me, except I knew. That was how my husband had addressed me, even while carrying on serial adultery with a variety of women from other countries while I was home with our baby girl.

"The sauvignon blanc, please." Her voice was barely audible, and she didn't look at me.

"I'll have the same, Cece," Greg said.

I poured both glasses and set them on the bar.

"Hey, I know you two." Ed smiled and raised his nearly empty glass. "*Salud, amigos*."

"Cheers, Ed," Greg said.

I held up the pinot noir bottle to Ed. "Another splash?"

"Don't mind if I do. *Gracias*, Cece."

"Dane, let me offer you my stool." Ed stood.

"Thanks, but I'm fine." She shook her head. "Seriously."

"You two going over to the gallery?" Ed sat again.

"We are. She wants to check out the competition." Greg squeezed Dane's shoulder.

She winced and took a step away from him. "That's not why. I like to support other artists coming up."

"A laudable sentiment." Ed gazed at Greg. "How's the business, man?"

"Excellent."

"You should join the Main Street business association."

"Not the chamber?"

"No," Ed said. "Our chamber of commerce is a bit dysfunctional, as a matter of fact."

"That's what my sister says, too," I said.

Dane didn't comment. Her knee jiggled at a fast pace.

Two customers at the other end of the bar waved their hands.

Mooncat approached the area carrying a tray full of empty glasses and baskets as well as order slips.

"Excuse me." I smiled. "Enjoy your wine."

"Cece, it looks super busy in here," Dane said in a quick spurt of words. "Do you want me to help?"

Did I? "Thanks, but that's okay." I regarded her. "You're not on the clock, and you're having a nice evening out."

She glanced away—from me and from Greg—with a pained look. *Huh*. Was she enjoying her date? Maybe the budding relationship with Jardis had already soured, and she wasn't having a nice evening at all.

"We can manage, but I appreciate the offer." I slid down to the other end of the bar. I poured, I schmoozed, and I rang up tabs. I loaded the dishwasher and fired it up. Ed, primo schmoozer that he was, held his own with Greg and Dane. Every time I glanced down there, she continued to shift from foot to foot or jiggle her knee. She didn't smile at Greg but engaged with Ed when he spoke to her. Something was definitely up with her.

At about ten before seven, business quieted. No new customers had entered since Greg and Dane, and a number of customers had paid and departed. I was focusing on opening a new bottle of the pinot when the group of town employees trouped in.

"Madam Mayor," Ed's voice rang out. "Join us, please. *Ven*." He lifted his still mostly full glass.

Malia did a double take. She squinted at the three of them. I watched as her lips pressed together. Surely not at Ed. What wasn't to love about him? She straightened her spine, plastered on a mayoral smile, and strode toward the bar.

"*Ola*, Ed." She extended her hand and shook Ed's. "Evening, Greg. Are you enjoying the wine here?"

Of course Ed and Malia knew each other, and I wasn't surprised she at least knew Greg by sight and by name. He had bought a popular local business. I expected Malia and Dane had met before, as well.

"Very much, Malia," Greg said. "You?"

The town clerk joined them. "Say happy birthday to your elected mayor."

Dane raised her glass. "Happy birthday, Malia." Her expression was grim.

Why?

Malia blinked at Dane. "Thank you, Dane." Her tone dripped with sarcasm.

Ed stood. "*Feliz cumpleaños*, Malia. Will you join us?" He gestured toward his stool.

"Thank you. I was on my way out, but I can stay for a few more minutes. I'd rather stand, though."

Greg wished her a happy birthday, but gave Dane an inquiring look. She ignored him.

The clerk shifted down to me. "Can you ring us up, please?"

"Sure." Our system was that we ran the credit card of a customer who wanted to open a tab and cashed them out at the end. Nobody had ever tried to skip out on their bill. If they did, the only thing we'd lose would be a tip. In general, folks who'd imbibed a glass or three tended to tip generously, and I directed all tips to my employees. I pointed toward the screen, which was open to the tips page. "You can sign there."

After he left, I finished what I was doing. Mooncat was busy clearing the patio. I checked out what was going on with Ed and company, super curious about the conflict between Dane and Malia. The mayor stood speaking with Ed. Dane and Greg faced each other, talking in low voices.

I headed to that end of the bar. "Would anyone like another glass?"

"No, thanks." Ed spoke first. "The opening reception starts soon, and I want to get over there."

"What reception is that?" Malia asked.

Ed explained about Yolanda's art. "It's her first show, and Henry thinks her work is quite good."

"I think I'll join you," Malia said. "So, no thanks on the wine, Cece."

"No worries." I gave a glance to Dane, who faced away from me. She shook her head, hard, at Greg.

Mooncat returned from outside and got busy at the other end of the bar.

"Are you coming, Cece?" Ed asked.

"You bet. Let me check in with Mooncat and pop into the back room for a second. I'll be ready in two minutes."

"Great, he said. "I'll wait for you."

"I'll see you both at the gallery." Malia headed for the restroom.

Dane and Greg were off in their own apparently confrontational world. I was happy to leave them to it.

Chapter 47

Blessedly, Ed and I had the short walk across the courtyard to ourselves. The evening was mild, and solar-powered lights were little beacons lighting the path.

"I texted Kelly Daniell that all her persons of interest will be at the reception," I said. "But did I lie? Greg and Dane seemed to be having an argument when I went into the back room to get ready."

"They'll be there. They apparently came to an agreement about at least stopping by the art show. They left while you were getting ready, and Malia made her exit before them."

"Good. Did you pick up on the spark between Dane and Malia?"

"Who could have missed it?" Ed asked. "I'm not sure I've ever seen them together in the same room before."

"I don't think I have, either. So, what were you going to tell me?" I slowed my pace as we neared the lit-up open door of Acorn Fine Art and Sculpture.

"I heard a tidbit at the diner from—"

"Hello, friends." Kelly Daniell strode up. "What did you hear, Mr. Ramirez?"

"Nada." He batted away the thought. "It was inconsequential, Detective. Have you come to peruse fine art or to make an arrest?"

I tried to hide my smile at his quick thinking.

"You never know," she said. "Cece, thanks for the heads-up."

"Any time." I stopped walking and lowered my voice. "Kelly, a few minutes ago in the wine bar, Dane and Malia were openly antagonistic toward each other. Ed saw it, too."

"I did," he said.

"Any idea what it was about?" Kelly asked.

"No." I shook my head. "Not a clue."

"Dane and her date, Greg Jardis, also seemed on the outs," Ed added. "That is, she was disgruntled with him, more so."

"Got it," Kelly said. "They haven't been going out long, am I right?"

"I think that's correct," I said. Depending on whether Greg had been double dipping at Hoppy Hills last week. Maybe he'd already been seeing Dane and arranged a date with a different woman, as well.

"Have you heard anything from Richard Flora?" Kelly asked.

"Not this afternoon. Late this morning I stopped by the hospital, and he was about to be discharged to his nephew's home in Cloverdale."

"It's good he won't be alone as he recovers," Ed said.

I nodded, gazing at the gallery. Yolanda passed by the doorway. I spotted Zeke, cup of wine in his hand, talking with someone I couldn't see. In the background, others moved about peering at the artwork, holding small plates of appetizers, sipping wine. It was like watching a movie with the sound off.

I shook myself. Having Kelly out here was an opportunity not to be missed.

"Have you or the Colinas PD figured out who the would-be intruder at my house was?" I asked. "And if they were who whacked Richard on the head?"

"Sorry, no info yet." Her lips pressed to the side. "I wish we had."

"You never seriously suspected Richard of murdering Regan, did you?" Ed asked.

"Not really," she said. "But we had to check him out."

A man sauntered up, hands in pockets. Kelly gave him a sharp look, but I smiled at Gareth Rockwell.

"Gareth, are you here for the art opening?" I asked.

"I am, and it looks like all the best people had the same idea. Good evening, Ed." He extended his hand to Kelly. "Hi. I'm Gareth Rockwell."

"Kelly Daniell." She shook his hand.

"That would be Sonoma County Deputy Sheriff Detective Sergeant Daniell," I added. "Gareth was a big help when push came to shove last winter, Kelly. Jim Quan was on that case while you were on leave."

"Yes," Kelly said. "He briefed me about it on my return."

"Good to meet you, ma'am." Gareth smiled at her.

"A heads-up, Gareth," I said. "Mayor Guttierez is in the gallery."

"Great." He frowned. "Well, whatever. We're all adults. I'll get my permits eventually."

"Permits for what?" Kelly asked.

"It's a new low-cost housing development, something this town desperately needs," Gareth said. "Malia seems to be opposed to it, which I can't figure out."

"I have a thought on that." Ed raised his index finger. "You know how Regan Greene thought she could lord it over everyone? Now that she's gone, may her soul rest in peace, Malia might feel she finally has the space to do the same to others."

"That's pathetic," I murmured.

"It doesn't make it right, but acting like that is human nature, I'm afraid," Ed said.

Kelly had been following our conversation closely. "I'll keep an eye on the mayor. We wouldn't want someone else doing to her what they did to the deceased."

Unless Malia herself was the killer.

"I'd better get inside and pay my respects," I said. "I still have a couple of hours on the clock in the wine bar."

"I heard that Cece Barton lady runs a tight ship." Gareth grinned.

"She's a tough boss, all right." I returned the smile.

"Shall we go in?" Ed gestured toward the gallery.

I hung back a little with him. After Gareth and Kelly neared the door, I whispered, "Text me, okay?"

"Will do."

Chapter 48

Trouble was brewing at the gallery. I sensed it when I entered. Sure, it was well attended. Nicely dressed art lovers circulated gazing at the paintings and conversing. I recognized several from the wine bar. Others were probably from out of town or folks I hadn't met yet.

The drinks table featured white wine, prosecco, bottles of seltzer, and a pitcher of water—a smart move by Henry. Nobody wanted red wine spilled on original art or sculpture, especially not the owner. The finger food appetizers were all in little individual paper cups so guests could help themselves without spreading germs to others. I liked that approach.

But, scattered here and there, interactions were tense. Dane seemed to be continuing her cold-shouldering of Greg. He stood with arms folded on his chest, studying one of Yolanda's pieces, while Dane huddled alone in a corner, working on her phone.

Gareth passed by Malia, giving her an unsmiling but polite nod. She had her mouth open to respond when Kelly approached. It might have looked like a casual encounter, but I knew Kelly better than that by now. Gareth moved on.

Yolanda, meanwhile, looked both glamorous and artsy. She wore a black one-piece sleeveless jumpsuit that was formfitting on top and wide-legged beneath, the silk fabric shimmering in the light. A beret at a rakish angle topped the outfit. She held a cup of bubbly and chatted with a small cluster of women.

I sidled up to the drinks table and selected an already poured cup of a pinot gris from Oregon. So much for supporting local wineries. I thanked the server standing behind the table and joined Henry where he stood in front of his retail counter.

"She has a good turnout," I said.

"Yes. I put the opening in my newsletter this week." He bussed my cheek. "Thanks for coming, Cece."

"You're welcome. I do have to get back to work soon, but I wanted to support you."

"I appreciate that," he said. "We haven't sold any of her pieces yet, but the night is young."

When a couple approached Henry, I excused myself and surveyed the room. Zeke was talking with Greg, and they were both involved in the case, whether directly or tangentially. I headed their way.

"Yolanda drew a good-sized crowd," I said to Zeke.

"Yes." Zeke gave me a faint smile. "Although seeing that detective here kind of spoils the effect."

Kelly must have interviewed him. "Maybe she likes fine art."

"Maybe," Zeke said.

"Has your sister sold many pieces?" Greg asked. "I might need to acquire one."

"I don't know."

"What's on the schedule for our next class, Zeke?" Greg asked.

"We're going to get into the fields and talk about the stages of growing and harvesting. And Cece here asked about blends. I'll save time for that, as well."

"Great, thanks," I said.

"Here comes trouble," Zeke muttered.

Kelly sauntered up to our trio. "I'd like a little chat with you, Mr. Cruz, if I might."

He gave her an icy stare. "At my sister's art reception, ma'am?"

"You've been a bit elusive until now. So, yes, at this very reception. If you'll excuse us?" She glanced from Greg to me.

"Of course, Detective." Greg gave a shallow bow and turned away.

Had he looked relieved not to be the subject of the little chat? Possibly.

I also stepped away. The women who had been talking with Yolanda moved on. I made a beeline to replace them.

"Great show, Yolanda." I smiled.

"Thank you." Like her brother, she barely smiled.

"Cheers." I held up my cup.

"And to you." She didn't make an effort to touch glasses.

Plastic wouldn't clink, anyway. I needed to get back to work and decided to plunge into the deep end.

"As a colleague of Regan's, have you heard about a service of any kind for her?" I asked.

"No."

"Does she have family in the area or elsewhere? I would think they'd be organizing something."

"I don't know."

"One more question, and then I'll leave you to your adoring fans."

Her lip curled, but she didn't stop me.

"At the car show last week, I overheard Regan say she was allergic to something," I began. "I wondered if you know what it was."

"I don't know anything except that she seemed to have a lot of allergies."

Kelly Daniel approached on pussycat feet behind Yolanda. She wiped her finger across her lips in what I thought might be a casual signal not to let Yolanda know she was there.

"It's that I heard her death might have been an allergic reaction," I went on.

Did alarm flash in her eyes? Whatever emotion it was passed quickly. "Where did you hear that?"

"Somewhere. I can't remember."

"What was it a reaction to?"

"No idea," I said.

"Listen, Cece. This is my big night, and I'm not going to spend it hashing out my former boss's death with you. Have a good evening." She turned, only to meet Kelly face-to-face.

"What are you doing here?" The artist's mouth turned down as if she'd tasted moldy cheese.

"Ms. Cruz, I'm going to spoil a few more minutes of your big night." Kelly gestured toward a quiet corner of the room. "If you please."

"Do I have to?"

"No," Kelly said. "But I would like to clarify several things with you."

"I have nothing to hide." Yolanda strode in that direction, chin high.

Dane came up to me, her head twisting to watch Yolanda. "What's up with her? Isn't she the celebrity tonight?"

"When a detective wants to have a word, it behooves you to say yes, celebrity or not."

"Ugh. I guess."

I took my last sip of wine. "I'm heading back to Vino y Vida. Mooncat's there alone."

"I'll walk with you." She drained her cup and held her hand out for mine. She set them on a tray for used cups near the door.

I pulled it open. "After you."

Chapter 49

"I was afraid the detective was going to corner me, too," Dane said as we strolled along the path.

"Why would she?"

"She's onto the argument I had with Regan. That doesn't mean I murdered the woman, you know?" She gave her head a shake. "Seriously. Half the population would be gone if people went around knocking off a person who rubbed them the wrong way."

"True."

"I mean, right now Greg's kind of rubbing me the wrong way, but I'm not about to kill him."

"That's good." It might explain their distance lately, but I didn't need to pry into what it was about. That was her personal business, not a homicide. We walked a few more paces. "Did you know Regan before she became director of the association?"

Dane didn't answer. We neared the wine bar.

"Dane?"

"I did, okay?" She faced me and folded her arms on her chest.

"When was that?"

She let out a noisy breath. "Back when she ran for state representative. At first I liked what I heard about her positions, and I signed up to volunteer on her campaign. But, Cece, she was the worst. She treated everyone like her personal servant. She ordered us around and became irate if any tiny thing wasn't as perfect as she wanted it to be. It was like working for a tyrant, and I wasn't even being paid."

"Did you quit?"

"You better believe I did. She didn't like that, either. Too bad."

"Sounds like the right thing to do," I said. "Before the reception, it looked like you don't care too much for Malia, either."

"I don't. Our daughters went to school together, and Malia gave my girl the cold shoulder more than once."

"I'm sorry to hear that. Listen, I do have to get inside. Thanks for being honest with me."

"No worries. I think I'll come in for a glass. I'm all done with the art reception."

"And with Greg?"

"Yeah. I told him at the reception." She barked out a laugh. "I mean, don't get me wrong. Greg's a nice guy. He's smart and funny and good-looking. He's generous with his considerable money, and he means well, but he really likes to have a beautiful woman on his arm. This week I've realized I'm not the right one. Heck, I don't even fit the beautiful part."

"Of course you do, but I'm sorry it didn't work out for you. Anyway, you're always welcome at the bar." We headed inside.

By the time I emerged from the back, apron-clad and with clean hands, Dane was well ensconced on a barstool with a glass of red in front of her. She'd already struck up a conversation with the woman next to her.

The place looked about half full. Mooncat stood behind the bar polishing clean glasses.

"Thanks for covering for me," I said.

"Sure. How was the opening?"

"Interesting, mostly because Kelly Daniell was going around pigeonholing people she wanted to talk with and not taking no for an answer, including the artist of the evening."

"How did Yolanda like that?" she asked.

"She wasn't happy, for sure. Any fireworks or crises here while I was gone?"

"Nope. Pretty quiet. Well, if you don't count the party of underagers with fake IDs."

"You caught them out?"

"Amateurs, every single one. I shooed their little behinds out the door and told them to go have a malted milkshake or a cherry Coke at the corner drugstore's soda fountain." She grinned. "I'm sure they had no idea what I was talking about."

"I understand the concept, but I haven't actually been to a soda fountain. Are you old enough to have?"

"Sure, especially in Julian."

"Where's that?"

"It's a sleepy little town in the mountains outside San Diego, although I heard it's gotten touristy recently. The drugstore had an old-fashioned counter for the soda fountain. I had the creamiest, best milkshake of my life there. It was so thick they served it in a tall glass with a long-handled spoon."

"Sounds heavenly." I gazed around the wine bar. "Any particular table or customers I need to know about?"

"No, everybody seems happy at the moment. A foursome is on the patio, but they're well behaved."

"Cool. I can work the front if you want bar duty."

"You got it."

I puttered around, clearing empty tables and taking refill orders, which gave me a little time to think. Hadn't anyone liked Regan Greene? All I'd heard this week were reports of what a difficult person she was. She must have had a difficult childhood to put up such a wall against being caring and considerate. It made me sad to think of the kinds of traumas kids go through at home or at school that carry over into their adult lives.

I'd struggled growing up with dyslexia and feeling inferior to my high-achieving twin sister, but love and support were never lacking in our home. I knew how lucky I was, then and now. I'd tried to reflect that love and support to Zoe, as Allie and Fuller did with their boys.

I pulled myself out of my reverie and carried a tray of used glasses to the bar, glancing over when the door opened. Gareth pushed through. Maybe we were the after-party to the reception, except he hadn't seemed all that interested in the art. Why had he shown up to the opening?

I smiled at him. "Continuing your evening, Gareth?"

"Yes. It was getting hot over there." He glanced around and lowered his voice. "And I don't mean the temperature."

"That sounds interesting. What would you like to drink?"

He checked the day's list of pours. "I was sipping prosecco at the gallery. But I'd like to taste the cab sauv on your list."

"It's yours." I poured for him. We already stood at the end of the bar with no one else nearby. I had time for a quick chat with Gareth.

"Can you give me a nutshell of what happened?" I asked.

He leaned in. "Yolanda was steaming by the time Kelly was done with her. Then the detective focused on Malia. After a few minutes, our esteemed mayor lost her cool and said Kelly would have to speak with her lawyer."

"Whoa."

"Right? It was pretty shocking."

"Did you catch why Malia was upset?" I asked.

"Not really." He smiled. "Believe me, I tried."

Chapter 50

Mooncat was about to lock the door at nine thirty when Ed knocked on the glass. She glanced back at me.

"Henry's with him," she said. "Let them in?"

"Please," I said. "And lock the door after them."

Ed thanked Mooncat.

"Amigos." I waved from the bar. "Come and chat while we clean up."

Ed ambled up and sat on a barstool, but Henry hung back.

"Come on, *querido*, you know Cece," Ed said in a gentle voice. "She doesn't bite."

Henry, his face drawn and lined, sat next to his husband.

"What's going on, guys?" I asked. "And would wine help?"

"Not for me," Ed said. "I've had enough, and I'm driving. I'll get myself a glass of water." He headed over to the water table.

"Anything white, please, Cece," Henry said. "Thank you."

I slid a hefty glass of Viognier in front of Henry. He looked like he could use it. I poured a half for myself.

"Forgive us for cleaning around you," I said. "So, the reception was that bad?"

"Worst I have ever hosted." Henry took a big swig of wine. "For one thing, Detective Daniell has a lot of nerve. Who thinks it's okay to grill the guest of honor at her own opening?"

"He's right," Ed slid onto his stool again. "And she kept going. I mean, isn't that why they have places like police stations? An interview room lets them question suspects in an official space that isn't out in public. For her to grill those people in the gallery was totally out of line."

"I agree, although I'm glad Kelly isn't letting up on the case." I took a sip of wine.

"Well, she shouldn't be doing it in my business." Henry, usually the most dapper man around, was showing the strain. His normally neat short white hair stood on end as if he'd run his hand through it, and the silk pocket square in his charcoal gray blazer sagged as much as his shoulders.

"Did either of you hear any of the questioning?" I asked. "The details, I mean."

"I didn't," Ed said.

"Only toward the end." Henry frowned. "When I approached to extricate Yolanda from Kelly's clutches, the detective seemed to be pressuring her about answering a question. I heard Zeke's name and something about wine. Yolanda refused to say any more."

"Kelly had talked with Zeke earlier," I said.

"Do you think he was involved in the homicide?" Ed asked me.

"I can think all I want." I began loading glasses into the machine. "Unfortunately, I don't know anything for sure."

Mooncat approached holding a tray of dirties. "I assume you all are talking about Regan's murder?"

I nodded.

"Earlier tonight, Gareth told us Malia was also questioned," she said. "He mentioned that she finally told the detective she'd have to go through Malia's lawyer."

"Indeed," Henry said. "And for me, that was really the last straw. I told Kelly she had to leave, that she was upsetting my guests. Fortunately, she saw the wisdom in that idea and cleared out."

"You were great." Ed gave Henry a fond smile.

"Well, it is my place of business, and I'm proud of it." He sniffed. "I should have a say in the mood, particularly at a special event."

"I agree," Mooncat said.

I held up a bottle of pinot noir to assess if it was over half full. It wasn't.

"An end-of-day taste, Mooncat?" I asked.

"Hit me."

I poured and slid the drink down the counter to her, then set to work on the glasses she'd brought.

"Thanks. So, what else do we know?" Mooncat gazed at the three of us.

I held up my hand. "As we headed back from the gallery, Dane told me she had worked on Regan's campaign back when she ran for office."

"For state representative, right?" Ed asked.

"Yes," I said.

"We were still bringing down the big bucks in New York at the time," Ed began, "but I stayed in touch with the local news back home here."

Henry had worked in finance, and Ed had been a high-power editor for a publishing house. They'd both wanted a quieter life, plus Ed wanted to be closer to his mom. They'd started new lives here in Colinas, Henry opening his gallery and Ed buying the diner. Neither had ever expressed a speck of regret about their move away from the giant metropolis to our modest tourist town on the opposite coast.

"And what did Dane say about the campaign?" Mooncat nudged me to finish my story.

"Right." I gave myself a little shake. "No surprise, she said Regan was awful to work for. She was demanding and critical and never happy with her staff. On paper, Dane had liked her political positions, but putting up with that baloney as a volunteer was too much, and she quit."

"As any reasonable person would," Ed said. "I didn't see Kelly corner Dane, did you?"

"No," I said. "I think she made her exit before that could happen."

Henry nodded his agreement.

"Did the detective grill Greg after I left?" I asked.

"She sure did," Henry said. "He didn't look happy about it, but he maintained his cool."

"That bit I heard at the diner that I wanted to tell you earlier, Cece?" Ed said. "Greg donated a big chunk of money to renovate the area's food pantry. They're going to build out the facility to make it like a regular market and not a warehouse of canned goods. People will be able to select the food they want instead of the volunteers handing them a bag of groceries."

"That's fabulous," I said. "The last thing folks down on their luck need is the indignity of being given food they don't like or want to eat." I'd thought he had something about the homicide to tell me. I supposed this qualified, kind of. Greg was a person of interest, after all.

"It is," Ed agreed. "They're going to have a fresh produce section and everything."

"It's a generous gift on Jardis's part," Henry said.

"I agree," Mooncat added. "Listen, Cece, I thought Dane and Greg were dating. She came in alone for wine and he stayed at the reception?"

"She told me she ended it, that she doesn't think she's the right person for him, or something like that." I raised a shoulder and let it drop. "The relationship was new. These things happen."

"He doesn't seem to lack for women, that's for sure," Ed said. "Seems like every time he comes into the diner he's with someone else."

"To each their own," Mooncat murmured.

"Speaking of that, Mooncat," I said, "it looked a lot like you and David Zelma are going out together. Am I right?"

"Girl!" Ed grinned. "Have you been holding out on us?"

"Hey, my romantic life is my own business." She blushed. "But, yeah, we are."

"Hey, honey," Henry said. "More power to you."

"Thanks." She grabbed the spray bottle and rag and began wiping down tables on the other side of the room.

Ed leaned closer. "It's about time she got lucky."

"Absolutely." I poured the last inch of a couple of bottles into our vinegar bucket and lowered my voice to a whisper. "As long as he's not involved in the murder."

"What?" Henry looked shocked. "David?" His voice rose.

Mooncat raised her head. "David what?" She covered the space between us in a few long strides.

Oops. "Um, Kelly told me the poisoned wine that killed Regan was a Zelma vintage."

"And?" Mooncat flipped open her hands. "You think he personally fills and corks every single bottle that his vineyard produces? That's crazy stuff, Cece."

"Of course he doesn't." I tried to keep my tone soothing. "But he was here this afternoon when Kelly texted me that tidbit. It doesn't mean anything about him personally."

"No, it doesn't." She turned her back and stalked back to her work, taking the spray bottle and rag out to the patio.

Ed touched my arm. "You're only concerned about his involvement because you care about her."

"You got that right." I gazed at the patio door. "I'll figure out a way to tell her. Anyway, she's right. Anybody can buy a bottle of Zelma anywhere. Including here, as a matter of fact."

Chapter 51

I didn't care that it was ten thirty at night. I was glad to be home. To let down my hair, take off my shoes, and change into loose pants and a T-shirt soft from many wearings. To feed and stroke my eager kitties. To savor a piece of toast with peanut butter and honey while they ate. To pour a little cognac and sit in the quiet of my living room with nobody around. I let out a long breath and tucked my feet up next to me.

What a day it had been. It began with the production facility tour, seeing those giant sharp screws and learning about chemicals. I learned from brainy, cute Tino about the poison being in a bottle of wine. At the market Zeke said he made wine at home. He obviously had access to corking equipment. Greg had access, as well, through what he stocked at the hardware store.

Kelly told me the poisoned wine was a Zelma vintage, and the idea of an allergic reaction to sulfites had reared its head. In Vino y Vida, Malia and Gareth had argued. So had Dane and Greg. And I was sure there was more I wasn't remembering at the moment.

As if all that wasn't enough, who knew a simple art reception would turn into a serial police interrogation? Poor Henry. I hadn't asked him if the detective pulling various guests aside to grill them had hampered sales at all. I hoped it hadn't.

The bit about Dane breaking up with Greg didn't seem pertinent to the murder investigation, at least.

Martin jumped up and snuggled next to me. Not to be outdone, Mittens made a beeline for my lap. Each cat was in their preferred place. Fine with me.

These sweet felines didn't know anything about homicide, unless one of them had killed a spider or tracked down a mouse in the crawl space. The cats hadn't been outside all day, but I would let them play in the garden in the morning. Neither was fast enough to catch a bird or a lizard. They seemed to enjoy a taste of the wildlife in the fresh air, and I didn't have to worry about them getting out and falling prey to either a coyote or a speeding car.

I pulled out my phone, which had been on mute for hours. *Uh-oh.* I'd missed two texts from Allie.

Sorry to ask, but can you keep boys tomorrow AM for a few hours? Fuller has to go for a test.

I can bring them there if you want.

Benjamin and I had a date to spend the day together, but we hadn't made any concrete plans. I was pretty sure he wouldn't mind hanging out with two great kids for a while tomorrow as long as I was part of the package.

I wrote back that I'd be happy to and that dropping them off here would be great.

Despite the late hour, she replied that she'd bring them at nine and thanked me from the bottom of her heart. She didn't need to do that. I already knew I occupied a corner of her heart, just as she held a place in mine.

We would have fun tomorrow. The boys loved visiting with the cats, but Arthur was too allergic for them to have one at home. In fact, Mittens had adopted the twins at the farmers market last year and had lived in a very nice setup in their shed at home until I moved into this house and offered to adopt her. With or without Benjamin, we could make waffles and garden together and walk to the playground in the park.

But . . . Fuller needing a test on a Saturday sounded serious, as if it couldn't wait until Monday. My heart broke all over again for him, for Allie, and for the boys.

I resolved to stash those feelings in a mental lockbox for now, as was my habit. I couldn't help my twin and her family with a broken heart, and I couldn't change the course of Fuller's diagnosis and treatment. What I could do was help find an at-large murderer to keep my loved ones and the rest of the community safe.

Where to start? Learning more about sulfite allergies might help, just in case that was the poison that killed allergy-prone Regan.

Digging into the topic made my eyes pop. People with allergic reactions to sulfites could have wheezing, a stuffy nose, or hives. But the rare serious reaction included anaphylaxis, with difficulty swallowing and breathing, tachycardia, dizziness, and vomiting. All of which combined could lead to death.

OMG. I sat back. If the toxin was sulfites, the person who increased the amount already present in the Zelma bottle must have been aware Regan was allergic to the stuff. Every single person on the "Hated Regan" list had to have known her well enough to have learned that factoid about her.

An anaphylactic reaction sounded like a horrible way to die. Not being able to breathe? Having your heart race as you vomited, maybe while falling over from dizziness? The poor woman. She was difficult, but nobody deserved that kind of death.

Chapter 52

By seven thirty the next morning, I was in my yard with a cup of hot, strong coffee dosed with cream. Martin alternated zooming around with crouching, ready to pounce on prey, real or imagined. Mittens maintained a sphinx-like pose in the dappled shade on the patio, watching. The morning air was fresh and cool but held a promise of warming up as the day went on.

I called Benjamin. When he didn't pick up, I texted him that I would have the twins for the morning and he was welcome to join us. I was about to add an apology for the change of plans but stayed my hand. Allie often reminded me that I apologized way too often, as did many women. The new arrangement was what my family needed, and all I could hope was that Benjamin would be able to adjust to it.

For the time being, I enjoyed the garden. As early June was well past the primary rainy season, I turned on the drip irrigation to my herbs and vegetables in the raised boxes and to my precious peach sapling. I'd loved picking juicy, fat peaches from the mature tree in my Pasadena backyard, but it might be too dry up here for one to thrive. Still, I was giving it my best effort.

I pulled a few weeds and rescued a tomato vine swooping outside its cage, tucking it back inside. I ran my hand over the top of the rosemary bush, inhaling the pungent scent, and greeted a lizard doing push-ups in the sunshine. When Martin sprang at it, the reptile wisely made its exit.

All of this made me miss Richard. We greeted each other nearly every morning out here and often had a morning visit in his yard or mine. Was he all right? Was he restless and champing at the bit in Cloverdale to get home? Or maybe his fall had affected his mental acuity more than any of us would want.

I pulled out my phone and tapped his number. I wanted to know how he was and let him know I was thinking of him. He'd answer or he wouldn't.

"Cecelia, dear, how lovely to hear from you," he said over the line.

A broad smile split my face. "Good morning, Richard. I'm out in the garden, and it's not the same without you here."

"Believe me, I can't wait to be home."

"How are you feeling, my friend?" I asked.

"Better every hour, thank you. Say, Peter is still away. Would you mind very much heading next door and turning on my drip hoses? I'm terribly worried about everything drying out."

"I'll go over right now. Keep the water on for an hour?"

"That should do it." He cleared his throat. "Now that we're talking, I thought you'd want to know that my memory seems to be returning."

"That's great." I waited.

"I think I recall a person coming up behind me that morning as I was hand watering the Meyer lemon tree. You know it needs the right amount of water. Not too much, not too little."

A person? My heart chilled. "Yes, you've said that." I had to restrain myself from pressing him to get back to this remembered person.

"I didn't see a face or hear a voice, alas," he said. "I only detected a moving shape, but it might have been the shadow of a passing cloud. And that's the last thing I remember until I woke up in the hospital."

I thought for a moment. "What about scent? Did you detect, you know, anything like a perfume or aftershave? Garlic breath?"

He chuckled. "That would provide an all-important clue, wouldn't it? I can't think of a smell off the top of my head but let me ponder it. I'll surely let you know if I remember something like that."

What else could provide a hint to the person's identity? "What about how they walked? Did they scuff the wood chips in the path? Maybe they breathed heavily or with a wheeze." I was really grasping at the proverbial straws, but I had to try.

He didn't answer for a few second. "I'm not sure. I feel that a memory is dancing around the edges of my consciousness. Cecelia, I promise I will sit and let it make itself be known. You will be the first to know."

That was all I could ask.

"Now, here's some good news," Richard went on. "Peter will be home tomorrow, and my nephew has promised he will return me to Colinas tomorrow afternoon, as well. They've been quite good to me here. But I miss my own place."

"Of course you do. I can't wait to see you, Richard."

"Likewise, my dear, likewise. Now be a gem and start my watering, will you, please?"

"You bet. See you tomorrow."

I disconnected with a big old smile on my face. Maybe back in the comfort of his own place, my neighbor would remember one or two key clues to his attacker's identity. It might also be a comfort to know that it wasn't being over ninety that caused his fall, but instead the act of a malicious intruder. Not that it was a comforting thought. Next time I saw Peter, I would urge him to add a fence and a locked gate on the other side of Richard's house. No one should be attacking him in his garden.

I headed to my gate. I had no intention of neglecting his watering. With my hand on the latch, I paused. What if the person who'd assaulted Richard was still there? His house was empty of humans. Maybe they had broken in to take refuge, or . . . *No.* The police had checked everything outside and in after Richard's fall. Hadn't they?

I couldn't let Richard's garden die. Still, I grabbed a heavy shovel leaning against the fence. I opened the gate, shovel in hand, and slipped inside. I glanced around, not seeing evidence of anyone. There weren't any cups or food wrappers on the patio. The sliding doors to the house looked firmly shut. I tried them anyway, and they didn't budge. *Good.* I turned on the hose and noted the time.

Back in my own yard, I locked the gate but left the shovel at hand. A text came in from Benjamin saying he could use a couple of morning hours for errands but would be over around eleven. I replied with a simple *XXOO*.

After I set a phone timer reminding me to turn off Richard's water—and my own—in an hour, I finished my coffee, then made my way inside to shower and prepare for two energetic boys arriving soon.

Chapter 53

The twins helped mix up and cook a big batch of whole-wheat waffles, which we devoured with yogurt, maple syrup, and sliced bananas on top. They moved on to the fun of a long session playing with the cats, both indoors and in the garden. At about ten thirty, we headed out to the playground. I texted Benjamin where we'd be.

I convinced Franklin to leave his book at my house before we left. It was fine to be a brainiac bookworm, but I thought good old-fashioned playing and running around would do him good. I was surprised when he agreed.

"As long as you push us on the merry-go-round, Auntie Cee," he said.

"I promise, honey."

Arthur, who was skipping ahead, turned around. "I like it when we go so fast we almost spin off. It's wicked awesome."

"I'm confused. What's wicked about it?" I asked.

"We have a classmate who moved here from Boston," Franklin explained. "Wicked is all she says. Everything is wicked this or wicked that. It's an intensifying adjective, you know."

"I can tell." I tried to hide my smile at his grammatical explanation.

"I like experiencing the merry-go-round's centrifugal force,"

Franklin added as his step grew more springy. "Don't you find the physics of it interesting?"

"You bet." I reached over and tousled his hair.

We were almost to the park when Franklin grabbed at my sleeve and pulled me to a stop.

"Wait for us at the gate," I called to Arthur. I gazed down at his twin. "What's up, sweetie?"

"Daddy's sick."

"Mmm," I murmured, not wanting this conversation.

"Mama won't tell us what it is, but I think it's serious. Do you know what he has?"

I knelt, my throat thick with emotion. "Franklin, your parents are going to have to explain that. What I can say is that he has expert, skilled doctors, and he's getting the best of care." I wanted to say that his father was going to be fine, but that was way, way above my pay grade. "Modern medicine does wonders. You know that, right?"

He nodded somberly. "But why won't Mama tell us anything? And Daddy seems like he's away on a trip even when he's in the same room as us."

"I don't know why, Franklin. I do know it's hard being sick. I'll talk with your mom. I agree that you should have more information."

"Okay. Thank you, Auntie Cee. If I can handle anything, it's information. Maybe I can help research the best treatments for his condition." His eyebrows went up and his shoulders relaxed.

The prospect of helping with medical research seemed to be enough for the boy, and he dashed ahead to join Arthur. I marveled at the resilience of kids.

Twenty minutes later, I stood watching my nephews. Benjamin strolled up, model handsome in summer Bermudas and a pink Bodega Bay road race T-shirt. He gave me a side squeeze and a cheek kiss. In turn, I leaned into him, wrapping my arm around his waist.

"Looks like they're having a grand old time," he said, gesturing with his other hand at the red-and-white multifaceted climbing structure.

"We all are."

Franklin methodically worked his way up the simulated rock-climbing side, carefully finding each handhold and foothold. His brother swung wildly from monkey bar to monkey bar, using his legs as leverage. Arthur jumped down at the end, then ran to another side of the structure and clambered, monkey-like, to the top.

"Benjamin!" Arthur waved wildly. "Come and play with us."

Franklin glanced over and grinned, then returned to his focus on climbing.

Benjamin returned the wave. "Hey, dudes. Give me a minute," he called to them. To me he said, "Not into climbing this morning, my sweet?"

"Not a bit. I need to keep an eye on both of them at the same time. Thanks for accommodating the change of plans. Did you get your errands done?"

"Most of them."

"Hey, while we have a minute?" I glanced up at him.

"Ask me anything."

"A few days ago, you said you might know something about Zeke Cruz, but we never got a chance to talk about it again." I looked around, but no adults stood nearby. "Can you tell me now?"

He gave a slow nod, as if he was thinking about how much to share. "You know I can't talk about a lot of my work."

"I do, and I respect that." He'd said he consulted on various kinds of crimes, cyber and otherwise, with law enforcement agencies as well as certain large firms. The secrecy used to bother me. It didn't now. I trusted him with my feelings and knew he was a law-abiding person. That was enough.

"Well, I came across Cruz's name in the last year," Benjamin said. "He has an advanced degree in agrochemicals."

"Which could be chemicals used in growing as well as processing?" I asked.

"Yes. One firm asked me to look into possible malfeasance."

"And?"

"Briefly," he pointed at Arthur jogging toward us, "we couldn't pin anything on Zeke Cruz, but he's worth keeping an eye on."

My light-haired nephew screeched to a stop and held up his palm. Benjamin tapped it with his.

"Come and push us on the spinner," Arthur urged. "We know you can make us go wicked fast."

I shook my head, smiling, and went along.

Chapter 54

By eleven thirty, the four of us were seated at a booth in Edie's Diner. Ed beamed at the kids after handing us all menus.

"You folks smell like fresh air," he said. "Where have you been?"

"At the playground!" Arthur bounced in his seat. "Benjamin pushed us so fast, I nearly flew off the spinner."

"The merry-go-round thing?" Ed asked.

"Yeah. It was great!" Arthur's face filled with wonder. "I've never had to hold on so hard."

"You too, Franklin?"

"Yes, sir. The centrifugal force was quite strong. It made me wonder what it would be like to be weightless."

"An astronaut in the making." Ed winked at him.

"And we got to drive in Auntie Cee's car with the top down," Arthur added.

What kid doesn't like a convertible? The sixty-six was the first year Ford had included rear seat belts, but I'd converted the front and back lap belts to three-point harnesses so the boys would have a safer ride. Mine was safer, as well.

"That's always fun," Ed said. "Now, what can I get you for lunch? Milkshakes all around?"

"Yes, please," Franklin said. "I'd like chocolate, and my brother prefers strawberry."

Arthur nodded.

"A pilsner for me, Ed," Benjamin said.

"Is it too late for a Bloody Mary?" I asked.

"For you, never," Ed said. "Have you decided on food, or should I come back?"

"No, we can order now," I said. "Right, boys?"

Franklin and I went for the fishburger, while Benjamin and Arthur were a match ordering hamburgers, with the works for the adult, but bun and meat only for my nephew.

"Coming right up." Ed turned to go.

"Off to wash your hands now, kiddos." I pointed toward the restroom at the end of the aisle.

They scooted out. Ed reversed direction.

"While they're gone, let me tell you about something interesting I overheard this morning," he murmured as he slid onto the banquette the boys had vacated. He leaned toward us. "Zeke and his sister were in earlier for breakfast. He seemed tense and worried. She acted both blasé and maybe a touch defensive. I was straining my ears to listen, but I couldn't catch what he was saying to her. She told him to mind his own business."

"Interesting," I said.

"I did hear him say, 'Don't make it worse,' but it wasn't clear what he was talking about. Also, last night after you left the opening, Cece, and after the detective finished questioning people, Yolanda was pestering Zeke about something."

"You couldn't hear the details?" Benjamin asked.

"Afraid not. Henry might have. I didn't think to mention it last night in Vino y Vida, and this morning I had to leave early as usual to open here. I didn't get a chance to ask Hen. Seeing those two arguing in the next booth reminded me of what went down in the gallery." Ed stood. "Let me get your order in before two hungry boys come back."

"Thanks," I said.

Soon enough, the twins were back, and I had no time to think about what Ed had said. Arthur slid in, followed by his brother. Both boys sported damp hair slicked back off their foreheads and were barely suppressing giggles.

"Looks like you washed your faces along with your hands." I smiled at them.

"Getting cleaned up for your first school dance?" Benjamin asked.

"You mean with girls?" Arthur's expression turned from mischievous to horrified.

"He does," Franklin said. "Our school doesn't have dances, Benjamin. That's not until middle school."

"Which you'll be in next year?" Benjamin asked.

"Yep," Arthur said. "It's sixth grade through eighth."

"I'm thinking it might be nice to dance with a girl," Franklin said. "Sometimes my friend Luwana and I play a Taylor Swift album and practice dancing."

Arthur wrinkled his nose. "Frankie, that's gross."

Franklin gave me a "What can you do?" look, an expression mature way beyond his years.

"Everything in due time," I said.

Ed approached holding a tray full of drinks. Benjamin thanked him.

"Food will be out shortly," Ed said. "*Buen provecho*."

"*Gracias*," Arthur's accent was perfect.

"Have you been studying Spanish behind my back?" Ed grinned at him.

"No, but Luis, one of my friends on the soccer team, doesn't speak very much English yet. I've been learning from him."

Ed gave him a thumbs-up. "I like it."

"Artie is way better than I am at languages," Franklin explained.

A bell dinged from the kitchen. "Enjoy your drinks." Ed bustled away.

"Cheers." I held up my loaded glass and clinked with a pint glass full of beer and two classic milkshake glasses.

We were halfway through our hearty lunches when Franklin's face lit up. I twisted to look at the door to see none other than Allie. Franklin hurried down the aisle.

"Mama!" Arthur called and dashed after his brother.

Both boys hugged her. Ed handed her a big paper bag.

"Is Daddy in the car?" Arthur asked.

Allie nodded, and the twins raced outside. She moved down to our booth and sank onto the banquette, setting the bag on the table.

"Take-out lunch?" I asked.

"Yes." She rubbed her face. "I'll give them a minute with their dad."

"Tough morning?" I kept my voice soft.

"It's a tough time right now."

"Cece briefly filled me in, Allie," Benjamin said. "I'm so sorry. Whatever help you need around the house or with cooking, please hit me up."

"I appreciate that."

I squeezed his hand under the table.

She eyed my half-empty drink. "Can I have a swig of that, sis?"

"Finish it." I pushed the glass toward her.

Ed sauntered up. "Can I get you your own drink, Allie, on the house?"

"Thanks, Ed, but I'd better not." She took a long swig from my glass.

"Let me know if you change your mind." Ed gave me a glance. "Anything else for the rest of you?"

"I think we're good, thank you," Benjamin said.

Ed laid the check facedown on the table and headed toward the kitchen.

"How did it go at the appointment?" I asked Allie.

"It was okay. But listen—and I have to make this quick—

did you hear that Kelly brought Malia into the station for questioning?"

"What? No," I said. "Did you get that information from your infamous grapevine?"

Allie smiled. "I did. It came from the cousin of a sister-in-law who works for the CPD."

"Is Malia under arrest?" Benjamin asked.

"I don't think so," Allie said. "And I don't know why the detective took the extra step of wanting the mayor in an official interview room."

"Kelly was at Henry's gallery last night talking to all kinds of people," I murmured. "Including Malia."

"That was Yolanda Cruz's opening reception, yes?" Allie asked.

"It was."

She drank down more Bloody Mary and stood. "I have to get Fuller home and fed. He's really tired. Okay if I send the boys back in?"

"Please," Benjamin said. "They need to finish their lunch, and we'll keep them occupied for the afternoon. Will that help?"

Allie's eyes welled up. "I love you guys."

I held up my arms for a hug. Allie hugged me and blew Benjamin a kiss before she turned away.

"Allie, your lunch."

She grabbed the bag, shaking her head with a rueful smile before hurrying away.

The poor thing. This health situation had to turn out okay. It had to.

Chapter 55

Somehow I was able to avoid dwelling on homicide or on Fuller's health for the rest of the day Saturday. Being with my nephews and then alone with Benjamin had helped, a lot. He and I had cooked dinner together at my house and gone for an early-evening stroll, holding hands and telling each other our worst jokes.

After we'd returned home, he did have a bit of intel for me that he'd shared as we sat together.

"I did a little asking around about Regan Greene," he'd begun. "It seems she had a rough childhood. Her father abandoned the family when she was in kindergarten, and she had an older brother who died in an accident when the two kids were playing together. Her mother mistreated Regan badly after that. Regan was also a peanut, slight and prone to illness, so the other children were mean to her, too."

"It sounds like she's one of those people who succeed despite their upbringing."

"Yes, but she also had a deep need to be right, to be in power, and to step on others as she went."

No kidding. Regan had done all of that, and more. How she'd been treated explained—but didn't excuse—why someone had lost it and killed her.

"Do you know if Kelly Daniell has that background on Regan?" I'd asked.

"I let her know."

"Thanks."

Now, at eight thirty Sunday morning, he'd driven home to go for a long run in the hills and get ready for a business trip to Chicago. Some might find it odd that we spent so much time apart, but the arrangement seemed to suit both of us. We had work and busy lives, not to mention children in their twenties. We were in early middle age and divorced. While I cared for him a great deal, neither of us had a strong need to move in together, at least not yet. We enjoyed each other's company when we were together, and we kept in touch by text and phone when we weren't. For now, that worked.

My day of rest stretched out in front of me with nothing on the schedule except church and the farmers market, and even those were optional. Richard said he'd be home in the afternoon, so I would check in with him then. That and a bit of sleuthing were all I really wanted to do today, although I wasn't going to call on my trusty sidekick Allie. Not today, when she had her man and her brood home together. Their family time was way more important.

I forced myself to hold off on digging for information about the murder investigation until I'd fed the cats, puttered in my garden, and completed my Pilates workout on the patio. The weather had turned cooler, with a brisk breeze coming in over the hills from the ocean, but the sun shone and the air wasn't too cold for me to enjoy the fresh air. Fleece sweatshirts and leggings were made for exactly that.

In an effort to still my over-busy mind, I often spent time meditating in the morning, but I skipped it today. Instead, I grabbed another cup of coffee, fixed a piece of avocado toast and half a sliced mango, and brought breakfast and my tablet back outside. It was time to catch up on the news—world, local, and murderous.

I fired up streaming for the Sonoma County NPR station and started an internet search on "Regan Greene homicide" while I listened. I was mostly curious whether Malia being brought in for questioning had been noticed outside of Allie's grapevine sources, whatever they were.

Whoa. It sure had. A headline read, COLINAS MAYOR SUSPECT IN UNSOLVED HOMICIDE. Below it was a link to video from a county television affiliate. I wasn't surprised to see Nan Tsujimoto speaking into the microphone in the opening shot.

I read the text article first and didn't see mention of Malia being booked. Did I want to watch the probably sensational video reporting? Not really, but I thought I should.

It was as I expected. The reporter had almost nothing of substance to say in her breathless, dramatic delivery. The mayor had been seen being escorted out of the police station yesterday afternoon. Malia had refused comment. A short press briefing conducted by Chief Fenner revealed only that the investigation was continuing and the county sheriff's detective was checking out all leads pertinent to the case. *Blah, blah, blah.* That was it. No news is no news.

Except it made me wonder if Kelly had brought in Greg or the Cruz twins or even Dane for additional grilling. Maybe she had, but Tsujimoto hadn't found any of them newsworthy in the way the town's mayor was.

Martin gave up on catching an acorn woodpecker and curled up near me in a spot of sunshine out of the wind. I didn't see Mittens anywhere. She might have claimed a spot on the comforter covering my bed or somewhere else equally as cozy.

I perked up my ears at the radio news update on the half hour. They ran through national headlines first, all depressing, then turned to local news. The first item was that the fire north of Cloverdale was blessedly 80 percent contained.

"Colinas residents are rightfully concerned about the week-long unsolved homicide in their sleepy town," a male reporter went on. "A number of persons of interest have been called into the police station for further questioning this weekend. Most notable among them was Mayor Gutierrez, but a local business owner, two artists, and another person have also been seen being escorted into and out of the CPD station. More at the noon hour."

I sat back, ignoring the weather report that followed. Based on the reporting I'd just heard, the whole group of possible suspects had been hauled in, with the exception of Richard, thank goodness. Kelly herself had admitted she'd never seriously considered him. The two artists had to be Dane and Yolanda, the business owner would be Greg, and I couldn't imagine who else the additional person would be if not Zeke.

I'd been in the station's interview room once. It was no fun for the interviewee, but the advantages to the authorities were several. The person being questioned invariably grew nervous, which could lead to slips and story discrepancies. The interview was audio- and video-recorded for future analysis and evidence. And the front door was in full view of the public as well as news agencies with their cameras and microphones.

Of course, if a person was guilty of murder, all that pressure shouldn't be enough to prod them into a confession, but I'd read about certain vulnerable or naive people who made up any story simply to get out of there. It was a tactic that usually didn't go well for them.

Chapter 56

After tidying up the house and showering, I set out for the Sunday farmers market on my bike at around eleven. I'd decided to skip church this morning. The thought of using my free day to nail down this case seemed more important.

The air was still on the cool side and forecast not to get much warmer. I'd stuck with cropped jeans and my fleece over a San Francisco Giants T-shirt. With a public-facing job, it was a relief on a day off to dress more casually than I did when I poured wine and ran a business.

I rode slowly and carefully, considering motive. Who among the four or five possible suspects had the worst animosity toward Regan? Or maybe I should be looking at the person with the least reason to kill, which had to be Dane. Regan hadn't been a good candidate to volunteer for, but her run for state office was a long time ago, and Dane had gotten herself out when she realized the relationship wasn't working for her.

Greg, Yolanda, and Malia had more complicated, entwined, and apparently fraught histories with the victim.

I'd never found out why Yolanda had continued working for Regan if she was miserable being mistreated on the job. Maybe the reason she stayed was as simple as needing the income and not being able to find another position that paid as much or better. Lots of people remained in jobs they didn't like. Expenses were up everywhere. A steady paycheck was important.

Could I learn about her feelings and reasoning? I wasn't going to go knock on her door and ask, not that I knew where she lived. What I could do was stop by the art gallery after the market and see if Henry had any ideas.

I knew Greg also wouldn't take kindly to me questioning him again. I doubted he'd be working at Colinas Hardware today, anyway. Now that Dane had broken up with him, maybe she'd confide in me about his past—if she was even aware of it. She had her usual Sunday afternoon shift at Vino y Vida. I knew where to find her.

Malia? She didn't seem sorry her difficult former opponent was dead, her pro forma words at the town picnic notwithstanding. With any luck, she'd be doing mayoral schmoozing at the farmers market and I could find a way to tease out more details about her past with Regan.

I passed the gourmet shop. My pedaling slowed. *Zeke*. He was on the list. If Yolanda was the guilty party, her brother—who knew wines inside and out—might have helped her finish off the woman who had been horrible for his twin to work for. I didn't know of any independent motivation to kill that he might have had, but I did know plenty about the deep and lifelong connection between twins, including fraternal ones.

I rode on with a full brain, then hopped off at the entrance to the already bustling lot full of white and green pop-up tents. I hung my helmet on the handlebars and walked my bike through the aisles. Despite having eaten, my mouth watered at the sights and smells of delectable veggies, fruits, olives, baked goods, and cheese.

The Cheese Man waved back, but I didn't stop. I hadn't finished the cheeses I bought last week. I did pick up a baguette, and two stalls down I bought two dozen corn tortillas from Ed's cousin, who had continued her mother's tortilleria. I couldn't help myself from eating one on the spot. Even unadorned, a fresh tortilla held a special place in my heart, or maybe it was my stomach.

Despite the town's unsolved homicide, Paul Fenner was at his wine booth. I waited until the customer paid for their wine and turned away before greeting the chief.

"I'm surprised to see you here," I added.

"I'm at the market every week, Cece." He folded his arms. "As you well know. Can I help you with something?"

"The merlot I bought from you last week was excellent."

"Thank you."

I glanced around and lowered my voice. "Too bad about the lack of progress in Regan's case."

"There's a lot going on behind the scenes that civilians don't hear about." He gave extra emphasis to "civilians."

"I'm glad to hear that. Good luck with it all."

"Luck has very little to do with it."

"Okay." It was time for me to move along. "See you later."

When he didn't respond, I walked my bike down the aisle. The man had been more taciturn than usual, but at least he'd stopped short of outright chastising me for my amateurish investigatory efforts.

I stopped to purchase a half dozen plump early apricots. As I paid, I heard a familiar voice at the pistachio stall next door.

"A bag of the chili-lime flavor, please." Malia handed a twenty-dollar bill to the proprietor.

I joined her in front of the table. "Those are good, but they're spicy, Malia."

She whipped her face toward me. "Good morning, Cece. Yes, I know they're hot. I like them that way."

"Awesome." I picked up a bag of the Indian-spiced nuts, which had a mild curry flavor, and handed the nut man exact change.

Malia thanked him, beaming her best mayoral smile. I waited. When she moved on, I kept pace with her.

"I was chatting with Paul Fenner a minute ago," I said in a low voice. "It's too bad Regan's killer is still at large, isn't it?"

Malia stopped and faced me. "Yes. And I hope you're not butting into their investigation again." She shifted her market basket from one arm to the other.

I flipped open my free hand. "I wouldn't do that."

She made a scoffing sound in her throat. "Sure, Cece. You have a good day, now." She reversed direction and picked up her pace.

Gee, who else could I get on the bad side of today? I reviewed my purchases and decided I'd shopped enough. It was time for my favorite part, a stop at Tia Tamale.

Chapter 57

Yes, there was another person I could alienate. Tino Ribeiro was at the end of the Tia Tamale ordering line. He hadn't yet seen me. Did I want to avoid him and skip my weekly taste of heaven? I did not.

I parked my bike near the truck and smiled at the cute librarian as I approached. I stood next to his chair so he didn't have to turn around. A full bag of market produce hung from a hook near his shoulder, with small artichokes and a bunch of spinach poking out the top.

"Best lunch in town, am I right?" I kept my tone light.

"It is," he said. "I get one every week."

"So do I. There's no way I'd try to make tamales at home."

"Same here. I do make a mean Brazilian feijoada."

"That's black beans, right?" I asked.

Tino laughed. "It's so much more, but you're correct. The base is black beans."

We moved up as the line did.

"Where's the boyfriend?" He gazed at the food truck, not at me.

"He's home getting ready to leave on a business trip tonight." I cleared my throat. "So, it's too bad there's still no news about any arrest in the case."

"No kidding."

"I was trying to talk with Paul Fenner about it a few minutes ago, but he basically refused to engage."

Tino smiled. "I'm not surprised. The man's as tight-lipped as they come, which is appropriate. Nobody wants a gossipy police chief."

"True. Speaking of law enforcement, Kelly Daniell says you consult with the sheriff's department from time to time, and that she's tried to hire you. That's pretty cool."

A faint blush came to his cheeks. "Thanks. I do like being useful, but my professional heart belongs to the library."

We moved up again. The one person ahead of us was now ordering at the window. The order taker was the same person as last week, which made sense. Richard had told me Pete wouldn't be back until this afternoon.

"What kind of tamale do you like to get?" I asked.

"They're all good, but today I'm going with the chicken-chili filling. You?"

"I'm a vegetarian, so I always order the veggie option."

He gave a hearty laugh. "Then you definitely wouldn't like my feijoada. I make the traditional recipe I learned from Vovó—my grandma—and it includes pig's feet and other bits of pork."

"Yeah, no." I smiled at him. "I'm not going there."

After the man in front of us moved to the side, the woman in the window emerged to take our orders. We each said what we wanted and paid, then slid out of the way. They must know Tino and that he wouldn't be able to reach up to the window to tap his card.

"I'm a regular here," he said. "They're great about accommodating all their customers."

"Want to eat with me in the park?" I wanted to stay friends with this guy. I hoped that was possible.

He thought about it for a moment. "Sure. That's what I usually do."

After a couple of minutes, the person who took our orders carried them out to us instead of calling out the numbers from the window.

"Your meal, sir, all dosed up," they said to Tino.

"*Gracias.*" His trilled "R" was perfect.

"*De nada, querido.*" The person grinned at him and hurried back into the truck.

"This place is great. They always remember I like extra green salsa and sour cream." He nestled the food in his lap on top of the several paper napkins that came with it.

I grabbed my bike, settling my own lunch on the top of the purchases in the bike basket. We wheeled together on a paved path into the park until we reached an empty picnic table where Tino could park at the end and we could enjoy tamale yumminess.

After plowing through several bites, I came up for air. Tino wiped a drop of green sauce from the corner of his mouth. He raised his eyebrows and made a little wiping gesture on the end of his nose.

"Need a napkin?" He quirked a corner of his mouth into a smile.

"Got one." I used it to swipe at my nose. "Can't take me anywhere." I returned the smile.

"How's your digging into the homicide going?" he asked. "Other than trying to grill the CPD chief, that is."

"Not that great." I scrunched up my nose. "But as I rode over here, I was thinking about motive. It seems like three people—Yolanda Cruz, Greg Jardis, and our esteemed mayor—had the most complicated and sticky pasts with Regan."

"It appears so. Any progress with the recorked wine bottle angle?" He forked in another messy bite of tamale.

"No, although Ed told me Yolanda and her twin, Zeke, were arguing yesterday morning at the diner."

"He could have abetted her with the wine bottle thing. If anybody knows wine stuff, it's Zeke Cruz."

"I had the same thought." I popped more cheesy, starchy, Mexicany goodness into my mouth.

"You know, I might have picked up something from a few avenues of inquiry Kelly asked me to trace." He frowned, drumming his fingers on the wooden table.

"And?" I asked, when he stayed silent.

"I'm trying to figure out how much I can tell you."

It was my turn to wait quietly.

"All right," he began. "Do you know about anyone's alibis?"

"I do not." I shook my head. "Malia lives with her family. I'd imagine she has an alibi, at least for overnight. I don't know who Yolanda or Zeke lives with, and I expect Greg lives by himself."

"Correct on the last and the first. Yolanda has an apartment in Las Madres not far from the AVDA offices, and Zeke rents a room in Cloverdale."

"So, all but the mayor has no one to vouch for them?"

"For the night hours, yes," he said.

"I sense an impending 'but.' Yes?"

"Exactly. Any of them could have delivered a bottle of wine dosed up with a toxic substance in the afternoon and been back home in time for bed, whether alone, with a bedmate, or in the company of family."

"Good point," I said. "What about door-cam footage of Regan's entryway, or information from neighbors who might have seen a delivery?"

"I don't know about any of that, although Kelly did say she planned to be in touch this afternoon." He finished his last bite and wrapped the detritus into a tidy wad. He took aim at the trash can several yards away and neatly sunk a three-pointer.

"Nice basket." I clapped.

"I happen to be the captain of the Alexander Valley wheelchair basketball team." He squared his shoulders in pride, relaxed them, and laughed.

"That's awesome."

"It's fun with friends. Everybody needs that, right?"

"Absolutely."

Like this lunch, for example. I was serious about wanting to stay friends with him, and I felt he sensed that.

Chapter 58

I pedaled home and unloaded my market purchases upon my arrival, feeling happy I'd been able to catch up with Tino and be confident we could stay friends. I set out again. Five minutes later I locked my bike in front of Colinas Hardware. Inside, an employee directed me to the winemaking supplies.

Six-gallon glass carboys sat on the floor. Shelves held clear plastic tubing, several kinds of thermometers, long-handled bottle brushes, curvy things labeled air locks, containers of something, bags of corks, and more.

It was the corking devices I was interested in. The store stocked several sizes of red tabletop corkers with double levers. A sleek stainless steel model had a single handle. A red corker about thirty inches high sat on the floor.

"Planning on making your own wine, Cece?" Greg Jardis asked from behind me.

I faced him. "I was thinking about it. There's a lot involved, judging from all this equipment." I had no intention of actually making my own wine, but he didn't need to know that.

"Yes, it's not a simple process."

"Do you make your own?" I asked.

"With so many great wineries in the valley? No way."

"Too bad." I gestured at the shelf. "I wondered which of these corking devices you would recommend."

"They're all good or we wouldn't carry them. Each has a different price point." He pointed at the biggest red device. "For example, I doubt you'd want to invest in the floor model if you're only a beginner."

Interesting. He didn't react at all to my question. His ready answer was exactly what an informed business owner would say. Greg didn't appear to be aware of the poisoned wine. Or maybe he was a super smooth liar. At least he didn't seem suspicious of me checking out the supplies.

"Thanks," I said.

"Let us know if you need help with anything."

"I appreciate that. I must say, I'm surprised to see you working on a Sunday." I smiled. "I would think the business owner would give himself a day off. I certainly have."

"I guess I'm married to my work. Have a good day, now." He turned away.

"You too."

Was there anything here I did need? As I headed for the exit, I passed the gardening section. I could always use a new pair of gloves to save the skin on my hands and my nails from dirt and thorns. I grabbed a three-pack of stretchy gloves in pink, green, and yellow and paid for them at the counter.

My next stop was Henry's gallery. He was busy with a customer but smiled at me and held up a finger, as if he wouldn't be long. I wandered along the gallery walls, taking a closer look at Yolanda's work. The labels next to several of her paintings were marked "Sold." That had to be a good sign for an artist.

After the customer headed out, Henry joined me. He taped a "Sold" sticker on the label for another painting.

"It looks like Yolanda's art is doing well," I said.

He nodded. "She's had a few nice sales. Tell me, what are you doing around here on a weekend?"

I laughed. "Guess."

"Trying to track down a murderer."

"Exactly. Without much luck."

"Are you still thinking my current exhibitor is the guilty party?" he asked.

"It's possible. Do you know where she lives? And if she's married or in a relationship?"

"You're looking at alibis. I certainly do know where she lives, although I'm not aware of her personal life beyond art and her day job. I'm heading out to her place as soon as I close at five today. I have to deliver something to her."

"Can I come?" I asked at the same time as he asked, "Keep me company?"

We both laughed.

"Great minds and all that," I said. "I'd love to."

"I'll pick you up."

"Thanks."

Two couples strolled in with wind-mussed hair and flushed cheeks. Henry called out a welcome.

"We were just at the cutest wine bar over there, and the lady said we had to check out this gallery," one of the women said.

"I'll see you a little after five," I murmured to Henry and slid past the newcomers. It was now two o'clock. They must have hit Vino y Vida right at opening. I didn't have anywhere urgent to be. I might need to drop into that cute wine bar of mine for a glass of something light. Maybe I could grab a chat with Dane if it wasn't too busy.

Chapter 59

When I emerged outside, I heard familiar voices from the bocce court. Fuller and Allie stood a couple of yards away from the twins, who squatted peering at two different-colored balls in the sand.

"Mine is closer," Franklin said.

"No, mine is," Arthur insisted.

Fuller caught sight of me and waved me over. "Aunt Cece is going to be the referee," he told them.

I was the lucky recipient of two hearty boy-hugs, an embrace from Fuller, and an eyeroll from my twin.

Arthur pulled me over to the balls in question. I folded my arms and gazed straight down.

"It's clearly a tie," I declared. "You both win."

Being the good-natured kids they were, the twins exchanged a high-five slap.

"You can play next game, Auntie Cee," Franklin said.

Fuller gave me a thumbs-up when I rejoined them. "Thanks for wrangling that." His dark face bore lines it hadn't had a few months ago, and his hair had sprouted a new crop of silver.

"Hey, I remember what twin rivalry is like," I said. "How are you guys?"

"We're having a family fun day." Allie looped her arm through Fuller's and gave him a fond smile. "His idea."

"I like it," I said.

"Stacking up the memories," Fuller said.

I didn't want to think about the implications of needing to bank memories now in case there wouldn't be any in the future.

"Allie told me about your diagnosis." I kept my voice low. "It sounds like you're in good medical hands."

He nodded, his gaze on his sons. "We're intending a good outcome, and I plan to be an excellent patient, if not an entirely patient one."

"Sounds like a plan."

"Daddy," Arthur called. "Your turn to throw."

Fuller joined them.

"What's next on the fun-day agenda?" I asked Allie.

"We already played mini-golf and had burgers and milkshakes at the diner. After this we're headed out to the beach for banana splits and seashell hunting."

"Mama!" Franklin beckoned to her. "Your turn."

"Talk to you later, sis," she said. "Love you." She hurried over to the game.

"Love you more." I turned away when my eyes filled. Fuller sounded positive. It was on the rest of us to maintain the same attitude.

And I had a homicide I wanted to get to the bottom of so I could focus on normal, nonmurderous, joyous life again. To that end, I headed into Vino y Vida.

Dane was pouring at the bar. Three men were standing at one end, and only two tables were occupied. I perched on a stool at the other end.

"Just so you know, I'm not checking up on you." I smiled.

"Hey, it's your business, Cece. You can check in on us any time you want. Do you want a glass?"

"Sure." I checked the board. "I'll take a glass of the Melon."

Dane poured and slid the glass toward me.

"Thanks. Is Dev on the patio?"

She frowned. "He had to take his dog to the vet this morning. The silly beast swallowed something he shouldn't have. But Dev texted that he'd be here by three, three thirty at the latest."

"Are there folks outside? I can help if you need me."

"Only one couple is out there, and it won't be long before Dev gets here. I think I'm good."

"Okay. If you get a rush while I'm here, I'll stay." I sipped the cool, complex white.

Dane loaded a few glasses into the machine and wiped down the counter.

"Dane, did Greg ever mention making wine at home?" I asked in a low voice.

"He did. How did you know?"

"Just curious." It was also interesting that he hadn't told me the truth about that.

She tilted her head and squinted at me for a second. "Right."

"Did you see winemaking equipment at his house?"

"I didn't see anything like that. He lives in a condo, or rather a town house, and it's a pretty roomy one. On the other hand, he told me he has a workshop on the lower level, and I never went down there. He could easily have a winemaking setup and I never ran across it."

Her answer was entirely inconclusive, unfortunately. It couldn't be helped.

"Why do you want to know?" Dane asked.

I shrugged. "He stocks quite an array of winemaking equipment at the hardware store. I thought maybe he makes it himself at home." *Liar*. Oh, well. White lies in the pursuit of justice had to be acceptable in the wider scope of things.

Dane slid down to the other end of the bar to help the three gentlemen. I sipped and thought. Kelly Daniell pulled open the door and pointed to me, then strode over.

"Can I talk to you in the back room?" she asked, her voice low and gravelly.

"You can." I grabbed my glass and led her through the swinging door. I waited to speak until it closed behind her. "It looks like something's up."

"Do you have any idea where either Cruz twin might be? Yolanda or her brother?"

"No." I thought back to the market. "I haven't seen them today, but I usually wouldn't. I mean, I met both of them only in the last week or two. It's not like we're friends or anything."

"The thing is, Yolanda seems to have gone underground since Friday night, and her brother with her." Kelly's frown seemed permanently etched into her brow.

"You did kind of grill them at the opening reception. That was Yolanda's big night and her debut as a commercial artist, from what I understand. Under normal circumstances, I wouldn't blame her for avoiding you after that."

"But these are hardly normal circumstances, Cece."

"They're not." I took a sip.

Kelly gave me a second glance. "Aren't you working?"

"No. I take every weekend off. I stopped in for a glass, and you lucked out finding me here."

"Oh. Sorry." She drummed her fingers on our worktable.

"No worries. So, have you come up with evidence against Yolanda? Is that why it's urgent to locate her?"

Kelly let out a long breath. "Sorry, can't tell you that."

Rats.

"But if you see either of them, please text me on my cell ASAP, okay?" She tugged down her blazer, which revealed the bulge of a weapon in a holster under her arm.

"I promise."

"Thanks. Later." She slipped out the back door in as much of a hurry as when she'd come in.

I'd gotten into this amateur investigating thing, but no way would I want her job as my livelihood. Like Tino, I wasn't a law enforcement professional, and I wanted to keep it that way.

Chapter 60

By three o'clock I was pedaling home. Once there, I shed the fleece, which was too warm now that the sun was stronger, and drank a big glass of water.

Playing with the cats outside was next on my schedule, and it was as relaxing and fun as always. I'd hoped to also visit with Richard, but neither a knock at his gate nor a text yielded any reply. He must not be home yet.

I dragged the comfiest chair on the patio into the shade and settled into it, putting my feet up onto a low table. I pulled out my phone, sure there was more investigatory digging I could do, but first I indulged in watching funny cat videos. Their lives, and those of my own kitties, seemed simple compared to the sticky complexities of what humans get themselves into.

I moved on to photos of the young heirs to the British throne. Some might think I'm silly to follow an archaic institution like the monarchy, especially one that had its own share of sometimes public dysfunction. But I knew how fortunate I was, to have a loving relationship with my immediate family. Many families weren't so lucky, for all kinds of reasons, including generational trauma and misfortune. I counted my blessings pretty much every day.

Soon enough, though, my idle thoughts turned to Kelly

Daniell. She'd shown up at the wine bar urgently looking for two of the possible suspects. I wasn't able to help her, and she refused to tell me why she needed to see them. That part wasn't surprising, but it did make me wonder what new information she'd uncovered, not to mention where Yolanda and Zeke were hiding out.

That got me thinking about why Yolanda harbored such animus toward Regan Greene. Everyone has had a difficult boss. To wish them dead or to be glad they were dead took it to another level. Had Yolanda's childhood been problematic? Maybe she herself had been mistreated in a way that made being talked down to as an adult intolerable.

Who would know? Zeke, but his loyalties would lie with his twin. He'd never divulge his sister's past traumas, if she had any. *Huh*. If they'd grown up in Colinas, Fuller might have an idea about her past. He was older than Zeke and Yolanda, as I was, but not by much, and he'd lived in town his whole life. Colinas even had a public park named after his public service–minded grandfather.

I wasn't going to call and ask him during his family day. Instead, I shot a quick text to Allie wondering if she could ask him when the time was right.

Yolanda might not be the murderer, though. Greg told Dane he made wine at home, although he specifically said he didn't after I asked him. He definitely had a past with Regan. He seemed to want to make up with her at the car show, but she wasn't having it, which could have turned his emotions to homicidal. I had to admit that was a stretch, though.

Malia, who had past and present rivalries with Regan, was also capable of poisoning and recorking a bottle of wine.

I yawned and leaned back, folding the phone into my hands and resting them atop my stomach. I wasn't going to solve the murder here and now on a sunny afternoon in my garden.

Henry wouldn't be here until after five. I had time for a bit of relaxing.

What? A ringing noise sounded in the distance. It was followed by banging. *OMG.* Was the killer trying to break down the door? My insides turned to ice.

CHAPTER 61

I sat up straight, making something fall to the ground. Whatever it was began buzzing. I glanced around, then down to the concrete of the patio. Oh. It was my phone that fell. I grabbed it, my heart racing.

Henry's face was on the display. I jabbed at the device.

"Cece?" Henry asked. "Are you okay? I've been ringing the doorbell and knocking. It's five twenty."

"It is?" Sure enough, that was the time on the phone. I swiped away drool at the corner of my mouth. "I'll be right there." I hurried to the front door and unlocked it. "I'm sorry. I fell asleep out back. Come on in. I'll be ready in a flash."

"No rush, Cece. I'm glad you're okay. I was starting to worry. I'll wait out here."

I headed for the bathroom and made myself presentable. Cats inside and fed, and with the back door locked, I grabbed my bag and a sweater and rejoined him.

"Ready to roll." I made sure the front door was firmly locked after me and climbed into the panel van he used for transporting artwork and around-town errands.

We headed out the same way I'd driven to the AVDA offices a few days ago.

"What are you delivering to Yolanda, Henry?" I asked.

"It's a little bit of a ruse. She left her portfolio in the workroom. I do want to get it back to her, but it's not like she's been asking for it." He glanced over with a grin.

"I like it. Does she know you're coming?"

"I texted her that I was. And what's your ulterior motive?"

"I'm not sure," I said. "See how she reacts, maybe? Kelly Daniell found me at Vino y Vida this afternoon and said both Yolanda and her brother seem to have disappeared. That is, neither is responding to her efforts to contact them. Since you aren't the cops, I don't suppose she'll try to evade you."

We drove past the winery. The parking lot looked full, which made sense on a sunny Sunday afternoon.

"I'm glad the place is thriving, after what happened." I said.

"It is."

"Do they serve food along with the wine?" I asked. "As in lunch or dinner?"

"Only charcuterie boards, which can certainly be a light meal. Ed and I were wondering if you wanted to join us for dinner tonight if you're free. We haven't decided on a place. Shall we try Holt Vineyards?"

"That sounds great."

"I'll text Eduardo once we reach our destination, and he can meet us there."

A few minutes later, we cruised into downtown Las Madres.

"Let's see." Henry slowed, peering at the numbers over various doorways. "Her address is on the main drag here. Ah, there it is." He pulled to the curb a block beyond the Rifle Club in front of the Steppe Up consignment shop.

"Looks like there are apartments upstairs," I said.

"That's what she mentioned." Henry climbed out and extracted a large, flat, black case with a handle from the back of the van.

I joined him at a doorway between the consignment shop, whose windows were dark, and the Green Leaf pot dispensary beyond. It was still open, judging by the lights within.

"There's no bell or intercom." He tried the door, which pulled open. He frowned. "That doesn't seem particularly secure. Shall we go up?"

I was seized with a sudden panic. "What if it's not safe? How about you text her and ask her to come down?"

He turned his face to gaze at me. "You're worried about us being alone with a killer."

"Kind of, yes."

Would he go along with my fears? Either way, I had no intention of heading up those dark stairs. He could go alone. Yolanda had nothing to worry about with Henry. He wasn't the one asking questions about her former boss's murder.

"You're being extra careful." He let the door swing shut. "I like that. I'll call her." He pulled out his phone and did exactly that.

With the phone to his ear, he nodded at me. "Yolanda, it's Henry from the gallery. I'm on the sidewalk in front of your place. Can you come down and grab your portfolio?"

She said something I couldn't hear.

"I'd prefer it if you came down. My van doesn't lock, and I don't like leaving it on the curb." He gave me a sly wink, listened, and disconnected. "She'll be down in a minute. Let me explain why you're with me, okay?"

"Please."

I shifted from foot to foot. This whole plan suddenly seemed like the worst idea, ever. But I was here. And, when the door began to open, it was too late to run and hide elsewhere.

Today the artist was in her own version of Sunday casual, wearing leggings and a paint-spattered oversized sweatshirt. She began to smile and opened her mouth. She closed it and her brow furrowed when she caught sight of me.

Henry extended the portfolio. "Here you go."

"Thanks." She mustered the smile again. "Hello, Cece."

I half raised my hand in greeting.

"Cece and I are headed out to dinner," Henry said. "She didn't mind a bit of a detour."

"I won't keep you, then."

"Yolanda," I began, "how is Zeke?"

"He's fine." Her smile, which had been lukewarm at best, slid away. "Why?"

"He said he was going to stop by the wine bar again, but we haven't seen him."

"I'll tell him you were asking about his welfare." She held up the case. "I appreciate this, Henry."

"I hope you know your work has been selling nicely." He smiled at her. "We'll do an accounting at the end of the show."

Her expression lightened. "That's great. Thanks for letting me know." She turned and disappeared through the door.

Henry turned to me. "That wasn't too scary, was it?"

"Not at all." I exhaled. "Sorry for the moment of panic."

"Hey, you were being prudent. I get it." He tilted his head. "Were you really expecting Zeke in Vino y Vida, even though you don't work on weekends?"

"Of course not." My smile to him was genuine.

"I'm going to give Eduardo a call about dinner." He strolled away past the consignment shop.

I had my hand on the van's door when Jared emerged from the dispensary.

"Hey, Cece." His face lit up. Jared himself might also have been a bit lit. "Slumming it again, are you?"

"I was in the neighborhood. Do you live nearby?"

"I do. I share a house with friends over by the tracks. I'd rather live in H-burg or Colinas, but who can afford that?" He grinned. "I'm young. I have plenty of time to get serious and make a lot of money."

His good cheer was infectious, no matter if it was caused by cannabis or his personality—or both.

"You do," I said.

Jared's gaze lifted to the building's upper floor. "You'd better be careful around here, Cece."

"Why?"

He lowered his voice and leaned toward me. "Remember when you stopped by the office last week?"

"Yes."

"One of the people you were asking about lives up there." He drew his expression into one of concern or maybe alarm. "I'd be careful where you tread."

"Do you mean Yolanda?" I whispered.

Raised eyebrows and a slow nod was my answer.

"What do you know about her?" I asked.

"She hated Regan Greene with a white-hot heat. I'm going to resign from AVDA if she doesn't. What if I'm next on her hit list?" Sweat broke out on his forehead.

Henry bustled up. "We're all set."

"Great. Henry, this is Jared. Jared, my friend Henry Cruvellier."

"Ooh, of the Acorn art gallery in Colinas?" His mood doing a one-eighty, Jared beamed and stuck out his hand to Henry. "I love your place. I'm Jared Lamott."

"Good to meet you, Jared." Henry smiled as he shook hands. "Stop by any time."

I fished a business card out of my bag. "Let's be in touch, okay?" I handed it to the younger man.

"For sure, Cece. Thank you." He said goodbye and sauntered in the other direction.

Henry stared after him. "Was he as high as a kite, or is he always like that?"

I laughed. "Some of both."

Chapter 62

At Holt Vineyards, Ed was already ensconced at a table on the patio. I wondered if it might be too cold to sit outside, but he'd picked a table near a wall that was out of the wind. One of the tall propane heaters, which had sprung up with the necessary flourishing of outdoor dining during the pandemic, sent its blessed warm air down on us.

The view of the valley from where we sat was delightful. Vines in their full flush of green stretched out before us. The patio umbrellas in primary colors on the level below us were all furled at the moment so they didn't block the landscape. A few puffy clouds blew by, and a hawk circled ever higher overhead.

Ed studied the short food menu. When a woman came to take our wine orders, he glanced up at her.

"We'd also like the large charcuterie board, with extra breadsticks, and the full crudité platter, please." He flashed her his warmest smile.

"You got it, sir." She headed back inside

"That'll be enough for now, right?" Ed asked both of us.

"It's plenty," I said.

Henry nodded. "The breadsticks alone are worth it. They have a garlicky rosemary crust that's made in heaven."

"Now, what good trouble did you two get into over in beautiful downtown Las Madres?" Ed asked.

"Our friend here was afraid we'd get into bad trouble, not good, by going up to Yolanda Cruz's apartment," Henry said.

"He indulged me by staying on the sidewalk and asking Yolanda to come down. We both might have engaged in tiny white lies." I smiled at Henry.

Our server arrived with three fat glasses of pinot noir. "Your food will be right out."

"Salud." Ed lifted his glass.

After cheering and clinking, followed by swirling, sniffing, and tasting, I set down my glass.

"Ed, you grew up in Colinas," I began. "I know the Cruz twins are a lot younger, but did you know them at all while they were growing up?"

"Not to speak of, but I was acquainted with their parents. Their children got hassled and bullied for being 'beaners'—a slur certain low-minded folks like to use for people whose families are from Mexico."

"That's a nasty one, although there are worse," Henry said. "And it doesn't seem to matter if the targets are recent immigrants or have been here for centuries."

"Like Malia's family, apparently," I chimed in.

"Yes," Ed said. "Her grandfather was one of the many orange farmers in the valley."

"I wonder if Regan Greene included ethnic insults in her treatment of people like Malia and Yolanda." I traced a line around the rim of my glass until it sang.

"It's possible," Henry said. "Although I never witnessed it. Did you, hon?" He gazed at Ed.

"Not brazenly, no, but I would have been included. Except if Regan was eating at the diner, she wouldn't dare insult the chef." He flashed a wicked grin.

Our groaning platters arrived, and I didn't get a chance to ask Ed to clarify. I'd heard of kitchen staff spitting on plates of rude customers before the food went out to the tables. I hoped that was the stuff of myth, not reality, but common civility was becoming rare recently, certainly from customers. I'd been treated rudely in Vino y Vida more than once.

The three of us fell silent except for crunching and murmurs of appreciation for the next few minutes. I finally came up for air.

"This is all fabulous." I gestured at the food. "The cornichons are perfectly crisp, and, Henry, you're right about those breadsticks. They're tasty, especially with this soft cheese."

"Try dipping one in the dilly sour cream." Ed pointed to the middle bowl of three on the platter of raw veggies.

Henry dipped and munched. "Oh, yes."

I sat back and sipped my wine.

"I can see wheels turning in your head, Cece," Ed said.

"You can?" I asked.

"You bet. You're thinking about the case, am I right?"

"Actually, I was enjoying the excellent provisions, wine, and company." I smiled. "You know me too well. I mean, I am loving all this, but I'm also still thinking about the murder. Ed, did you know Malia growing up? Or her family?"

"I didn't. I believe she spent her formative years in Healdsburg and moved to Colinas when her children were young. And that was about when I moved to New York." He swiped a slice of jicama through the dip and popped it in his mouth.

"It seems the police and the sheriff's department aren't making much headway this time," Henry said. "Do you get that impression, Cecelia?"

"For sure. But neither am I."

"It's not your profession, *querida*," Ed pointed out.

"No, and I wouldn't want it to be." My phone rang with the ringtone I'd set up for Benjamin, the refrain from "All You Need Is Love" by the Beatles. "It's Benjamin. Excuse me for one sec?"

"Do it," Henry said.

I twisted away from the table and connected. "Hi, sweetie."

"Hi, yourself. Listen, I can't talk, but I heard something you might want to know. Apparently Greg Jardis has been helping Chief Fenner on the case."

My eyebrows flew up. "Helping, as in exchange for a lighter sentence?"

"No. I don't believe he's been charged with anything. Jardis has been acting as an informant of a sort, on a professional basis. Sorry, that's all I know."

"Thanks for cluing me in."

"Any time. Love you, hon."

He ended the call before I could return the endearment. I turned back to my friends.

"That sounded interesting," Ed murmured.

"It was." I told them what Benjamin had relayed.

"Does that mean Jardis is off your suspect list?" Henry asked.

"I have no idea."

Would Greg help the police if he was guilty? He could be trying to lead them astray from the truth by doing so. Would that make it worse for him if he was discovered to be the actual killer? Or maybe he was innocent, and his intentions were to help the police catch a murderer. It all made my head spin so much I resolved to give up—for now—and enjoy the evening out with my friends.

Chapter 63

Henry dropped me at home by eight thirty as the sun was setting. I puttered around, visiting with my kitties, tidying, and getting ready for a new work week, as one does on Sunday nights.

I savored a square of dark chocolate, since our supper excursion hadn't included dessert, and chased it with a tall glass of cold milk.

By nine fifteen I was on the couch with my little glass of cognac and my thoughts. I shot Allie a text.

Thinking of you all. Hope the beach was fun. XXOO

A message from her came back within the minute.

Free for a call?

Instead of sending a response, I called her.

"That was fast," she said in lieu of a greeting.

"I always have time to talk with you. So, how are things?"

"It's quiet around here, finally. Two happy but exhausted boys are clean and asleep. Their father is, too."

"Good," I said.

"Listen, I had a chance to ask Fuller about Zeke and Yolanda. He's about five years older than they are, but he was friends with Jimmy, their oldest brother at Colinas High."

I sat up straight. "And?"

"He said all the kids, Jimmy on down, got a lot of flak because their parents were born in Mexico."

"Ed told me something similar. But it's not uncommon to be second-generation Americans around here, is it?"

"Not at all. Doesn't prevent children from being brutal to their classmates, though."

"You're right." I had been made fun of because I had trouble reading.

"Fuller had his own share of bad treatment, being one of the only Black kids around," she said. "One thing he said tonight struck me. He mentioned that Zeke was mean to younger kids, and that's not all. Once he was accused of shooting pellets at a cat."

"That's awful."

"I know," she agreed. "I guess nothing happened because the owners couldn't prove it."

"In the limited contact I've had with Zeke, he's seemed like a congenial and gentle adult."

"Good to know."

"Did Fuller say if he knew Malia when he was young?" I asked.

"No, but she's about a decade older than we are. Unless she babysat for him and his brother or something, they wouldn't have known each other."

"Right. Oh, wait. Ed told me over dinner that she grew up in Healdsburg. Never mind."

Allie laughed. "Get your stories straight, Cee."

"I'll try. So, when is Fuller's next treatment?"

"Wednesday, I think. I'll have to check the calendar."

"Listen," I began, "I haven't had a chance to tell you, but yesterday Franklin was asking about his dad's illness. The kid knows something is wrong."

"Yeah." She let out a noisy breath that might have been half sob. "He doesn't miss a beat. And we owe him and Artie the truth. I was hoping we could explain it to both of them today, but I didn't want to spoil the glorious day. I mean, Fuller isn't suffering from the treatments or the cancer yet except for being tired and worried, but he will soon, from both."

"I get it, sis. You wanted them to have unspoiled memories of today."

"That's it. Anyway, I'll talk with Fuller in the morning. We'll sit them down tomorrow after school and tell them everything before this goes any further."

"Good." I glanced at my phone. "Oh, Zoe is texting me. Do we have more to say right now?"

"No. Talk to your girl." She clicked off.

I tapped into Zoe's text. If she wanted to talk now, I was ready. Instead, she said she would call in the morning, which would be her Monday night. I responded that that would be perfect and that I loved her.

I'd better get myself to bed. Japan was sixteen hours ahead of us, which meant she'd probably call at six or earlier.

Except I stayed put, absorbed in my thoughts about bullying and meanness. Why did people mistreat each other? I hated to think there was a core of cruelty in each of us. Maybe it came down to power. Those who felt powerless exerted a small bit of power over others they saw as weaker. Or was it love? If a person, no matter their age, felt unloved and criticized, they passed that way of interacting along to whoever was nearby.

The thought of Fuller being treated badly as a child because of the color of his skin both broke my heart and made me furious, as did bad behavior toward people whose family's roots were in another country or toward anyone whose abilities were outside the norm. I imagined Tino had also been harassed or made fun of in the past.

Benjamin had mentioned how damaged Regan Greene was by her upbringing, which apparently led her to be so hurtful to others. That someone killed her was understandable—in a way—but that didn't make it right. Murder was still a crime.

CHAPTER 64

After I talked with Zoe from the comfort of my bed the next morning, I tried to slide back into sleep, but it proved elusive, and I gave up. By seven o'clock I'd downed my first cup of coffee and carried my second in a travel mug outside to the garden. The chilly, foggy morning made me zip my fleece all the way up.

A whistled tune from over the fence made me smile. "Good morning, neighbor," I called.

"Cecelia! Please pay me a visit."

I unlocked the gate and went through. Richard, wearing his cool-weather gardening jacket, held a hose in one hand and leaned on a cane with the other.

"Welcome home, Richard." I joined him where he stood watering the lemon tree. "It's good to see you up and about."

"Thank you. It's terribly good to be in my own digs again."

"I hope the garden looks okay."

"It's fine. Thank you for your efforts, my friend." He lifted the cane and pointed at the faucet. "Would you mind turning off the water for me? I feel the need to sit."

"I'm on it." I hurried over to shut off the supply. He'd had a new-style lever handle installed. It was coated in soft yellow plastic and was super easy to use, no matter how strong or weak one's grip was.

I joined him where he sat on his patio. "Are you feeling back to good health?"

"Close enough, I'd say."

"I'm glad." I took a sip of coffee.

"My memory seems to be returning. I've recalled something important from that morning when I fell."

"Seriously?"

"Yes," he said. "I was wandering among the raised beds puttering. A larger than usual lizard ran across my path. It startled me and I became tangled in my own feet. The next thing I knew, I was on the ground and you were calling my name."

Which meant nobody malicious conked him on the head. What a relief.

"I'm glad your memory is returning," I said.

He nodded. "Now, then, I hear the murder of the week still isn't solved."

"Not at all. I mean, not that I know of."

"Fill me in on what you do know, will you, please?" he asked. "I could use a good mental puzzle about now. This old brain needs a challenge to stay sharp."

"There's nothing dull about your brain, Richard." I smiled. "But I'm happy to oblige."

He'd researched and written about Regan, after all. He might be the key to finally figuring this thing out.

"As I understand it, here are the persons of interest." I ticked off the five names on my fingers. As I did, I realized I'd barely been thinking about Dane lately. I didn't want her to be guilty, but I couldn't take her off the list. She hadn't been cleared of suspicion—yet. "What do you think?"

"First, that I'm relieved not to be among the suspects." He gave a low chuckle. "I expect you find the fact that our mayor is on the list to be as disturbing as I do. An elected public servant. What has our society come to?"

I nodded my agreement.

"Her father was part of our ROMEO lunch club until dementia took his mind. Now he doesn't recognize any of us." Richard gazed at me. "My body might be growing frail, but at least I've kept my wits about me. I think that's far preferable to the alternatives, one of which is being in the ground."

"Absolutely." He'd told me earlier in the year about the Retired Old Men Eating Out group. I loved the acronym.

"At any rate," he went on, "despite Malia's success in civic government, her father told me that she had had trouble in her past."

"What kind of trouble?"

"He described it as a lack of impulse control. That sounds like a modern term, but he was a psychiatrist ahead of his time."

"I wonder if that means a lack of control in what she said or in striking out," I said. "I know a couple of people who don't seem to have a filter between their thoughts and what they say, which can end up being destructive in its own way."

"That, but she might possibly also have been physically violent."

"Was it when she was young? If she had a police record, you'd think it would have come out during campaigning."

"Agreed," Richard said. "Her father can no longer be relied on to relate the facts, I'm afraid."

"Do you know anything about Yolanda Cruz or her twin brother, Zeke?"

"She's an area artist, isn't she?"

"Yes," I said.

"I can't say that I do." He caught sight of one of the ubiquitous acorn woodpeckers attacking his back fence. He shook the cane at the bird and yelled at it to be gone, slipping in a couple of four-letter curses.

Last year my friend had lobbed acorns at the pest. It was an indication of his frailty that all he threw now were words.

"Cursed beasts," Richard muttered. "Now, where were we? Ah, yes, homicide suspects." He gazed at me. "I'm afraid your employee Dane Larsen might not have an entirely clean past. Did you know that?"

"The only thing I know is that she had clashes with a guy when she was trying to get through a course to become an electrician. She dropped out of the program because of it. By not a clean past, do you mean something criminal?"

"Possibly." He tented his fingers.

"Then, no, I don't know about it. I admit my hiring practices have been built more on trust than on background checks." Which might have to change. "What did Dane maybe do?"

"Well, she was rumored to have sabotaged a campaign to bring mural art to town."

"Seriously? She paints big pictures herself that are almost murals."

"That was the issue," Richard said. "She wasn't accepted as one of the artists. The organizers wrote a grant proposal to bring in farmworker and immigrant artists. People who hadn't benefited from an art education but who painted scenes from their own lives."

"And that excluded Dane, with her pale skin and Nordic last name."

"Exactly."

"Was there violence involved?" I asked.

"No, thank goodness, which possibly makes the whole thing irrelevant to the current situation. Also, in the end, I don't believe she was charged with committing a crime."

My shoulders relaxed. The last thing I needed was a violent person working for me.

"As for the other persons of interest, I don't believe I can be of help," Richard said. "But I shall keep my eyes and ears open to new information."

"I appreciate that." I stood. "Can I help you with anything before I get on with my day?"

"No, thank you. Peter will be up by and by and he has a list to work through."

"Great."

We said our goodbyes, and I made my way back through the gate with new thoughts swirling in my brain.

Chapter 65

I drove into the lot at JJ's Automotive at nine thirty. The fog had lightened, but the air remained cool and damp. I was glad I'd opted for yoga pants and my beloved jeans jacket, which was well broken in from years of use, and hadn't put the roof down.

Thank goodness for digital calendar reminders. I had an appointment for Jo to change Blue's oil, but it had slipped my too-busy mind entirely. Old cars burned through oil way faster than new models, and it was important to switch out the lubricant at least every three thousand miles if not earlier.

The bay door was open, and a battered vintage Volkswagen bus sat on the lift, with Jo standing straight under it. I paused to give Ouro a scritch on the head before I headed inside. He gave a little whine but didn't budge from his spot near the door, his head on his paws.

I greeted Jo and pointed to the vehicle on the lift. "Is that Dane Larsen's van?"

"Hi, Cece. It is, and it's having issues."

"Too bad. It looks like a seventy-three."

"Close," she said. "Seventy-four. VWs were so popular, I think the company stopped caring about quality that year. You brought Blue?"

"She's out front, and the keys are in the ignition."

"Great. How's the investigation going, by the way?"

"Not great, as far as I can tell," I said.

A thought struck me. Dane drove a vintage vehicle, as did Greg. Jo was pretty much the only mechanic around who was an expert in cars of the pre-computer age. It would be too weird of a coincidence if all suspects owned fifty-year-old rides. Wouldn't it?

"Say, do you have any customers with the last name of Cruz?" I asked. "Yolanda or Zeke, maybe?"

"Doesn't ring a bell."

"How about Mayor Gutierrez?"

"In fact, she bought a baby blue VW bug I had on the lot a couple of weeks ago. I helped the owner sell it, and Malia seemed determined to own the thing, although it's a bit of a wreck. The valves tap, and it needs a new muffler. She bought it anyway."

"She said her family owned one like that when she was younger," I said.

"She told me that, as well. It was kind of strange. I swear I saw the same Beetle being driven around a neighborhood out at the edge of town as I was heading home from the car show Saturday. Except, as far as I know, the previous owner didn't ink the deal until Monday."

My alert radar went up. That area was where Regan Greene had lived. Maybe Malia took possession of the VW sooner than Jo was aware. I would let the detective know as soon as I could.

"I was going to wait while you do the service," I said. "Is that still okay?"

She stuck the wrench she was using in her back pocket and grimaced as she wiped her hands on a red rag.

"Well, this job is taking longer than I expected. Also, the pooch isn't feeling great today. If you have a few extra minutes, would you mind dropping him at my place? By the time you come back, I should be finished with this and can do your oil change in short order."

I thought about my schedule. "That's fine. I don't have anything specific going on in the next couple of hours. What's wrong with Ouro?"

"I'm not positive. It seems like he has a cold or whatever they call it in dogs. I don't think it's anything serious, but you know how you're more comfortable in your own bed and yard when you're under the weather?"

"For sure, and your yard is fenced. He's safe being outside. I'm happy to run him over."

"Thanks so much. Here's a house key." She handed me a key on one of her own branded key chains. "Do you remember where I live?"

"I do." I'd been to her place a couple of times.

"The oil change is on me."

"Nonsense. This is your business." I glanced outside. "Does he need to be belted in?"

"Nah. Well, probably, but he never wears a seat belt in my truck." She walked outside with me and knelt in front of Ouro. "Hey, buddy. Cece's going to take you home, okay?"

His head perked up when he heard the word "home." Then he sneezed.

I opened the passenger door. Jo led him over, and he happily hopped in. She shut the door.

"I can't thank you enough," she said to me. She blew the dog a kiss.

"It's not a problem," I said. "See you in twenty minutes."

CHAPTER 66

I cracked the window a few inches. Ouro liked to taste the wind, and this way the opening wasn't wide enough for him to jump through. A friend in Pasadena hadn't secured her small dog in the front seat of her car, and he'd leapt through the open window and was killed by another vehicle. No way was I letting that kind of tragic accident happen to Jo's beloved canine companion.

Regan Greene's neighborhood was more or less on the way to Jo's place. I wended my way through the residential streets, but since I didn't know her address, I couldn't stop and gaze at her porch, imagining someone dropping off a murder weapon disguised as a gift.

I steered back onto the larger road leading to Jo's property. After a couple of minutes, a glance in the rearview mirror showed a flash of a light-colored car following several vehicles behind me. It wasn't white. Could it be Greg's silver Porsche? Maybe I'd passed Regan's home without knowing it, and guilty Greg had been parked nearby watching for who came to investigate. Or maybe he was police informant Greg, according to Ed. I wished I knew what information Greg had.

The turnoff to Jo's approached on the right, a gravel roadway through the trees ending at her five acres. I shook off my nerves and left the pavement. I'd be able to hear if anyone followed me.

Ouro yipped at the familiar surroundings. I gave him a quick look. Can dogs smile? This cat person didn't know, but he certainly looked alert and happy. I could probably let him out now and he would beat me to the house, even though he was under the weather. Instead, I kept driving, raising a cloud of dust behind me.

I pulled up in front of Jo's yurt and switched off the engine. The cylindrical structure with a shallow conical roof was about thirty feet in diameter. Ouro panted at the car window and laid his paw on the door.

"Just a sec, doggie." I opened my door but paused to listen. The surroundings were quiet except for the hammering of a woodpecker in the woods and the drone of a small plane somewhere overhead. I made sure I had the house key in hand and my phone in my pocket before I went around and opened the passenger door.

Ouro dashed out and raced to the nearest tree, then lifted a leg to deliver liquid marking. He trotted to the door of the yurt. I had to laugh at his typical teen expression of, "What's taking you so long?"

"Be right there, bud." I had the key pointed at the lock when the sound of tires crunching in the distance slowed my hand. In contrast, my heart sped up. The crunching grew louder.

Ouro's ears went on high alert. I grabbed his collar. He was mostly golden retriever. He also had a mix of some other breed in him, and Jo had mentioned he was a good guard dog.

I doubted this vehicle was bringing a package delivery. Jo kept a post office box in town for letters. She had all parcels, both business and personal, delivered to JJ's Automotive.

I thought fast about who the driver could be. Who followed me down this private lane? I didn't know what kind of car Yolanda drove, or Zeke, for that matter. It might be Greg in his antique Porsche. Not Dane in her van, but she could have borrowed a car. It could be Malia in her new/old Beetle.

"Ouro, sit." I pointed down, using the same firm tone Jo did. He finally settled his haunches on the ground. "Good boy. Stay."

When he obeyed, I pulled out my phone, but I was seized with indecision. Did I call Kelly? Jo? Maybe I should go straight to 911.

No. Until I saw who it was, I wasn't calling in an emergency. I tapped Jo's number. Blessedly, she picked up.

"Did the lock stick, Cece?"

"No. I'm at your place, and somebody is driving in after me. Call Kelly Daniell. I'll text you the number now." I disconnected as she was speaking and quickly forwarded her the detective's cell number.

My heart now beat in my throat. I could barely swallow as I cast through my options at lightning speed. I could lock Ouro and myself inside the yurt, but we'd be trapped. I could persuade him to go in to keep him safe and close the door after him, facing this threat on my own. But if he was a good guard dog, we both might need him.

Time slowed. The usually adorable quail on the fence stopped running and stared at the entrance to the woods. The hammering of the woodpecker now sounded like a warning, as did Ouro's low growl. A brown-and-white spotted hawk glided down to perch on a branch near the yurt, glaring down at anything that moved.

I had no evidence the person driving the approaching vehicle was dangerous. Every instinct in my body signaled they were.

CHAPTER 67

I was right. When a pale blue VW with a noisy muffler that sounded like a hot rod came around the bend into sight, my decision was made. I cursed the driver under my breath and hit 911, even though I'd already asked Jo to contact Kelly. A dispatcher answered, and I put the call on speaker.

"This is Cece Barton at Jo Jarvin's home off North Palito Road in Colinas. The person who killed Regan Greene just drove up. I'm here alone. Send help." I muted the sound but kept the call open, sliding the phone into the front pocket of my denim jacket.

The bug idled for a moment, its valves tapping, after its driver parked the vehicle crosswise close behind Blue. The engine shuddered when Malia shut it off. She climbed out.

"You're not much of a detective if you can't detect someone following you, Cece," she sneered.

I mustered my imaginary calm inner adult. I tried to keep my smile from wobbling. "I'm not guilty of anything. Why would I care if someone was tailing me?"

She barked out a laugh. "As if. You think you're not guilty of playing amateur PI? You've been asking questions all over town, trying to malign my character and put me out of a job. It wasn't enough that the self-appointed Queen of the Valley did it. You had to follow in Regan's footsteps." She wore low black heels and strode toward me, nearly turning her ankle on the gravel.

Ouro quivered with tension. My car was blocked from moving unless I backed into the VW. Nobody but the dog could help me escape. In the tennies I wore, I could easily outrun the mayor. So could Ouro. But what if she escaped and managed to evade the authorities? The homicide case would still be open, with nobody having to answer for their crime.

I could try to stall her from attacking by asking for more of her story, except stalling was a tactic used in novels, not in real life. Malia wouldn't be here wearing a mask of fury if she didn't intend to harm me. What was her plan?

"I've had to struggle my whole life." She waved one hand in the air as she spoke. "As a Hispanic kid, in college, at the hands of my piece of crap ex-husband. I barely won the election for mayor. But the worst was that witch Regan, and she never gave up trying to lord it over me."

Uh-oh. Her other hand was in the pocket of the loose black linen blazer she wore over a black-and-white-striped dress. If I wasn't mistaken, she gripped something with that hand.

"But I showed her, didn't I?" Malia ranted on. "When you grow up making wine with your granddad, you know a thing or two and happen to have a box full of equipment." She'd been almost talking to herself but now turned a laser focus on me. Her eyes burned. "And you're not spoiling my victory, Barton."

My own hand still held the house key. I maneuvered it between two knuckles and squeezed my fist around the sharp metal key. It was to my advantage that I kept in good shape with Pilates and bike riding. Malia was shorter than I was, and she was wearing heels on a gravel driveway. I could get away, unless—

Her pocket hand began to move. Ouro uttered a louder low

growl. Malia pulled out a knife handle. The blade snicked open. A sharp, lethal-looking blade. She reached for me with the other hand.

I leaned away. Ouro leapt. With a snarl, he sank his teeth into her bare calf and hung on. She cried out, trying to slash at him with the knife.

No! I couldn't let her hurt him. I swept the edge of the key across her exposed neck, etching the tender skin.

Malia gave a yell of pain. She dropped the knife and collapsed to sitting, holding her hand to the deep scrape on her neck but trying to kick at Ouro.

I skirted her and picked up the knife. "Ouro, stop."

He gave one last growl but let go of her leg. Her dress was now black, white, and red with her own blood.

"Don't move, Malia." I pointed the knife blade at her and stepped away, standing between her and Blue. "The police are on their way." That is, I prayed they were.

Ouro yipped, gazing up at me.

"Ouro, come here." I patted my leg. "Sit."

He gave Malia one last growl, then trotted over and sat at my side, still alert.

"Good boy." I stroked his head. I couldn't see any cuts on him, thank goodness. "What a good dog you are."

Our attacker twisted to her feet faster than I thought possible. She lurched at me, reaching for the knife.

"Ouro, go," I commanded.

Chapter 68

Malia's eyes flew wide. She whirled and began to run. Ouro jumped at her, knocking her down on her front. He glanced up at me.

"Good boy." I took two long strides and set one knee on her back. I grabbed her closest flailing hand, twisting it up behind her back. Ouro crouched and placed both front legs over her ankles. This mayor wasn't going anywhere.

"Get off me!"

I ignored her. My shoulders relaxed as I finally heard the up and down of a siren growing ever louder, the best soundtrack I could imagine for the rest of this sad story.

A moment later, a black Colinas police cruiser sped up in a cloud of gravel, followed by a white Sonoma County sheriff's SUV. A couple of Colinas PD officers jogged up. Chief Fenner and Kelly Daniell weren't far behind.

I pulled my phone out. "The police are here." I disconnected the call.

One of the CPD officers pointed a gun with both hands at Malia. "Stay where you are, Ms. Gutierrez." To me, she added, "I've got this, ma'am. You can get up."

Ouro quivered again.

"It's okay, Ouro," I told him as I pushed up to standing.

"They're friends. Stay. Lie down." I pointed to the ground and couldn't believe that he obliged, crouching into a sphinx pose. "Good boy."

"You okay, Cece?" Kelly asked.

"Yes." I gestured toward Malia. "She parked me in, accused me of some stuff, and pulled out a switchblade."

"Cece and the dog attacked me!" Malia said from where she sat.

On the contrary, but I wasn't going to engage with her. My work here was over.

"Do you mean that knife?" Kelly pointed her chin at my hand.

Oops. "Yes. After Ouro bit Malia's leg, and I used Jo's house key to do a bit of damage to her neck, she dropped the knife, and I picked it up. Here." I extended it, haft forward.

Fenner slid on a glove and pinched the knife between thumb and index finger. He handed it to a different patrol officer, who secured it in a paper evidence bag.

"You probably want the key, too." I handed it over.

The chief repeated the evidence-securing process. He turned toward Malia. Fenner recited the Miranda rights to her. The guarding cop held up handcuffs.

"We'll wait on that until the ambulance gets here." Fenner gave Malia a stern look. "The mayor isn't going anywhere."

Kelly and I watched.

"Did you know she killed Regan?" I asked her in a low voice.

She opened her mouth to speak. At the sound of another vehicle, she clamped it shut. Posture alert and right hand on her sidearm, she stared at the drive.

Even before Jo's truck was visible, Ouro was off and running. I could glimpse the red through the trees.

"It's Jo," I murmured to Kelly. "Not to worry."

Jo pulled into the clearing from a different direction and exited her truck, Ouro at her side. I hadn't realized there was a loop off the main way in and out.

She jogged toward us and took in the scene. "You okay, Cece?"

"Yes, thanks to your most excellent pooch. He was a very good boy. But I'm afraid Chief Fenner has your house key for now."

"No worries. That was my spare, and I have other copies."

An ambulance pulled up behind the sheriff's vehicle, and a couple of EMTs joined the party.

"Will you be at the wine bar this afternoon?" Kelly asked me. "I can find you there to get your statement."

"I guess." Did I want to go home and dwell on the attack for the rest of the day? Not really, and it was only ten thirty. I had time to recover my nerves. "I need to be at Vino y Vida by twelve thirty. Am I free to go now?"

"Yes." The detective pointed at me. "And thank you."

"You're welcome." I gazed at Jo. "I think I'll postpone that oil change if you don't mind."

"I can understand why," Jo said. "Bring her in any time. Make your escape by way of the loop if you want."

I would, on both counts. When I did bring my car for its service, I'd also bring a big box of treats for Ouro. He was the hero of the day.

Chapter 69

Even though I'd bathed earlier that morning, I took a second shower and stood under the hot water for a long time, grateful for the on-demand water heater. Water wouldn't wash away the memory of being threatened by a killer, but it helped in the short term.

In case Benjamin had heard the news about the morning's events, I sent him a text saying that I was safe and that Malia had been arrested, adding that I'd be at work by midday onward. I called Allie, who didn't pick up. I sent her essentially the same text.

By twelve fifteen I walked over to Vino y Vida and began doing all the preopening things. I doubted too many sippers would want to be on the patio with the high temperature barely pegging sixty. If the sun wasn't out by now, it wasn't coming out. Still, I wiped down the tables. You never knew with tourists. Many wanted to be outdoors as much as possible in California.

Back inside, I set out baskets of crackers and lined up clean glassware. When someone tapped on the window, I glanced at the entrance, expecting Kelly.

Instead, it was Zeke peering in. He held up his index finger. I could take a minute to speak with him. I unlocked the door.

"Can we have a quick word, Cece?" His tone was tentative.

"Sure. Come in, please. We're not open to the public yet." I locked the door behind him and gestured at a chair, but he shook his head and stayed on his feet.

"Thanks." With his shoulders hunched and worry lines creasing his forehead, he slid his hands into his pockets. "I'll only take a minute of your time. I heard the mayor was arrested for attacking you. Did she say she murdered Regan Greene?"

"She did."

He blew out a breath and his shoulders relaxed. "My sister and I are going to be happy the detective will no longer think we did it."

"Understandably. But why did Yolanda say that thing about being glad Regan was dead?"

"You'd have to have known us as children. Yoli has really come into her own, but as a kid she had a terrific overbite and got called Rabbit. Plus both of us and our siblings were harassed by other kids. They called us wetbacks and illegals even though we were neither."

"There are so many in California with roots in Mexico," I said. "I'm surprised that still goes on."

"Unfortunately, it does. Anyway, my sister is extra sensitive to being bullied, and Regan was nothing if not a bully." He held up a hand. "If you're wondering why she didn't quit working at AVDA, it's because she's really trying to make it as an artist, and the association paid well. She knew she wouldn't make anywhere near as much money waitressing or doing another low-end job."

I thought about what Benjamin had said about Regan's own past.

"I learned that Regan herself was badly mistreated as a child," I said. "She's an example of how that behavior gets passed on."

"For sure. My sister and I are both doing our best not to mistreat others despite our childhood. I'll let you get on with your job, but thanks for listening, Cece."

"I appreciate you dropping by. See you in class tomorrow."

He gave me a thumbs-up and left, his step considerably lighter. That chapter was done and I was glad of it.

I was about to relock the door when Benjamin hurried up the sidewalk. I stepped into the comfort of his open arms and stood there embracing him for a long minute.

"I would have come sooner," he said into my hair, "but I was locked in an important meeting, and I'm afraid I have another one in a few minutes."

I pulled away. "I'm fine, truly. And I love that you hurried over."

He set his hands on my shoulders and gazed into my face. "You're sure you're okay?"

"Yes."

"And you'll tell me all about it tonight after work? I don't care how late it is."

"I will." I bobbed my head.

"I'll pick you up here." He gave me a smile full of love, then pulled me in for a long kiss before hurrying away.

I was still feeling warm as I locked the door and headed back to my tasks.

Chapter 70

No more than two minutes later, I smiled at my twin's face peering in through the glass. I hurried to the door.

"Cee, you had quite the morning." She pulled me in for a different kind of comforting hug before stepping back. "You're okay, right?"

"Now that you've released your death grip, yes, I am." I decided to leave the door unlocked. "Come on in. I'm setting up for the day."

Allie followed me to the bar. "I need to know every single thing."

"And you shall. So—"

Mooncat sailed in from the back room. "Look who I found poking around the back door." She pointed her thumb over her shoulder.

Kelly Daniell flipped her hands open. "I wasn't poking, exactly. Just thought the front wouldn't be open."

"It's a hen party!" Mooncat grinned as she tied on a store apron and scrubbed her hands.

"The more, the merrier," I said. "I was about to tell Allie what happened. Now I can tell all of you at the same time, but let me relock the front door first."

"I'll do it." Mooncat sashayed over to the door and turned

the bolt. "You totally don't want the thirsty public in here listening to Cece relate the last deranged act of a homicidal mayor."

Kelly had met Mooncat before but perhaps hadn't seen her in all her glory. The detective gave her head a little shake as she perched on a barstool next to Allie.

"'The Last Deranged Act of a Homicidal Mayor' sounds like a great book title," Allie said. "You've been thinking of writing a novel, Cece."

I shuddered. "I have, but not that one."

"Excuse me, ladies, but I actually have reports to file," Kelly said. "If you wouldn't mind, Cece?"

"Okay. Here's the thumbnail sketch. I brought my car to Jo's garage for an oil change, and I was going to wait. She asked me to run Ouro home while she finished up a job because he wasn't feeling well. Apparently Malia was following me."

"Did you know she was?" Kelly asked.

"Not really. At one point I thought somebody was on my tail, but then I figured I was mistaken. I should have trusted my instincts on that, but it's too late now."

"Please go on," the detective said.

"I was about to unlock the door to the yurt when Malia parked crosswise behind me. She came close and said she knew I was onto her. Ouro was the one who was onto her. When she pulled out a knife, I told him to get her. He bit her bare calf and hung on. She tried to slash him, but I gave her neck a deep scrape with Jo's house key." My voice trembled at the memory as I rushed through the rest. "Malia dropped the knife and sat on the ground, except then she grabbed it, jumped up, and tried to attack again. Ouro knocked her down. He and I made sure she wasn't going anywhere. The police came. End of story."

Mooncat and Allie clapped.

"Three cheers for Cece and the dog." Mooncat gave two thumbs-ups.

Allie, her eyes instantly full, reached across the bar for my hand and squeezed. I squeezed back.

"You left out the part about asking Jo to call me," Kelly said. "And you called nine-one-one yourself, smartly keeping the call open."

"Just trying to stay safe." I gave a quick shrug. "Kelly, can you say anything more about the other people you were considering might have killed Regan, like Greg Jardis and the Cruz twins?" I didn't want to mention Dane.

"Of course. I owe you that." Kelly glanced at Allie and Mooncat. "I'm sure both of you know everything Cece does and thinks about doing."

"Mostly." Allie smiled. "Please don't hesitate because of us."

"Very well," Kelly began. "Yolanda Cruz has been open about her deep dislike of the victim, and she seems to be hiding something, but we couldn't find any evidence linking her to the murder, nor her brother. Jardis has been cooperative, although we hadn't ruled him out entirely. Now we can."

"And the homicidal mayor?" Mooncat asked.

"Isn't she the only person who had an overnight alibi?" I added.

"Yes." Kelly nodded. "But the poisoned wine bottle was delivered in the late afternoon. Where anyone was during the night hours ended up not mattering."

Hadn't I said the same thing to somebody? Or maybe I'd only thought it.

"Malia must have confessed to the murder," Allie murmured.

Kelly nodded. "She actually did, which surprised me. She must have realized that after being caught attacking you, plus your testimony, her prospects of not being convicted were slim to none."

"As they said in days of yore, all's well that ends well." Mooncat uncorked a bottle of pinot noir.

"Not for Regan or Malia," I said. "But certainly for the rest of us."

"One more thing, Cece," Kelly said. "Your crowbar-wielding friend? It turned out to be a misguided teenager in search of electronics and cash. A couple of other residents caught him on their door cams, and Paul Fenner's people were able to apprehend the kid. Hopefully, he's young enough to straighten himself out, but it wasn't a murderer coming after you."

"What a relief," I said. "Thanks for letting me know.

A new tapping came on the glass door. Greg Jardis peered in and gave a grinning wave. I glanced at the clock.

"It's opening time, friends." I headed for the door and let Greg in.

"Look at this." He beamed. "All the loveliest faces in town, and the best minds as a bonus. I've won the lottery."

Kelly rolled her eyes and stood. "You all take care. I'm off to my next stop."

"Don't leave," Greg said. "Was it something I said?"

"Lucky for you, it was something you didn't say," Kelly said. "More accurately, something you didn't do."

"Did I hear correctly that poor Regan's killer is behind bars?" he asked.

"You did," Kelly said.

"I know I was kind of on your suspect list, but with the mayor locked up for the murder, that means I'm off the list, and that's a good thing."

"You are, and it is. Cece, good working with you. I hope we never do it again." The detective smiled and bustled out the door.

"How did you know Regan, Greg?" I asked. "I heard you calling her a nickname at the car show."

"We were lovers for a while." He smiled and shrugged with a sheepish air. "But I've had many, and she was in the far past.

Now, can I please get a glass of wine? Something cool and white would be perfect."

"You bet," I said.

Allie waggled her fingers. "I'd like a glass of whatever he's having. When my twin is a winner, which is happening a lot lately, we celebrate."

Mooncat poured a Vinho Verde for both of them, and an inch in cups for each of us.

"We have much to toast," I said. "For now, let's keep it to a simple cheers."

We tapped glasses or cups all around. I tasted the fresh white Portuguese wine. Its hint of bubbles was appropriate for a celebration, even if I couldn't indulge in more than a taste for now.

Allie was right. It was about time for me to toss my former lack of self-confidence in the trash can. I'd been having success after success ever since I moved to Colinas. My daughter had reconciled with me, putting her past hurts in the rearview mirror. I'd acquired a loving and decent beau, and I'd learned that I wasn't half bad at owning and running a business. And I'd found this odd ability to ferret out murderers, sometimes before the law enforcement folks did.

Still, Kelly was right, too. May we never meet again over a homicide. I'd be just as happy with nonmurderous successes going forward.